Bastille Day

A NOVEL

———

GREG GARRETT

Raven

PARACLETE PRESS
BREWSTER, MASSACHUSETTS

2023 First Printing

Bastille Day: A Novel

Copyright © 2023 by Gregory Todd Garrett

ISBN 978-1-64060-751-4

The quotation on page 4 is taken from "Fortunate Son," written by Bruce Hornsby, published by Zappo Music c/o Downtown Music Services, and is used with permission.

The Raven name and logo are trademarks of Paraclete Press.

   Library of Congress Cataloging-in-Publication data
Title: Bastille Day : a novel / Gregory Garrett.
Description: Brewster, Massachusetts : Paraclete Press, 2023. | Summary:
   "Garrett's characters wrestle with the ghosts of their pasts, as they
   long for love, and faith in the present: Our histories can damage us,
   but hope can heal us."— Provided by publisher.
Identifiers: LCCN 2022044089 (print) | LCCN 2022044090 (ebook) | ISBN
   9781640607514 (trade paperback) | ISBN 9781640607521 (epub) | ISBN
   9781640607538 (pdf)
Subjects: BISAC: FICTION / Christian / Contemporary | FICTION / Christian /
   Romance / Suspense | LCGFT: Christian fiction. | Novels.
Classification: LCC PS3607.A77 B37 2023 (print) | LCC PS3607.A77 (ebook)
   | DDC 813/.6--dc23/eng/20220913
LC record available at https://lccn.loc.gov/2022044089
LC ebook record available at https://lccn.loc.gov/2022044090

10 9 8 7 6 5 4 3 2 1

Published by Paraclete Press
Brewster, Massachusetts
www.paracletepress.com

Printed in the United States of America

FOR JEANIE

Je t'aime. Je t'adore. Now. Forever.

"Well I was always taught well, taught well
To be the strong one and keep it inside
But sometimes I sit beside the freeway
And howl out at the dark, dark sky"

Bruce Hornsby, "Fortunate Son"

PROLOGUE

Paris

—

July 14, 2017

My late father, Master Sergeant Calvin Jones, impressed on me that it was essential to always tell the truth, no matter the personal cost. He didn't know he was forming me into a journalist, or that he was shaping me to tell this story. Seriously, he was just one of those straight-arrow Army types who believed that George Washington really did chop down a cherry tree but at least he told the truth about it. My father could only see the world in terms of truth and lies, good and bad, them and us.

True story: I cheated on a geography test in seventh grade. Only once. I hadn't studied, and it looked like Dean Mottola was breezing through the quiz, so I looked over and stole his, although I ought to have known even then that Iran and Iraq were not interchangeable and that Saudi Arabia was not to be found in Europe. Dean Mottola was an idiot, and I was an idiot for copying his answers.

I cheated, and I got caught, and when I tried to lie my way out of it, my father beat my ass.

But it wasn't the whupping that made the biggest impression. It was the way my father's face crumpled as I tried to spin my ridiculous tale, as though I had failed him as well as my geography test.

Because I had.

Because I had.

I learned to tell the truth.

And to associate with a smarter class of people, for God's sake.

I didn't tell my father another outright lie until the biggest one, the ongoing one: that I didn't worry about him when he deployed to Iraq.

Truth: I worried about him every time he deployed, every day of his life.

Truth: I worry about him to this very day.

I went to see him in country one time, a year or so before he died. I had arrived three days earlier, hadn't been embedded with my unit yet, and I hitched a ride from the Green Zone in a Bradley with some guys I found out were heading to Fallujah. I was technically off the reservation and could have been sent home. This was not the unit I was going to be embedded with, just some decent Joes who wanted to help a guy see his father who was a career non-com, "one of the good guys," as they put it.

I found my dad walking a shattered street with his men, checking house to house. He wasn't surprised to see me; he was upset.

"You shouldn't have come here, Cal," he told me, right after he shook my hand. "This city is a powder keg. And if you get blown up, your mother will give me holy hell when I get to heaven." Anne Johnson, my mother, passed when I was small, and exists now mostly in old photos and in the moment before I drop off to sleep.

"Assuming you even get to heaven," I told him.

His boys thought that was funny.

"True that," one of them said.

My father was right, of course. Just being in Iraq put me in danger every damn day. The network was spending something like $15,000 a month on my life insurance policy, and it got more expensive as the country became even more dangerous for journalists. Some bean-counter at Aetna was already pretty sure that I was not going to survive this assignment, and going to the Anbar Province was an astonishing risk. Fallujah was the worst, even early on, and it got worse still, as you will hear. But I'm glad I went. I'd do it again, even though I caught holy hell from the network when I returned. My producer, Callie, threatened to replace me. Said there were a lot of people who would kill to be where I was.

"Or get killed," I told her, which shut her up.

It was worth it.

If I hadn't gone to Fallujah that day, I'd never have known that my father was proud of me.

"This is my boy," he said, introducing me to everyone we met, to his other boys and to Iraqi commanders and to the occasional shopkeeper. "He's here to tell the world about what's going on. He's here to tell the truth."

Well. True that.

That was over ten years ago. A lot has happened since that day, some of which I will have to tell for you to know the whole story. To understand what happened in Paris and before, and, maybe, after.

But all of it will be true.

You have my word.

As I write this, I live in Paris. Maybe I always will, although it's too early to say where telling this story is going to leave me, if the city is going to feel to me like a place I lost myself or found myself.

But you probably already know: this story isn't going to leave me or you where it found us, because that is the truth of all stories worth telling.

They always take us someplace else, always leave us trying to figure out what just happened.

So turn the page.

I've got a story to tell you, and it's time we got started.

1.

London

July 9, 2016
Saturday

I shouldn't be here.
And by "here," I didn't just mean the third floor of Selfridge's Department Store on London's Oxford Street, where I stood surrounded by wealthy Arab women in lavish veils and ornate burqas shopping for lingerie, although that had me feeling plenty uncomfortable. I haven't had many great experiences with Arab women. Many of them wanted me dead.

Some of them have said so to my face.

But that wasn't it, wasn't what I was thinking, exactly. It was more like:

I shouldn't even be alive.

A couple of days earlier, I had been face-down on a Dallas street, bullets flying over my head, people getting shot.

And someone died right in front of me.

Again.

Thinking about everything I had seen—or trying to stop thinking about it, I guess, which was what I had been doing for days—was maybe why I was standing, frozen, a lacy purple bra dangling from my hand for a length of time that probably made me an object of conjecture for others in the lingerie department.

Which was to say, a room full of Arab women covered head to toe in gorgeous fabric and, apparently, sporting push-up bras and lace panties beneath those coverings.

I didn't think I could be any more disconcerted by Arab women, but I discovered that, actually, once you added that fact, I could.

Someone slid in beside me and spoke: "You are buying this for your mistress, yes?"

The voice was soft, low, humorous, beautifully inflected, and it shook me out of my reverie. The formal syntax suggested English was not her first language, although the accent was classic Oxbridge.

I looked to my right, where the speaker stood, herself covered head to foot in black. Her Selfridge's badge, pinned to her shoulder, read "Anna." Two brown eyes twinkled back at me.

I don't know if it was her words—or her eyes—but I momentarily lost command of the English language. I put the bra down, then picked up another so my hands had something to do. "What? Um, no. I mean, I don't have a mistress. No. A girlfriend. I guess. Yes. A girlfriend."

Her eyes drifted languidly left and right to see if she was needed elsewhere, then she began refolding the lacy underthings in front of her.

"Perhaps you should be very certain of that before you make any purchase." Her eyes indicated the white push-up bra with breathtaking lace décolletage I was now holding. "Everything here is ... expensive." I guessed she was comparing my worn jeans and battered combat boots to my choices in lingerie and finding them wanting.

I sighed, nodded.

"That is how she prefers things," I said.

She was Kelly McNair, who made her debut in Houston before coming to Dallas to do interior design and generally enjoy life. We'd been dating for two years, more or less, and I didn't feel that I knew her any better than I did on our first date. Perhaps she'd say the same of me. I'm not easy to know, and it's probably better if you don't get inside my head and poke around too much.

"We make a nice-looking couple," she liked to say, which was true enough.

I was on TV; she was pretty enough to be on TV. Maybe she felt like that was enough.

"Will you marry her? This girlfriend with expensive tastes?"

Anna was still folding lingerie. She picked up one of the bras in front of her, held it up, turned it side to side, shook her head, set it down.

I shook my head along with her. "No. I don't think so."

She looked left and right again, still satisfied that nobody needed her more than me at that moment, and so she turned to look at me full on.

"Do not marry someone you do not love," she said. Two fingers on my forearm were punctuation. I could feel their imprint after her hand moved, after she turned her attention back to the lingerie.

"What?" I felt stunned, as though she had tased instead of touched me.

"Do not marry someone you do not love," she repeated. It sounded as if she might have some personal knowledge of the situation.

"Um, okay," I stuttered. "I mean, well, it doesn't look like anyone is getting married. I'm going to Paris to start a new job. The girlfriend is staying in Texas."

"Oh, Paris," she said. I could hear the smile, although I could not see it. "You will meet someone there."

"Of course," I said. "I have seen that movie."

A voice growled across the room: "Anna!" and both of us jumped.

An older Arab woman—guessing by her voice—clad head to foot in black, stomped across the room, looked at me with all the menace that two eyes can deliver, and took Anna by the arm. Judging by the heaping armful of lingerie, she was ready to check out. I looked right back at her, disdain for disdain.

I had seen those eyes before in the Anbar Province when American soldiers took someone's son or husband or grandson away. When I followed a squad through a shattered front door to find a family quailing, on their knees, but one strong mother or grandmother fixing these invaders—fixing me—with the evil eye.

The woman and Anna spoke to each other in Arabic. I understood a little. Enough to know I'd been insulted. Anna pulled her arm gently free, soothed the older woman, who offered me another scorching look and turned toward the checkout desk.

"Goodbye, American boy," Anna said over her shoulder as she walked away. "Remember what I told you."

"Boy?" I wanted to say.

When I was just a boy, I spent three summers lifeguarding. I saved people who were drowning. When I became a man, I stood alongside soldiers in combat so I could tell their stories. I've seen men, women, and children blown to pieces. I just held a man as he died, and that was not an action for boys, let me tell you, sister.

But what I said, instead, in creaky but technically correct present-tense Arabic, was "I thank you, Anna. Actually, I will purchase these."

And I followed her and the glaring woman to the checkout desk to spend a substantial part of my first paycheck from the new job in Paris.

2.

Paris

July 11, 2016
Monday

Rob, my new boss and my old friend, had proposed we meet at Harry's New York Bar to celebrate my first day on the job. He said it was one of his favorite bars, and it might be a nice way for this American to step into Parisian life. I agreed. I had read about Harry's in a James Bond story, "From a View to a Kill." The 16-year-old James had told his taxi driver to take him to "Sank Roo Doe Noo," as the ads have advised French-illiterate English speakers to do for a hundred years, and there had commenced what Bond described as "one of the memorable evenings of his life," culminating in the loss of both his virginity and of his wallet.

I took the Metro from my new apartment on the rue Edmond Valentin, in the Seventh Arrondissement near the Eiffel Tower. I had already discovered that if I took to a chair on my sixth-floor balcony I could see almost the entire Tower, although I don't think the network's insurance provider would approve, and honestly, I could see plenty of the Tower without climbing. Heights got to me.

I stepped off the subway at the Opéra Garnier, loitered for a few minutes on the front steps of the baroque gilded opera house people-watching, then made my slow and tentative way down through the narrow streets to 5 Rue Daunou carrying my notebook and my battered paperback of Ian Fleming's *For Your Eyes Only* to read while I waited, because I expected to wait.

I had never even been to Paris before I agreed to go to work for Rob. Truth to tell, if not for him, I would not have come. He'd told the higher-ups at his network that I had two years of French (which I did, indeed, in high school) to accompany the Arabic, Kurdish, and Pashto I'd picked up during three years' reporting in Iraq and Afghanistan. And Spanish, from growing up with bilingual kids on the base and doing news in Dallas, Texas, for a solid decade. Who better, he asked the higher-ups, to report on terrorism in Europe?

Well. I could have named a dozen people without stopping to think, all of them also more stable than me at this moment. But the timing was good—I had nothing to look forward to where I was— and I did want to work with Rob again.

If he ever arrived, since he was always, always late.

Harry's was all but empty at midday. I was supposed to arrive at 2, but as I stepped to the door of the bar at 2:15, Rob texted to say he was running late, 2:30 maybe. I suspected 3. Inside, the bartender, dressed in a white jacket, black tie, and white apron, leaned onto the bar talking to a young Arab woman with long lashes. She was wearing form-fitting running clothes and had a dog leash draped across her lap. A couple of beefy Americans, man and wife, maybe, sat in a booth at the back drinking what looked like a Bloody Mary and a French 75, both drinks reputed to have been created at Harry's.

I was disappointed. I had expected Harry's to be a party out of Scott Fitzgerald. Drinks should be flowing, a piano should be playing—didn't Gershwin write *An American in Paris* here?—but this was just a dark and frankly tiny bar that was not dissimilar to the dive where I used to drink after work in Dallas with my cameraman, Ted.

I took a seat at the polished bar, two chairs down from the woman. She glanced over, then turned back to the bartender. I flashed back to Anna in London, the almond brown eyes, sure, the fact that she was Arab. Saudi, maybe, but very Western. She was wearing yoga pants and an oversized white top, with the straps of an athletic bra peeking at her shoulders. That middle-aged shopper in Selfridge's would have slapped her silly for showing so much skin.

"Monsieur? What can I bring you?" the bartender asked, bringing me back to now. His English was accented. Eastern Europe. Maybe one of the former Soviet states. He had a thick black moustache, and unruly dark hair, cut short and spiky. The name badge on his apron read "Frederick."

"An Old Fashioned, Frederick," I told him. "With Bulleit, if you have it. And bring me another every fifteen minutes until my friend arrives."

Frederick raised an eyebrow. He knew from long experience that this was not a recipe for a successful afternoon.

"Always late," I sighed. "Our longstanding deal is, I drink on him. One drink every fifteen minutes. If he doesn't want to pour me into a taxi, he's got to arrive in some reasonable amount of time."

"Very good, monsieur," he said. "But almost you have to drink the whisky sour if you are going to sit on that stool," he said, indicating with his head as his hands washed glasses in the sink. "It is Mr. Hemingway's."

"Oh," I said, looking down at my seat. "Really? Ernest Hemingway?"

"Oui. Thirty whisky sours Mr. Hemingway would drink on an afternoon. Then he would go back to work." He wiped his hands on a towel, ready to serve.

"What? Thirty?" I looked down at the stool beneath me. It all seemed frankly impossible. But—Mr. Hemingway. "Okay. Whisky sour, then. You do have Bulleit?"

He nodded and pulled a glass from behind the bar and the bottle from a shelf behind him. I checked my phone. Nothing from Rob yet.

"*Quelle heure est-il?*" the woman asked me, leaning across the stool separating us.

I thought hard and stammered out, "*Il est deux heures vingt.*" I'm not sure even my high school French teacher would have known what I was saying.

She found my bad French charming for some reason. "*Américain?*"
"*Oui.*"

"I wasn't sure," she said. She indicated my James Bond. "I thought perhaps *Anglais.*"

"*Pardon,*" I said with a wry face. "*Je parle un peu.*" I was laboring. And her English was a lot better than my French.

"It's okay," she said. "I prefer to speak English."

"I also speak some Arabic," I told her. "But your English is excellent."

"It should be." She looked up from her drink and smiled at me, the camera pushed in slow on her face, and it was in that precise moment, I believe, that I was lost. Her lips were so beautiful that I had to concentrate to make sense of the words she was forming: "I have been living in the States for ten years."

"No kidding," I said, trying to keep my voice from shaking. I felt tased again. "Where?"

The bartender set down my whisky sour and I looked over at her. "Can I get you something?" She was sipping at a French 75—served in a tumbler rather than a flute—but had drunk almost none of it.

"No thank you," she said. "I'll have to go back soon." She made a sour face, as did the bartender. She ticked the following off on her fingers. "I went to Phillips Exeter Academy. Then Stanford. I did my Master's degree at Rice. Global Affairs."

"Wow," I said.

She shrugged. Maybe it didn't seem such a big deal when you were the one who had done it. "Can you understand me?" she asked in Arabic.

"Yes, very well," I told her in return. She nodded.

"Nadia," she said, offering her hand. A crisp, short shake. Her nails were red, lacquered. Her hand was as beautiful as the rest of her.

"Calvin," I said. "Cal." I let go her hand.

She leaned a bit in my direction. "How did you learn Arabic, Calvin?"

"I was a reporter in Iraq," I said. "During the last war. I spent three years in the Middle East—" I tried to remember. "Whew. That was ten years ago."

"I haven't been back for many years either," she said. "I enjoyed being away, I think." She looked closely at me. "Did you like it? Being in Iraq?"

"It did not work out so well for me," I confessed. Understatement is your friend. "But I did like waking up to the muezzin calling people to prayer, that is, if there were no snipers in the minaret. I did meet some people I'll never forget."

And I did get a headful of carnage I'll never forget. But there you go.

This was not a topic that invited further discourse. Neither of us cherished our memories of the Arab world. We sat in silence for a bit. Frederick clanked some dirty glasses in the sink. I sipped at my drink, took surreptitious glances at her, tried not to gaze directly at her bare shoulder for fear it would strike me blind.

"What do you like about James Bond?" she asked, at last, nodding at my book. It was a step backward, but it was at least a step. "The beautiful women? The brave man of action? The gadgets?"

"I like Bond in the books," I said. "And the Daniel Craig movies. He is brave. But broken. That's where the bravery is." I nodded. That sounded right. "He's broken, but he goes on." But Jesus, no more of that. At least not without about five more whisky sours. I put the book under my notebook. Another dead end. "What are you going to do with global affairs? That was at the Baker Center, right?"

"Baker Institute. James Baker, yes." Now she took a big sip of her drink, made a face, sighed. "I was to begin work on a PhD at Georgetown this fall. I wanted to make a difference somehow." She offered a smile that was simultaneously rueful and heartbroken. "Then my father called and said I have been educated enough. It is time."

I took another sip. "Time?" That sounded ominous. "What does that mean?"

She looked across at me and her eyes were sparkling, this time not in a good way. I looked away quickly, down at the bar, down at the bronze rail beneath my feet. "He meant that it was time for me to marry. That he had at last completed all the arrangements. That's why I'm in Paris." She sighed. "We'll have a ceremony here in Western formalwear. It's all the rage now, apparently. Take pictures on the Alexandre III Bridge or somewhere after in my Elie Saab dress so everyone can see how elegant his bride is." Now she looked down at the bar and said quietly, "I hoped to change things for my mother and sisters in Saudi. Now I'll go home and put on the burqa and make babies and no one will ever hear from me again."

Quel dommage. I was stunned. In the course of a minute, she had gone from gorgeous, brilliant, and available to unhappily married. But sadly this wasn't the first Saudi girl I'd ever met who'd been sent to the States to increase her marriage value. It was a thing.

And the last thing I needed was to take on someone else's pain. I should take a step back. Or, better, two.

"It sounds bad," I said, shooting for breezy. "But maybe he's a decent guy."

"Maybe," she said. "It would be nice to know before I marry him." She took a big gulp of her drink, returned it gently to the bar, stared at it, into it, maybe. "Everyone else gets something from this. I don't see any way it works out well for me."

And breezy or not, I had to agree.

We sat for a moment in silence. Life is heartbreaking, as I know better than most.

My phone buzzed and I took a glance. "There in five," was Rob's text. I predicted ten. But that meant he had, at the very least, left the office.

"Nadia," the barman proclaimed sadly, checking his watch, "it's time, my sweet."

She sighed and slid off the seat. "*Merci, Frederick.*" She took up her dog leash.

I turned to her, and although it would have been better to just let her walk out, I truly wondered, and so I asked: "What kind of dog do you have?" It had broken my heart to leave Grace, my loving Golden Retriever, behind in Texas, even though my aunt and uncle would be better parents than I had ever been. As bad as things may be, I thought, at least this Nadia has a dog who loves her.

She stopped beside her chair, looked up at me, and shook her head gently like I was an ignorant child.

"I don't have a dog," she said.

She could read the confusion in my face, looked down at the leash, smiled sadly. "I'm staying now with his mother at the Four Seasons on George V." She pronounced it "Sank," as in Sank Roo Doe Noo. "When she first arrived in town, I told her that I had kenneled my dog on the Left Bank. And every day, I tell her I am leaving the hotel to walk her."

That was pretty audacious. "I'm—aren't you afraid that she'll find out?"

She shrugged. What did it matter? "My mother-in-law doesn't want to talk to me," she said. "She's very traditional." She pursed her lips and decided. "I think, actually, that she hates me. She seems happy to see me leave the suite every day. She'd probably be happier to see me dead, but Ali seems to like my profile."

"Ali. Your—"

"Yes," she said. "Ali. My future husband. He's 44." She shrugged those beautiful shoulders, sighed. "Not ancient, at least. A prince, one of the great houses, richer than God, to my father's great relief. He needs the money." She reached over, emptied her drink, set the glass back down with a thunk. "I hope that works out for him."

"Have you met Ali?"

She shook her head and turned to go. This was not a subject she wanted to discuss any longer.

I indicated her leash. That part, at least, was brilliant. And some part of me couldn't bear to see her walk away.

"There's no dog," I said, putting it all together. "But you leave the hotel and you come here?"

"Not often enough," Frederick said. He was drying glasses and putting them away.

She inclined her head to him before turning back to me. "*Merci*, Frederick. Yes. I come here. I sit in cafés. I walk along the Seine. I stand on the Pont de l'Alma Bridge and stare down into the river and think about jumping." She smiled, as though this was normal talk. "I pretend like no one is making decisions for me for an hour or two." She turned to go, and said so softly I could scarcely hear, "What does it matter? He arrives on Friday. I marry on Saturday. And then—" Her smile faded. Her head dropped.

She turned back toward the door.

Today was Monday. Bastille Day was on Thursday. And Saturday—

She was getting married in five days.

I slid off of my seat as well. Mr. Hemingway's stool.

Papa would do something brave, especially after a brace of whisky sours.

"*Mademoiselle*," I said, and I touched her gently on the arm just to arrest her progress.

Perhaps my touch and my intervention were unwanted. Honestly, what was wrong with me? Just let her go. She has her heartbreak and you have yours. And yet, I spoke: "Someone in London told me something the other day: 'You should not marry someone you do not love.'"

She looked at me, and she smiled, sadly, beautifully, gratefully. "That is very good advice, Calvin," she said. "For someone who has any kind of a choice." She dropped her eyes and took another step toward the door.

"Nadia," I said. I fished my wallet out of my back pocket and pulled out one of my new business cards. Again, against my better judgment. Five days. She was getting married in five days. "Take my card. If you need—I don't know. Someone to talk to." I held it out. "A friend."

She looked at it. She looked at me.

"If you need help," I said. "Call or text my cell. Any time."

"You have helped me," she said, and she favored me with another sad smile. "I have decided. I will be James Bond."

"Brave," I smiled back at her.

Those eyes considered me, but she shook her head, and her smile did not reach as far as her eyes.

"No," she said. "Broken."

But she accepted the card, looked at it, looked back at me.

"*Au revoir*, Calvin Jones."

I took her hand again. "*Au revoir*, Nadia."

She walked out into the Rue Daunou, the saloon door swinging shut behind her with finality.

And that, I thought is that. I would never see her again.

I climbed back onto my seat at the bar.

"*Tant pis*," I said. That's "too bad," in French. Just so you know.

"It is sad," Frederick said. He sighed. "I am half in love with that girl."

"Well," I said. "She is—lovely." Those sad eyes, those lips, that formidable mind.

Frederick put his hand over his heart. "More than that, monsieur. She is kind," he said. "I see many sad people at this bar," he said. "Many of them are cruel. Angry." He shook his head, started making my second whisky sour. "That one," he indicated with his head, "wants to change the world, even though the world never wishes to be changed." He smiled sadly, slid the drink in front of me. 28 to go. "If she would have me, I would marry her this moment. Today."

"You should ask her," I said, indicating the swinging door with my head.

"Ask who?" came a booming voice beside me. "Ask her what? Frederick, how are you?"

"*Bonjour, Monsieur Rob*," Frederick said, and he suddenly had a big smile on his face. Rob has that effect on people. "I should have known you are this man who comes always late."

I slid from my barstool to offer my hand. "Your fame precedes you."

"Oh, the hell with that," he said, seeing my proffered handshake. He pulled me in for a man hug. He was the size of a bear now, so I guess let's call it a bear hug. Then he held me at arm's length and stared at me for longer than I liked. "You look good," he decided. "And you look like hell."

"That sounds fair," I said. I was physically in the best shape of my life. But I had backslid a fur piece on everything else.

"What happened in Dallas?"

"It was bad," I confessed. "I'm kindly a mess." I gave a shaky laugh. "Worst going-away party ever." I tried to smile, discovered that I couldn't quite get there. The world still seemed very unstable under my feet.

"I know," he said. "I know. We'll get through it. Do you want to talk about it? All I saw was that last broadcast. Holy shit. It looked like you'd seen a ghost."

I took up that second drink and gulped half of it. "All the ghosts," I said. I took a deep breath, tried to figure out how to say this. "It was supposed to be an easy last night. Simple shoot. Black Lives Matter rally in downtown Dallas. Peaceful march. Some b-roll and then a live feed back to the studio. Easy last night." I took another drink, and that was pretty much the end of that whisky sour. "We had already done my going-away party in the newsroom before I went out to shoot. White sheet cake from HEB. Crap frosting. Not even the butter cream. And in piped blue icing, 'Good luck, Cal.'"

Frederick brought a French 75 to Rob, indicated my almost empty glass with quizzical eyebrows.

"No," I said. "I'm working."

Rob raised his glass. "*Salud.*" I clinked with my empty glass. "How many dead?"

"Five local law enforcement. And the shooter. They blew him up with military ordinance, Rob. Blew him up. It was Fallujah all over again." My hand was shaking as I set my glass down.

"That bad," Rob said. He was watching me closely, like he was trying to gauge where I was. He'd be a fool if he didn't.

"Yeah," I said. "One of the cops who died bled out right in front of me." This was the first time I'd said this out loud. The most I had said out loud. There was more I hadn't said. And probably couldn't say. I looked across the bar. "Maybe just one more, Frederick."

"At once, monsieur," he said.

"He didn't have on body armor," I said. "Nobody did. The cops were in short sleeves, Rob. It was a hot night in Texas, nobody expected any trouble." I took this drink from Frederick. "Last one, I swear." I'm not sure who I was pledging this to. One more gulp. About right to relate at least part of the story. "We were at the back of a patrol car, kneeling at the bumper. 'Stay down!' the officer tells me. I'm still live. Producer in my ear, of course, what do you see, what's going on? The officer steps out from behind the car and gets one through the lung and then one in the neck. He holds up his hand to tell me to stay back even after he's down. Like I was going to just watch him die." Rob nodded; he knew. Watching is the worst. "I got pressure on him, but it wasn't enough. He bled out under my fingertips. Bullets still flying. I couldn't save him."

"This fucking world," Rob said. There were tears in his eyes. Okay, so Rob was a teddy bear now. He was not like this when he was at FOX.

He laid his big hand on my shoulder. "You could have taken a couple more days, Cal. I wouldn't have minded."

I let out a long whoosh of a sigh. "A couple more days would not have helped, Rob." I am not a person who cries. Not at my mom's death. Or my dad's. Or any other horrible thing. I just dig a deep hole, drop something into it, shovel dirt over it until it disappears from sight. "Nothing would have helped."

He nodded again. He knew all too well. You see, we went way back, Rob and me. Rob was on-air talent like me before he stepped up to producing. We reported together from Iraq, lead correspondents for rival networks, but we were under fire together a bunch of times, and both of us saw shit no one should ever have to see.

Rob was with me on July 14, 2007—Bastille Day, I suddenly realize—when I got the news that my father, MSGT Calvin Jones, was killed in a market square in Anbar Province, along with two of his boys and fourteen civilians, by a powerful Improvised Explosive Device.

I needed more than a couple of days when I got that news too.

Then I lost someone else I loved and I kind of completely fell apart, and the network sent me home for a rest, which was both a good thing and a bad thing. The end of something.

Back in Texas, living in my father's house where every corner held the echoes of that man, I swilled Jack Daniels like it was a magical elixir that could bring him back if I drank hard enough and fast enough.

I did some violence to others in bars and in alleys as a way, I now understand, to do violence to myself. Because, for true, I had my ass handed to me more than once by members of the American armed forces in dives near Fort Hood, and I came very near to permanently damaging my only real asset, my handsome face.

All of which was in the hard-drinking tradition of war correspondents including Mr. Hemingway, I guess.

I could have gone back to the Middle East and been yet another shit-faced face on camera while bullets flew, brave as anything because I couldn't feel anything.

I might in fact still be drunk, drunk as I felt myself becoming that afternoon on Mr. Hemingway's stool in Harry's Bar, which was drunker than I had been for a long long time.

Which is how and where Rob comes back in the story, and why, to tell the truth, I had to come to Paris.

When Rob told me, "I need you in Paris," I told him, "I'm on my way."

Because without him, who knows where I'd be?

I had never said this to him, that I owed him my life, although I think he knew.

Rob was still in country while I was drinking myself to death. But when he returned to the States, he flew to DFW, then drove to Killeen, where my father had lived off base, and sat down with me in my dad's kitchen, where I was already on my fourth or sixth or eleventh drink of the day.

He sat across the table from me then, his dark cold Shiner beer half-drunk in his mug, and at last, after I'd been vomiting out my rage at my father and at Sunni insurgents and at anyone anywhere who thinks God is telling them to blow people up or cut their heads off on camera, Rob set his mug on the table, and he spoke the words he had flown all the way across the world to tell me: "This doesn't fix anything."

"What?" I dragged my bleary gaze across the table to him.

"You can drink yourself dead," he said. "But you can't drink him back alive. Either of them, actually."

I raised my head and fixed him with a stare. "Fuck you," I said.

He shook his head. "This is not what they would want, Cal."

"Fuck you, Rob," I said. I got unsteadily to my feet, my chair toppling behind me, and my fists were balled. Rob was not such a good friend nor so enormous yet that I wouldn't stagger over there and take a swing at him. "What the hell do you know about my father?"

"I know what you told me." He looked me in the eyes. "That he loved you as well as he could. And vice versa." He raised his mug, took a drink, wiped his lip with the back of his hand, still looking at me. "Oh my God, this is good. What I wouldn't give for a Shiner when its 123 degrees over there." He set the mug back down on the table.

And he said, again. "And so I know, Cal. He wouldn't want this. To see what you're doing now. What you've become."

Thus: the moment.

A good friend might tell you something that will make you feel better.

But a real friend will tell you something you don't want to hear. Even with the threat of violence looming.

Rob was right. I couldn't go on the way I'd been. And I couldn't go back to what I'd been. So I quit the network. I took a weekend anchor job at the affiliate in Dallas, where the babies there fresh out of J-school regarded me like I was some legendary pitcher from the bigs, Sandy Koufax, maybe, who had wound up back in Double A. Lo, how the mighty are fallen. And hell, maybe they were right. I was a shadow of my former self.

But for ten years, I went to bed sober most nights.

I let go of some of the anger.

I stopped having the nightmares.

I got up and went to work, met a girl, made some kind of a life for myself.

And, up until my last night on the job, it had all been okay, if only just okay.

"Do you need more time?" Rob asked me now, point blank. "I can make that happen."

I shook my head. "No. I'm ready to go to work," I said. "I think maybe I need to."

"Okay," he said. "After lunch tomorrow, I'll take you into the studio. Introduce you around. You'll have a couple of days to settle in. I've scheduled your first shoots for Bastille Day. The military parade, and then that night, the fireworks to introduce you to viewers." Then something occurred to him, and his lips pursed. "Oh. I do hope you've gotten over that fear of heights."

"I am going to beat you," I told him, my eyes going wide. "What have you done?"

"Well," he said, "we're shooting from the tower of the American Cathedral Thursday night. Best vantage point in the city for the fireworks off the Eiffel."

"How would you know that?" My heart seized in my chest. "The tower of what? American Cathedral? What is that?"

"I'm on the vestry of the Cathedral," he said to my uncomprehending face. "It's my church."

"I don't even know where to start on that," I said. "Your church? Weren't you an atheist when we were getting shot at?" I glanced at the menu Frederick handed me. "*Croque monsieur,*" I said, handing it back without having to think about it. Who doesn't like grilled cheese?

"*Salade du chef,*" Rob said. "What?" he asked, sensing my disapproval. "I'm watching my calories. Not all of us run marathons."

"I don't run marathons," I said. I had run three or four miles along the Seine that morning, past the houseboats, back across the Pont de l'Alma Bridge, and then walked down the Avenue Bosquet and back to my apartment. "And I don't eat salad."

"Fine," said Rob. "You're in great shape. At least you won't be panting when you climb to the top of the tower."

"Hooray," I said. "My heart will be pounding with terror instead." It was already, in anticipation.

"Good lord," he said, shaking his head. "I thought that would be an easy first day."

"Okay," I said. "But I'm guessing it probably won't be."

"Oh," he said. "That reminds me. I know you were dating that society girl in Dallas. But Brigid and I have someone we want you to meet. Allison. Good Anglican girl. Drinks and reads books. You'll like her."

For a few minutes there I had forgotten I was dating that society girl.

Kelly. Her name was Kelly.

Because somehow at the moment, my mind was occupied by someone else.

"We're having dinner with Brigid and Allison tomorrow night," Rob said. "Okay?"

"I need another drink," I sighed.

So Frederick smiled, and nodded, and went back to work.

3.

Paris

July 12, 2016
Tuesday

The old dreams were back.

I hadn't had them for a long time—for years, actually. But since the Black Lives Matter shootings, and now in Paris, my windows open to the sounds of far-off traffic, sweat soaking the bed, I was back in country.

I was back watching people die.

The night was dark, and all I could see were moving shadows.

And all I could hear was the sound of things exploding.

Boom.

Boom.

BOOM.

The explosions got closer and closer. I told Khalid, my driver, and Waseed, my cameraman, to get down. And in my dream, as they always did in real life, they laughed at me.

"Don't be so scared, Calvin Coolidge," Khalid said. He really did say this to me. All the time. He was so proud that he had studied American history. He knew that our President Coolidge was also called "Silent Cal," and sometimes he called me that instead. It was not entirely inappropriate.

Khalid saved my life a hundred times. Seriously. He pulled me out of riots. He drove us out of jams where men with their faces covered by kafiyas were chasing us, or actually shooting at us. He persuaded people who thought they wanted to kill me to let me go, for his sake, for the sake of the Prophet. He told a sheikh who wanted to kidnap me and sell me to some bad guys that, first, he did not want to split the profits with him, that this would be dishonorable. And second, that his, Khalid's clan, was bigger, smarter, and tougher than the sheikh's, and that it would go badly for them if the sheikh made a stupid move now.

"What is he saying?" I asked. They had talked for ten minutes in low voices, and I had only picked up a few words yet that early in my tour. Later, Khalid told me everything, but he knew now I needed to keep my eye on the ball. He smiled and nodded and said, "He says he will talk to you about the insurgents."

When I complained about the shifting sides, about the dishonesty of so many of the Iraqis we met, Khalid pulled together a pile of videotapes from somewhere and asked me to watch them. They were torture and interrogation tapes from the Baathist prisons, Iraqis who had suffered and died under the gentle ministrations of the Husseins and their flunkies. I had to stop watching. It was as bad as the insurgent beheadings, and I got Khalid's point.

Don't judge us, if you haven't walked in our sandals.

If you or those you love haven't been tortured in Saddam's prisons.

Those people were seriously damaged, that whole country was seriously damaged, and I got it, and I forgave a lot, as much as I could, because I know what it's like to be seriously damaged.

I even got *Quisas*, the Arabic concept of revenge as justice. "A life for a life," they would say, and I came to want that myself.

But, in all things, through all the terrible events I reported, I trusted Khalid, and he trusted me.

He was more than my driver.

He was my friend, and I loved him, and I could not live with myself after what happened to him.

In the dream, the explosions come closer, always closer, like the footprints of a giant, pounding his way toward us step by step. The earth shakes. My ears hurt.

And in the dreams, as always, Khalid steps away from me smiling and then disappears in a flash of violent light.

I woke up, panting, still sweating, one of those crazy ooga-ooga French police sirens sounding in the distance. It might have been my head going off. I'd had way too much to drink the night before and still couldn't seem to sleep. Not a good sign, the drinking or the insomnia.

My phone was ringing. That's what had woken me up, and now my head swiveled and I found it on the bedside table.

My ringtone was The Clash: "Rock the Casbah, rock the Casbah."

If you can't name it, it has power over you, right? Don't say "He Who Must Not Be Named." Call him "Voldemort."

I picked up the phone to check the call. Rob, I figured. Like him to do an early callout. Parades and fireworks, my ass. But the phone said different: "Uncle Jack."

This was not going to go well for me. But I answered all the same. Jack was my only living relative.

"What time is it there?" I asked, trying to convey a lightness I did not feel.

"When were you going to tell me?" he asked, a counter question, and clearly he was pissed. "I had to talk to that girl of yours to find out where you went." That must have been quite a phone call.

"I told you I was thinking about taking the job," I said. Which was true. I had told him I had an offer. And then he had told me he thought going to Paris was a stupid idea, and that was where we had left it, and then I covered the BLM shooting. I only remembered telling Kelly McNair because she had immediately told me she would come over and visit me.

"What time is it?" I asked.

"Ten," he said. "I just went off shift."

"Anything happen tonight?" Easiest way to derail him was to get him talking about the job.

"A couple of traffic stops," he said. "Broke up a fight between some homeless guys. Got called to a domestic."

"Anything that would make the news?"

"Nada." He went silent long enough that I actually pulled the phone from my ear and checked to see if we were still connected.

"Are you okay?" he finally asked. "I know last week must have been—"

"I'm okay," I said.

"Really?"

Uncle Jack was my only living relative. He was my dad's younger brother, and a Dallas policeman, and he was actually the one who found me wandering downtown after my live report, my microphone in my hands. It—and they—were covered with blood.

He found me, and he bundled me into his squad car, and he drove me home.

The truth. Well.

"No sir," I said, shaking my head. "No. I am not okay."

His answer was immediate. "Do you need me to come over there? 'Cos I will, nephew."

I actually laughed at that. Jack Jones, in his white Resistol hat and cowboy boots, striding through the City of Light.

"Rob is here," I said. "That's a good thing."

"But—"

"No buts, Uncle Jack. I'm in a bad place now. It happens, as you well know. How are you holding up?" The Dallas Police Department must be reeling. Losing a single officer was a tragedy. Five was uncharted waters, the edge of the world.

"Sweet Baby Jesus, Cal," he said. "These funerals. They are breakin' my heart."

"I know," I said. I had covered plenty. The police sirens were closer now, and the sounds of traffic through my window were growing louder as Paris began to grow light. "I am so sorry." We sat in silence. I hadn't talked about this, but maybe it was time to say it out loud. "Officer Reynolds saved my life. I mean—"

"I know," he said. He let out a sigh. "He did his job."

"You go to that funeral?"

"Yup. Wife. Three children. I thanked her for your life. It seemed to mean something."

"Thank you, Jack," I said. "I hope I deserve it." I rolled out of my bed, walked over to the sink, drew a cold glass of water. I was silent long enough that he asked:

"Cal?"

"I'm having the dreams again," I told him. I drank to the bottom of the glass, and still I was parched.

"Ugh," he said. "Well, I'd be surprised if you didn't." He sighed again. "You know, maybe you should consider another line of work."

"I was thinking about being a checker in Wal-Mart," I said. "But that comes with its own distinct set of challenges."

"Oh my Lord," he said. "Enormous women in yoga pants."

"Jack," I said. I filled my glass again.

"That simply should not be allowed."

"Go home," I said. "Hug that wife of yours for me."

"I worry about you," he said.

I nodded. "Well. You probably should."

"The dreams?"

"Khalid," I said. There was a long pause.

"Son," he said at last, "you need to let that go."

I drank, put my glass in the sink. "I know I do," I said. "Yet here I sit."

There was no answer to that. I told Uncle Jack I'd call him later in the week, thanked him for checking in, sort of apologized for moving across the Atlantic without telling him. As I was doing that, my phone buzzed with an iMessage, filtered through the wifi maybe: "What'd you get me? Coming to see. Arriv this weekend!"

Jesus. Kelly, texting from Texas.

"What did you tell her?" I asked my uncle.

"Who?"

I waited. Nothing.

"Jack, Kelly McNair just texted me that she's coming to Paris."

"Well, hell," he said. His strongest cuss word. "I just told her that you could probably use some company. And she does seem to miss you."

"She misses being wined and dined," I said. "That's all."

"That's as may be," Jack said. "I just thought it might be nice to have someone to hold right now."

"Everybody seems to think so," I admitted. "Rob is trying to fix me up."

I looked down at Kelly's message. What should I tell her in response? Don't bother? See you soon?

I didn't want to see anyone just now.

My heart was three sizes too small. Like the Grinch.

My uncle laughed and I raised the phone back to my ear. "If you don't like either one of those, the missus has this sweet little girl from church she's got her eye on for you."

"Jesus," I said.

"Don't you blaspheme. You could do worse than a girl who says her prayers."

"I'm texting Kelly not to come." I typed out a message to that effect—"Not a good time, not free this weekend," hit SEND.

The sun was coming up. "Go to bed, Uncle Jack," I said. "I'll call you this weekend."

"Sooner if you need to."

Then I remembered what was coming. "Please pray for my dad on Thursday."

"I intend to. I wish you'd join me."

I sighed. "I don't have a single prayer left in me."

"I know you think that," he said. "But it's not true."

"It is for now," I said, for that was certainly how it felt. "Thank you for calling, Jack. I appreciate you."

"Same," he said, gruffly. "You take care." And he hung up.

I put on my running clothes, pulled on my shoes, grabbed my phone and headphones. I had run through Baghdad and Mosul,

Fallujah and Ramadi. Sometimes faster than at other times. I had been chased by starving dogs, and once, by a carful of Sunni insurgents who would have killed me if they caught me. Just a few days back, I had run at sunrise in Hyde Park along the Serpentine. Now it looked like I was going to get up every morning and run along the Seine.

Not everything about my life was awful.

My phone buzzed again. "Damn, woman," I said. "You do not like to be told no."

I picked it up and got ready to text back something somehow simultaneously witty and sweet and put out.

And then I read this from a number I didn't recognize, a 713 area code. Houston, I realized. Where Rice University is: "I don't know what to do. You saw that yesterday. I just prayed Fajr by the river, and it helped a little. I am grateful for your kindness. Nadia Al-Dosari."

I set the phone back on my bedside table, felt my hand rise involuntarily to my chest. "That's a damn good use of 144 characters," I told the room.

Fajr is the dawn prayer for faithful Muslims.

What had Jack said? A girl who says her prayers?

I paused, reached back out for the phone, sat there, my fingers poised. What to say?

"I can't seem to pray just now," I ended up typing, after three replies that tried to do entirely too much. "But if I could, they'd head your way. Let me know if you need help walking the dog."

Before I could stop myself, I sent it and waited to see if she'd respond.

Dot dot dot.

The phone buzzed. "You will be the first to know."

Smiley face emoji.

I smiled back, pulled up some music on my phone, and stood up to go running.

Down the stairs I went, two at a clip. We had a tiny little elevator, but I didn't imagine I would ever want to use it, even though I lived on the fifth floor.

"*Bonjour,*" my landlady, Fantine, said on the ground floor, where she was already up Windexing the front doors.

"*Bonjour,*" I said. I stepped outside, then picked up the pace. This morning, I ran down the Champ de Mars and under the Eiffel Tower, then back along the Seine and the Quai Branly to the Pont de l'Alma, over the bridge there and left, past the so-called Diana Memorial on the Right Bank, down some steps to the riverbank, and along the houseboats moored across from the Tower.

I was listening to U2 as I ran, the album *Songs of Innocence* that appeared on everyone's iTunes account a couple of years back. Some people were upset about that, but not me. Who wouldn't want a free U2 album? And they're so good for running, the rhythm section like feet pounding the pavement—or like a heartbeat.

The paving alongside the river was cobblestoned and uneven, and I stepped carefully as I ran. Uneven surfaces can wreck your knees, as I knew too well. Then up some stairs, along the Voie Georges Pompidou, across the Seine again at the Pont Mirabeau, and back home past the Tour Eiffel to 13, rue Edmond Valentin, where I panted up the front steps, past Fantine, now polishing the brass of the gateway—honestly?—"*Bonjour, bonjour*"—up the stairs to my apartment, took off my running clothes, and wedged myself into what was quite possibly the smallest shower in Europe. If I gained five pounds, I would find it impossible to squeeze through the door.

Then I put on my dark blue suit, a red and blue Repp tie Kelly had got me at Brooks Brothers, slipped on my cordovan Oxfords. I was a different person now. I could take on the world.

That lasted for all of about ten minutes, which was about how long it took me to walk from my apartment to the studio, near the Quai d'Orsay and behind the Assemblée Nationale.

"*Bonjour*," I told the security guard, Raoul, who had been at the desk the day before when Rob brought me back to get my keys and cards and meet the staff.

"*Bonjour, Monsieur Jones*," he said as I buzzed through the security gate.

I took the elevator up to five, bonjouring continuously past the front desk and down the hall to the bullpen where I'd be working with reporters and support staff. Rob had an office—a big one—with a view of the Seine and the Place de la Concorde. There were a couple of studios, an editing suite, and some gear rooms. We had the whole floor. It was a nice spread, much nicer than the station in Dallas, and not just because of the view.

I sat down at my new desk, a blank expanse waiting to be filled.

I had nothing to do yet, nothing working until the Bastille Day festivities. I pulled out a legal pad and began brainstorming leads for stories, how I was going to get them, who I needed to talk to. If I was going to report on terrorism in Europe, I had a lot of ground to cover.

For the first time in my life, I could not wait for the morning editorial meeting. At ten we sat down, Rob, the promo producer Edgar, the web content editor Rianne, and the other reporters. They all had pitches, were following stories that mattered. Politics and culture and—

And I would be going live tomorrow for our fireworks coverage. It wasn't exactly an awe-inspiring start. But at least Rob informed the table, "And after that, he's going to start digging on terrorism and counter-terrorism stories. He'll be talking to you about that in the coming weeks."

That was why I had come, what Rob had sold the network as my expertise. It was going to mean talking to Algerian separatists and Muslim clerics and French law enforcement and rabbis and politicians. It would be real news gathering, and I discovered that I was excited about doing that again.

About doing work that mattered.

But for today, I was just doodling on my legal pad. And dreading our dinner.

"Come over to the house at seven," Rob told me when the meeting broke up.

"Do I have to? Is this a condition of my employment?"

"No. And yes, you have to." He shook his head at me. "Come make a friend. And I want you to meet Brigid."

"I met Brigid at the wedding."

He laughed. "Cal, you weren't at the wedding. I was married before I left for Iraq."

"I could have sworn I met her at the wedding. I'm Facebook friends with her."

"Well, come meet her in real life. And Allison is smart. Funny."

"I notice you don't say beautiful." I had a vision of my uncle's enormous Walmart women in stretch pants.

He just smiled and waved goodbye.

"Great," I said. "Faaanntastic. I'll see you at seven."

4.

Paris

—

July 12, 2016
Tuesday

I left work at five, walked back to the Champ de Mars café down
the street from my apartment, and settled at a table on the corner.

"*Un kir, s'il vous plaît*," I said after my waiter dropped off the
menu.

I took a quick look at the menu, but we would probably have an
apéro—a drink with some nibbles—at Rob and Brigid's, then go out
for dinner itself, so I didn't need anything to eat. "*Juste un apéritif*," I
told him, handing the menu back.

He brought my drink, and I sat and watched the traffic, foot and
car, moving down the avenues. I took a sip. Kir is made with cassis—
raspberry liqueur—and white wine, so it's light and berry-flavored.
A Kir Royale is cassis and champagne, also good. The French think
hard liquor numbs the palate. Maybe they're right. It numbs plenty
of other things too, some of them, thankfully, things that need to
be numbed.

It had been just over six months since the terror attacks in Paris,
and it might have seemed to some as if things were back to normal
except for the occasional squads of four soldiers marching down
the sidewalks with their automatic rifles. The city was quiet, but
it was also plain to me that security remained high. Rob had told
me that the American Cathedral had hired armed guards for their
Christmas services, that the bishop had broken bread at the altar
while men in body armor patrolled the sidewalk outside. But at

this moment, an American couple—was this that couple from Harry's?—sat at the table next to me, waxing rhapsodic about the view from atop the Eiffel Tower in thick Midwest accents as they sipped their red wines.

An Algerian man, his wife, and their children, the females all wearing head scarves—France has outlawed the full burqa in public—were eating an early dinner. The boy was complaining that he didn't like *frites*. Who doesn't like French fries?

Behind me, a British guy in pressed khaki shorts and a pink Izod shirt was complaining about banking or the stock exchange or some other such financial thing into his cell phone. Someone had neglected to buy something—or had bought too much of something—and in his precise and civilized way, he was giving that other person holy hell. "When you call me back," he said, as crisply as starched linen, "I want it to be as though this never happened. Are we clear?"

Crystal.

And a father leading an enormous family—mother, wife, at least five children stair-stepped down from ten years old—slid into three unoccupied tables near me, chattering in Spanish, the father telling the kids to sit down and shut up, the mother saying soothing things about how they were going to have sorbet, wouldn't everyone feel better after they had some sorbet?

It was hard to imagine that this street scene could be shattered by violence—until I started imagining it.

You know, Iraq was not always a ruin. Once, people in Fallujah walked down the street talking and laughing. You could walk into a kebab restaurant without all conversation stopping like in an old Western movie, and no one in the room would be planning to kill you—or looking as if they were.

But just months ago, right here in Paris, people were dancing at a club, and sipping coffee at a café, and watching a football match, and suddenly death was there with them.

That car driving slowly past now—that car could be ready to explode.

That man on the sidewalk—he was Arab. And he was looking right at me.

Wow.

Jack was right. I needed to let this go.

And yet, there I sat.

I took another sip of my Kir. It was not nearly enough.

There were things to be said for hard liquor.

Alcohol was strictly forbidden in Iraq. Officially, any member of the military and everyone housed on military bases was barred from owning, making, drinking, or selling it. But unofficially, just like in Vietnam, people who were getting shot at wanted to take the edge off, so you could always get something. Sometimes we had "hajji juice," a clear local moonshine smuggled in for us by contractors or bought from Iraqi soldiers. You never knew how potent it would be; sometimes it hardly budged you. Sometimes it knocked you over. And a bad batch could rack you up.

You took a lot on trust with hajji juice.

Sometimes we bought gin and whisky and vodka on the black market, carried down from Europe or up from Africa. You could get your hands on Efes Beer from Turkey, a Pilsner that reminded me of Miller High Life, which is decidedly not a recommendation. Sometimes we asked friends back home to send gin or vodka in economy-size mouthwash bottles with a little food coloring to disguise it. Sometimes someone managed to smuggle something in their luggage when they came in country, although you could also get caught doing that.

A reporter would get sent home.

A soldier would get court-martialed.

At night we drank, soldiers with soldiers, reporters with reporters, and sometimes all together.

Sometimes you got a truer story if you liquored up the men.

And of course, sometimes you just got bullshit.

We called the guy who usually smuggled in our hajji juice Faisal, not because it was his name, but because one of the reporters who covered the Middle East in the beforetime thought he looked like old King Faisal of blessed memory—beak of a nose, bushy eyebrows, goatee, all that. Our Faisal was also graying, dignified, and took our money with hauteur, like he was doing us a favor in accepting payment.

I spoke with Faisal a lot. Like Nadia from the bar, he'd been educated in the States, gotten an engineering degree from Cornell, worked for Saddam, and he lost everything when the Baathists were thrown out. He knew people, and knew people who knew people, on both sides of the insurgency. Sometimes he gave me a lead when I needed one, and I paid him extra for our booze. He needed that money to take care of his family, his wife, their children and grandchildren, although you would not have known it from his manner, or from the things he said about Americans.

He never bothered to hide his contempt for us, his anger at our coming to Iraq. If he were younger, he told me, he would be an insurgent, fighting to take his country back. He would be trying to kill me, just like so many of his countrymen.

"One day," he used to tell me, "you Americans will be gone. Either we will throw you out, or you will get tired of us killing you. Americans do not have a stamina for being killed." And eventually, he was right. Folks back home got tired of seeing American troops on casualty lists, and we pulled most of them out of the Middle East. And didn't that just inaugurate a new dawn of peace and stability?

Not that Faisal was there to see it, or to celebrate it. One day he just didn't show up with our moonshine. I put out some feelers, made some visits. He hadn't come home the night before. No one had seen him for days. His wife was frantic, grabbing at me like a madwoman.

He turned up four days later, a bullet in his head, his fine nose broken, his face bruised and bloody. He'd been caught by some Sunnis—I actually interviewed them later—who killed him as a collaborator.

Or maybe because he was Shiite. It didn't matter, ultimately. Either way, he was dead as Herod. And we did mourn.

Him, for a moment or two.

Our reliable supply of hajji juice, until we found another guy.

That one died in a car bombing. Another was shot by men with their faces wrapped as he drove in toward the Green Zone. After that, I started buying alcohol from the men in my unit. It cost more, I couldn't get as much, but I didn't care.

I didn't want anyone else killed just because I thought I needed a drink.

I finished my Kir, checked the time. It was almost seven. I checked the Google map on my phone, saw Rob's place was about an eight-minute walk, and asked for the check: "*L'addition, s'il vous plaît.*"

"I do hope everything gets sorted," I said over to the British investment banking type, who was sitting, still, with his foot tapping, transmitting his fury to the Earth.

"It had better," he snapped, but then he realized that he had snapped at me. "Sorry, old boy," he said. "I came here to relax. To unwind. And you see how well that is going."

"I feel you," I said. "Cheerio and all that."

Rob had a high-floor apartment with a balcony. I actually saw him—or he saw me—on it, and he called down to the street, "Care for a drink?"

"Oh yes," I said. Someone buzzed me in, and I walked upstairs.

At 5A, I started to knock, but the door opened and a vaguely familiar buxom blonde woman threw her arms around me.

"Brigid?" I said.

"Of course, Calvin," she told me. "My goodness. Come in. We are so pleased you are here. Rob has talked of nothing else for a month."

"Oh, surely that's not true," I said. But I went inside, and there, on the balcony, stood Rob with a tall and not unattractive woman in her thirties, dark hair, gray slacks and a white silk blouse, who was introduced to me as Allison. She was British—I hoped she hadn't just been talking to the banker on his cell—had studied at Oxford Christ Church, was working for an international development agency in Paris.

Brigid had set out some green olives, some Camembert, some dark bread, a bit of *saucisson*, sausage. It was a fine apéro, and I plated a little of everything while Rob was finishing my drink, an Old Fashioned.

"With Bulleit," Rob said. "The way you like it."

"An extra dash of Angostura?"

"Even so."

Allison was drinking a gin and tonic with a slice of lemon, British style, and then everyone was seating themselves around the coffee table. Like every apartment in Paris, this one was cramped, although unlike mine, Rob's apartment had an easy clear view of the Tour Eiffel.

"So Cal has just arrived," Brigid said, "and we are celebrating." We toasted each other.

"Rob tells me you are the best reporter he ever saw in the field," Allison said, after we'd all offered our *saluds*.

"That's guaranteed to embarrass," I said. "I was just trying to measure up to the level of my competition."

I raised my glass to Rob, who had in fact been a kickass reporter back in the day.

"It's true," Rob told Brigid. "I've never seen anybody else who could keep his head and keep reporting when things went bad. And they went very bad toward the end."

"They did," I agreed. "But in Texas, I did more weather remotes and less car bombings. So it all evened out eventually."

An apéro in Paris is like a dinner party, except that it's a pre-dinner party. Dinner comes later, 8 or 9 in France. The highlight of an apéro is conversation, although the excuse is an aperitif and something to hold you over until you eat the genuine meal. The apéro is, someone said, the French religion, which might be true, since religion certainly isn't the French religion.

Brigid had managed to place Allison and me across from each other. Well played, I thought.

"Allison," I asked, "how do you know these good people?"

"From church," she said. 'Rob and I both serve on the vestry." She saw my blank look. "The governing board of the American Cathedral."

"I'm sorry," I said, looking sideways at Rob. "I thought you brought me to France. But apparently I am back in Texas, where the most important question you can ever ask is where someone goes to church."

"There's a big expat community that gathers around the American Cathedral," Rob explained. "Americans, Brits, Australians, Kiwis. Some are religious. Some aren't. But they all like having a little piece of home."

"It's a lovely spot as well," Allison said. "The Dean's Garden is one of my favorite places in Paris. Gorgeous hydrangeas. Very peaceful. Sometimes I just sit and think."

"Well, I can't wait to see it," I said. "Allison, are you by any chance watching the Bastille Day fireworks from the tower?"

"Of course," she said. "Never miss it. It's the best view in Paris."

"Of course," I said. I looked at Rob and then across at Brigid, both of whom had looks of smug satisfaction on their faces.

But see, it turns out Allison was all right. She was not a voracious manhunter, and if I had been represented to her as a possible prize, she did not seem to be trying too hard to collect it. Perhaps it was her British reticence, or perhaps she just got a good look at me and saw I wasn't much of a catch, but whatever it was, I was thankful. I liked talking to her.

Moreover, she was crazy smart, and as I mentioned, I now try to surround myself with the smartest people I can find to make up for my tendencies toward laziness and ignorance. Thanks, Dean Mottola. She was an expert on Russia and the former Soviet Union, and I had to ask only a couple of questions out of my ignorance to find that Russia was on the move, that Putin was as great a destabilizing force in her eyes as any fundamentalist terrorism around the world, and that the world itself could not be righted until he was reined in somehow.

"James Bond," I sighed. "We need you now."

Our dinner too was lovely. We walked to this neighborhood restaurant that apparently Barack Obama had made everyone's neighborhood restaurant in Paris. La Fontaine de Mars it was, and we were shown to our table at 8:30, on the terrace looking across a plaza with, I suppose, the titular fountain. "Another of my favorites is just up that street," Rob said, motioning with his head. "The former chef for the American embassy opened his own place. Excoffier."

"Escoffier? Like the chef from the Ritz?"

"No. With an 'x.' Philippe Excoffier. Brigid and I have date night there at least once a month. The soufflés are to die for."

"It is one of my favorites too," Allison said. "I eat there once or twice a week."

Dinner at La Fontaine was simple French country food, lots of it, and it was actually very good. Mr. Obama did us right. After opening with duck pâté for the table, Allison and I had duck confit, and Rob and Brigid shared a huge cassoulet, a duck, ham, sausage, white bean, and vegetable stew. Brigid was quiet, but funny; she had a way of listening and then reflecting back something someone had said earlier with a new twist, a new insight. Rob was jovial, at his hosting best, making sure everyone had enough and too much of everything. I was reminded again why we had become friends in Iraq. Some people make your life easier and better, and Rob was ever one of those people.

Allison looked across at me. "Rob and Brigid are my two best friends in Paris. Do you know anyone else here?"

I shook my head, although that was not quite true. I knew my landlady. A bartender. A beautiful woman soon to be headed back to Saudi Arabia with a new husband.

"I've never had a lot of friends," I said. I corrected myself. "Good friends."

Rob. Khalid.

And there was once a boy named David Marshall, whom I'd known since kindergarten. Funny. I hadn't thought of him for a long time, had maybe avoided thinking of him, but there at La Fontaine, sitting at a nice dinner, I remembered the meal where I'd last spoken to him.

"I was remembering," I told the table, "my best friend David."

"From Killeen," Rob said. He was the only one who knew this story.

"One night in college," I told the table, "David declared his undying love for me." My smile broke. "I did not handle it well."

That was, as usual, understatement.

"I'm sorry, Cal. That would be—a very hard thing to handle well," Allison said. She patted my hand—not like a date would, but like a person who wanted to communicate comfort.

"I'd handle it differently now," I said. "I hope. He deserved better."

When you were an on-air personality and even moderately good-looking—which was how I thought of myself, moderately good-looking—you had to turn people down. In Iraq, I got hit on by foreign correspondents all the time. I could have found a better way. Saved his feelings. Salvaged our friendship, maybe.

"Maybe you could have complimented him on his good taste," Rob said.

Allison chewed, swallowed. "Maybe you could have told him how sorry you were that you didn't feel the same way." Her smile bore a trace of sadness. She had heard similar words sometime in the not too distant past.

"Maybe," I said.

Allison was kind. She was smart. If I wasn't going to fall for her—and I didn't think I was going to—I thought she could certainly be my friend. And that was a valuable commodity at any time, but especially just now.

So at last the mousse and crèmes brûlées were cleared away, we were lingering over port, and Rob, who was pleasantly fuzzy, began telling war stories. All of us reporters have them, a store of them, for any occasion. Funny stories, sad stories, startling stories. The worst ones, we never tell.

Rob was telling a story about how his former network, FOX News, started turning their compound, one of Saddam's palaces in Baghdad, into a fortress. I remembered: They built concrete walls, higher and thicker. They hired security forces, then a security consultant to tell them how best to use those security forces. They bought a virtual armory full of weapons, "more Kalashnikovs than South Vietnam had in their best year," Rob said. They bought armored BMWs for when they ventured out of the Green Zone. They bought rafts, so in case the compound was overrun despite all these precautions, they could slip into the Euphrates and row across to the American base.

"Or get shot out of the water as possible insurgents," I interjected, since that had always seemed more likely to me.

It was a funny story, the level of precaution for a few American journalists, but what underlay all these precautions was not the least bit amusing. I knew that Rob had also lost Iraqis he cared about. I knew that another reporter from FOX had been snatched up in an alley by Sunni insurgents—we all agreed, better Shiites than Sunnis if someone had to take you—dressed up in an orange jumpsuit, Abu Ghraib style, and had his head cut off on camera. *Allahu akbar!*

Those were the stories you didn't tell. Still, even with the ones we did, people got to feel like they had experienced something outside their ken. We, the tellers, got to feel a tiny bit understood. And if you were swapping stories, you got to be reminded that you were part of a brotherhood or sisterhood, that you were not the only one who had seen and heard and smelled those things and lived to tell the tale.

There was so much you couldn't communicate because people couldn't grasp it, or because they didn't care. How you were never not miserable when you were in country. How everyone around you stank, reeked, actually, from perspiration and stress. How the MRE's that we sometimes ate for days on end left us so constipated we wondered if we would ever shit again. How the air smelled of burning tires, how the very sky was hazed from the smoke rising from them, how it was so hot—120 degrees F. and more—that it took weeks to adjust to it, if, in fact, you ever did. How when you traveled by vehicle, you hugged your vitals, contracted yourself in hopes of protecting your organs, how the whole time you were riding, you could not help from thinking, "I'm going to be in an insurgent video." How people switched sides in Iraq like a schoolyard game of shirts and skins. These guys were on your team today; next week, they might be playing for the other team. How no matter what we did in Fallujah, it was like we had the reverse Midas touch: Everything we did there turned to shit and ashes.

Those were the things you couldn't say to anyone who hadn't been there, because they couldn't take in those truths, and that was why war stories were at last so artificial. You wanted to offer some small semblance of what life in country was like to people who couldn't, at last, bear to hear what life in country was like.

I sometimes wanted to tell the story about how the unit I was traveling with discovered booby traps in trees the previous unit had planted as part of a neighborhood beautification project. Randy, a private from Kentucky, told me, after they'd removed all the explosives, we thought, that this had become an existential crisis for him.

"It would really blow," Randy said, sounding like the cornfed redneck he almost certainly was, "to die. And it would blow ten times as hard to die in Iraq. But Jesus, Mary, and Joseph. To die from an exploding tree in Iraq? If that happens, Bud, I beg you, lie to the world. Tell them that we were heroes. Tell them something—anything—besides that."

That was a great story, but not a good story. It did not show our boys off to their best effect.

And, besides, nobody got killed by an exploding tree. So where's the drama?

Rob finished his story about the FOX fortress and turned to me. I was tired, and a little drunk, but I did have something in the chamber. I told my story about the Minefield Butcher, this enormous Iraqi in a dirty apron and turban who stood around waiting for sheep to wander into a minefield and get blown up so he could lug out the carcasses and carve them up. Sheep, being sheep, did just that. Wander, that is. This guy then had to wander into the minefield himself, of course, but he told me he had memorized the ground.

"I will never die," he had assured me, his hand on his heart.

And he never did get blown up. That was the punchline, and it was important. You could not tell that story in polite company if the butcher too wound up as meat.

Everyone laughed, even Rob, who had heard the story often. Allison clapped. She was happy, her face a little red with drink, and the color and the candlelight made her beautiful. Brigid asked our waiter for the check, and after we paid, we lingered a little longer.

This was a lovely city.

No one had gotten blown up.

All in all, it was as successful a night as you could hope.

5.

Paris

———

July 13, 2016
Wednesday

In my dreams, the giant footsteps were drawing closer and closer—like the Stay-Puft Marshmallow Man in *Ghostbusters*, I sometimes thought—but, it was never funny. Like Egon, I was too terrified for rational thought.

Boom.

BOOM.

BOOM!

"Don't be so scared, Calvin Coolidge," Khalid said, as they approached, as our houses and offices rattled.

"We should be scared," I told him. "It's going to—"

And Khalid disappeared in a flash of light that threw me to the ground, stunned, weeping, desolate.

I stood up. I was covered in blood. I was shaking.

"Where's the fucking chaplain?" I was yelling. That's what people always screamed when there was a disaster in country. An ambush, a drive-by shooting, an IED explosion. At first, I thought it was funny because it was so profane. But when people are dying, bleeding out in front of you, there's no time to waste. Better to offend. There would be time to repent or ask for forgiveness if we survived. And meanwhile, for those who wouldn't—or didn't—survive?

We needed a fucking chaplain.

The morning light was coming through my window when I opened my eyes. Maybe that was what woke me. I checked my phone. 7:15. I thought about rolling over and going back to sleep, but that would just lead to more nightmares.

Where was the fucking chaplain?

I groaned upright, threw my feet over the side of the bed, lurched into the bathroom. I put on my running clothes, picked up my iPhone, plugged in my headphones, stretched, and jogged down the stairs. Fantine, my landlady, was sweeping the front steps, I swear to you. I expected one morning to find her power-washing the sidewalk at 3 a.m.

"*Bonjour, Monsieur Cal,*" she said as I erupted from the front doors.

"*Bonjour, Madame Fantine,*" I panted. I was listening to Mumford and Sons, *Wilder Mind.* Also good for running, and I intended a long one this morning to try and clear my mind, east to and through the Luxembourg Gardens, then north to the Seine, then back to the apartment. I had just gotten my first glimpse of the golden spire of Les Invalides, where Napoleon is buried, when my phone buzzed.

I stopped at the corner to wait for a traffic light, pulled it out of my pocket, and read the text.

"Calvin—Thank you for your kindness. It is all too much. I am sorry. When you can pray, if ever you can, please pray for my soul—Nadia."

I had started across the street at the green light and I stopped dead in my tracks.

Pray for my soul.

"Shit," I said. A car, then four, honked at me, blocking traffic as I now realized I was. I jumped back onto the curb, checked my bearings. The Four Seasons Hotel was over that way, just on the other side of the Pont de l'Alma Bridge.

I stand on the Pont de l'Alma Bridge and stare down into the river and think about jumping.

"Shit," I said again.

I texted back: "Where are you. Please don't do anything until we talk." I pressed SEND, waited, hopping from one foot to the next in my impatience, waiting for the dot dot dot. Nothing.

I broke into a hard run, turned right to head back toward the Seine, tried to text something as I ran, failed miserably, pushed the microphone icon to record a text.

"Please," I said. "Nadia. Please don't. I am coming to the hotel. Please don't."

SEND.

Nothing. I replaced my phone in my pocket, ran hard along the Seine, watching the early morning vehicle traffic pick up on both sides of the river, the barges and the first tour boats and water taxis on the river. Down some stairs and alongside the river. I was sprinting, and I had to slow down. I had a hitch in my side, was panting. If I wanted to get to her, I had to slow down.

I ducked through a crowd of tourists on rented bicycles, who, I swear to you, were taking videos of the river with one hand as they slowly pedaled. I may have knocked one or two of them over. I am not proud. Around two older women powerwalking, past an Algerian guy who was skipping rope. He looked like a boxer. I made very sure not to knock him over. Then, up some stairs to the Pont de l'Alma Bridge. I crossed the street at the light, over to the west side—that was where I would cross to George V and the Four Seasons—and leaned into a faster pace again. I was close now.

Closer than I knew. As I ran along the bridge, there a block away, surrounded by tourists taking pictures of the Eiffel Tower across the Seine, was Nadia. She was dressed in her running clothes, but she was not running.

She was pulling herself up onto the green metal railing of the bridge.

"Nadia!" I shouted. "No!"

People around us looked up, curious. My tone was not friendly. It was smack-full of fear.

She looked at me, her brown eyes awash with tears. Then she shook her head, pulled herself atop the railing, crouched wobbling there for a moment suspended between river and sky.

"No!" I shouted again. More people were looking at me. I broke into a sprint, gave it everything that I had, and I am a good runner, people.

She shook her head again. When I was just twenty feet from her, she dropped over the side, gracelessly, like a bag of potatoes instead of a beautiful woman.

She hit the water hard, went under, and disappeared.

People around me were screaming. And turning their cameras from the Eiffel to the river.

Me, I was thinking, so fast I couldn't have isolated an individual thought. I knew from my lifeguard training that you never dive into water when you don't know the depth, and while I thought the Seine was plenty deep here, I also wanted to get out toward her quickly. Stride jump was the best way, I thought, although it was going to hurt like hell. In our training they used to tell us, only use the stride jump if you are no more than three feet above the water. I was a whole lot higher than that, but I didn't want to take my eyes off Nadia—or where I thought she might be—for an instant.

And so I pulled myself up onto the railing. Someone next to me tried to grab my arm, was shouting at me in Spanish. I looked over, saw a mom, dad, and family. The mother was trying to restrain me. "You'll kill yourself," she was saying.

"Possibly," I agreed. I handed her my phone and balanced for a moment atop the rail.

Nadia broke the surface for a split second, then disappeared again, farther downriver. Too far.

I could not just stand and watch.

Not again.

I took a deep breath, then stepped forward, my front leg bent slightly, into the air.

"Stride jump" is precisely what it sounds like—like you're running into the water. It's great when you need some distance to get to your rescuee quickly, need to keep eye contact on the victim so you don't lose her.

It is not so great when there's a substantial distance between you and the water.

I prepared for the impact, which was painful but not quite paralyzing. As soon as I hit, I started kicking toward where I thought Nadia had drifted. She came back up, her head and one arm momentarily above water, then disappeared again.

The river was dark, fast, cloudy. I could not see her underwater. Or anything.

The Seine was not a good river for rescuing people.

I modified my intercept course, struck out powerfully for where I thought she might be now. I am a strong swimmer, and I knew now I had to get to her quickly or she wouldn't make it.

Because I had seen: she wasn't even struggling when she broke the surface.

She intended to die.

She bobbed up again. Her eyes met mine. They were wide, wild, sad.

I was so close. Twenty feet.

Ten feet.

She went under, and I submerged, kicked hard, felt a touch of something. A wrist. I clamped my hand around it.

She tugged back, trying to pull it out of my grasp. Once. Twice. She wanted to get loose, and she was pulling us deeper into the murky dark in the process.

Not a chance. I didn't ruin my running shoes for nothing. I rolled onto my back, kicked hard for the surface, hoisted her up and out of the water. She was coughing, spluttering, trying to say something, to protest, trying to pull away from me. But not today. I was strong. I had one arm tight across her chest, the other arm stroking hard toward the bank. The current was taking us toward the houseboats on the Right Bank, but I remembered from my morning run that there were steps in the stone wall between the boats if I could just get us there. I had seen a homeless guy bathing in the river and wringing out his wet clothes where he climbed out.

We bumped one of the houseboats. For a moment, I was afraid the current might tangle us in the mooring cables, but we were lucky. I pulled Nadia into the space between boats, found rocks beneath my feet, tugged her toward those steps.

I half pushed, half pulled her up the stairs and we collapsed onto the cobblestones of the pier.

"No," she said. "I can't." She was coughing and weeping. She lunged for the river. I grabbed her and took her back down onto the cobbles.

At first she was screaming, fighting. It took all my strength to hold her. Then she gave up, and lay there crying inconsolably, and somehow that was worse.

"You don't understand," she said, after a short barking cough. "I can't marry him." She coughed again, couldn't seem to catch her breath between the coughing and weeping. "It will be . . . the end of everything," she somehow got out.

I raised my head to look at her, gasped, "I thought your family would be ruined if you didn't marry him."

"They will be ruined no matter what." She coughed again. "And if I live, they will be shamed."

"Shamed?" I suddenly remembered the honor killings I'd reported on in the Muslim world, fathers or brothers who had killed a daughter or mother who had "shamed" the family. In Syria, an honor killing is not even considered murder; I remembered how a young girl in Syria who had been raped was killed by her own brother. Even after she had found a husband, "there was no other way to wash away the shame," he told the authorities—who let him go.

"You're not a virgin," I said.

She pushed herself up on her elbows to look at me. "I am 25 years old, Calvin," she said, looking at me like the prize idiot that I am. "Of course I'm not a virgin." Nadia looked down.

"Yes, that could be worrisome," I panted. "But jumping in the Seine?"

She shook her head firmly. "I told myself once that no man would ever make decisions for me again. And yet, here I am." Her hand indicated me, the dock, Paris, the world, and two big tears rolled down her cheeks.

"That is why I jumped," she said. "Why couldn't you just let me go?"

"I'm sorry," I said, because I suddenly realized: I had taken away her choice. But then I shook my own head. There was only one possible choice. "I'm sorry. I just couldn't."

I shut up, and then I got up, warily placing myself between her and the water. Nadia waved her hand at me airily, as if to say, don't worry. Maybe the moment had passed. She got to her knees, slowly, as if she were bearing the weight of much more than one slender young woman.

Up on the sidewalk, a pod of Segues rolled by, the helmeted family of tourists completely oblivious to us down on the pier. A petite Japanese woman powerwalked down the pier toward us wearing a surgical mask, walking poles splayed out to either side as she strode. She nearly speared Nadia with one of the poles, but so far as I could tell, she didn't see us either.

That was not to last. I heard the sound of people yelling, and the Spanish family from the bridge were at the front of a gaggle of bystanders running down the stairs.

"*Pobrecita*," the mother said, kneeling next to Nadia, cupping her wet face in her hands. She looked at me. "*Un hombre valiente*," she said, handing me back my phone and headphones. You are a brave man.

I shook my head. I did what I thought I had to, and now it seemed that even that decision was the wrong one.

"I will help her," I told them, trying to clear some breathing room. "She is my friend."

I extended my free hand to Nadia, and with the Spanish family's help, I pulled her to her feet. Some of the people who had followed them from the bridge or the street were taking pictures, streaming video. I stood in front of Nadia. "Put those away," I said in several languages, my stern face on display.

In the distance, I could hear a siren, the two-note alternation.

"It's the interval of a fourth," Nadia mumbled. "Like 'Here Comes the Bride.'"

I looked at her.

"We learned intervals in my music theory class," she mumbled. I thought she might be in shock.

"We have to get you out of here," I told her gently. "Before the gendarmes or the real media complicate this even more. Can you walk?"

She was bent over. I think the fall into the river had knocked the wind out of her. And then, of course, she had swallowed much of the Seine. I had gulped in a bit myself, and it was not pleasant.

I came to a decision. "My place is just on the other side of the river," I told her. "Come and get dry. We'll figure things out."

She raised herself enough to look at me, and improbably, she was smiling like the Mona Lisa. "Is this an elaborate American ruse to seduce me?"

"Yes," I said, pulling her upright and then bending over and trying to catch my own breath. "Clearly this is foreplay. I have never been so turned on in my life." That siren was getting closer. We had to get under the footbridge, then up the stairs on the far side and over. "Come on," I said. "I need you to move."

The Spanish father and mother helped us both stand upright, pushed us toward the stairs. "Quickly," they said. Like me, they heard the gendarmes approaching. "*Arriba! Arriba!*"

I hustled Nadia up the stairs, onto the pedestrian bridge, past the Algerians selling Eiffel Tower trinkets, and once we reached the Left Bank, I hustled her down side streets. People were staring. Two completely soaked humans—I guess I could understand their curiosity. You cannot legally swim in the Seine, and *piscines*— swimming pools—are few and far between in the city.

Squelch squelch went my shoes, *cough cough* went Nadia, as we dripped toward my building, where Fantine opened the front door for us, an expression of purest concern on her face.

"*Je pense qu'elle est malade*," I told her by way of explanation. I think she is sick.

To her credit, Fantine didn't bat an eye or ask why, exactly, it was that we were soaking wet. She asked if we needed a doctor, if there was anything she could do for mademoiselle.

"*Merci*." I shook my head. Not yet. I pushed the tiny elevator door open, wedged myself into it for the first time ever, Nadia now dead weight in my arms.

In my apartment, I helped her into the bathroom, set her on the toilet, turned the Hot on in the tiny shower, pulled out fresh towels. "Take those things off," I said. "I'll find something for you to wear." I closed the door, looked through my closet. I didn't have a robe, but I could give her a long-sleeve flannel shirt, maybe a pair of my running shorts. I found some wool socks. Not a stylish outfit, but warm.

"Here," I said, handing them through the cracked door. She passed back a mess of dripping clothes. I put them into my tiny dryer. They would take forever to dry.

I could hear her getting into the shower, the water pattering off her, and I tried without much success to get that image out of my head. After a time, the door opened and then she came unsteadily into the living room and fell into a chair.

"Holy shit," she said. "That hurt."

"Of course it did," I said. "That was like a thirty-foot drop. Worse than belly-flopping off the high board."

She looked at me, and even in her strange ensemble, she was beautiful. My flannel shirt had never looked so good before. "How did you do that?" She smiled ruefully, sadly. "I thought I was home free."

I shrugged. No mystery there. "I used to be a lifeguard," I told her. "For three summers, I stared at hot girls in bikinis."

"And you saved people."

"A few."

"Why did you save me?"

I looked up. She was still wondering. And since I had taken an option off the board for her—at least for the moment—she deserved an answer, not a glib deflection.

"I have watched so many people die," I told her. "I'm haunted by every one of them. If I had to watch one more, I just—I thought it might be me in the river next."

She nodded, slowly, then her lip crumpled and she was crying again, this tragic and beautiful woman whose clothes were tumbling in my dryer.

How could any of this be possible? "Of all the gin joints in all the world," I started to say. But it wasn't funny in the room, and I didn't know if she knew *Casablanca*, and it didn't seem the time to find out.

"Would you like some tea?" I asked, instead.

She nodded, tears streaming down her cheeks.

I got up, grateful for something to do. I put on the pot to boil, looked through my stash of stolen tea bags. I pulled out a bag of Fairtrade English Breakfast I had snagged from the Hilton in London, let it steep, sliced lemon, pulled milk from the door of my miniature refrigerator.

I carried it all in to her on a tray—and had a strange vision of myself as Jimmy Stewart in *Vertigo*. Nadia wasn't in my bath robe— and I hadn't stripped her naked to change her—but the situation was otherwise disturbingly on point.

"Do you know that movie *Vertigo*?" I asked. "Alfred Hitchcock? James Stewart."

She shook her head, confused. "Does it have a happy ending?"

"No," I said. "It does not." Understatement is your friend. "I watched it for a media class. Strange movie. Stewart pulls a girl out of San Francisco Bay."

She started, then caught herself. "San Francisco Bay?"

I nodded.

"And brings her tea?" she said.

"Something like."

"Strange movie?"

"Strange and sad."

She nodded. "Like life." She took the cup, put in two lumps of sugar, stirred. She took a sip. She sat quietly for a bit. Took another sip. Then she looked up at me.

"I cannot thank you," she said. At first, I thought she might say "enough." But she did not. "I wanted to die." She took another sip. "And yet, I suppose I have to. Thank you." She looked as though she didn't know whether to laugh or cry; either would have been horrifying in that moment.

"I'm sorry," I said again. "You don't have to thank me. I just thought—"

She arched an eyebrow at me. "Thought what? Thought for me?" Her voice had steel in it.

"I thought you might find a reason to go on living," I said. "We often do."

"We do have a habit of living," she said. She looked down into her tea, then back up at me. "Well. I'll think about it."

"You would dishonor the memory of my poor running shoes if you tried to throw yourself in again today," I said, setting them in the sink. I tried to keep it light, but I found I couldn't. I turned back to her. "Please. Don't."

She set her cup down. "I saw your texts. Before I jumped."

"But you went ahead and did it."

She shrugged. "I didn't know you so well then." She gave me a tiny smile. "I understand, Calvin. Your intentions were good."

My phone buzzed with a text. Rob. "Where are you? I need to talk."

"Excuse me for a moment," I told Nadia. "My boss. My friend."

"Following a story," I texted him. "Can we talk later? Office? Drinks?"

A short pause, then a buzz. "Harry's at 4?"

"Deal." I put my phone down turned to her, took her in, her wet hair, her running mascara, the tears still glistening on her cheeks.

"I want to do a story on arranged marriages in the Arab world," I decided, on the spot, and turned to Nadia. "About the way someone's fate can get decided for her. Could we meet tonight to talk? Maybe over dinner?"

"Dinner? With you?"

"Your story could help other people. Or you can talk on background, if you want." I looked at her imploringly. "At least help me understand what it's like to have so little control over your life that jumping in the Seine seems like your best option."

She considered. "I suppose," she said, at last.

"Okay then. Can you get out this evening?"

She considered some more, pursed her lip, then nodded.

"Meet me at Fontaine de Mars," I said. "Do you know where that is?"

She nodded.

"8:30 or so?"

"I suppose," she said again. She looked down at my flannel shirt, fingered it experimentally. "Are my clothes dry?"

"Finish your tea," I said. "And I'll check."

They weren't. So she had another cup of tea. I made us some eggs, scrambled, served them with a little of the precious salsa I'd brought over. We turned away from the act I'd caught her in, from the river, as though it were an indecency someone was committing in an adjacent apartment. She asked me about the upcoming American presidential election, whether I preferred Trump or Hillary, what I made of the Brexit vote a few weeks earlier. She asked about the new job that had brought me to Paris, about Rob.

So I told her a little about Iraq, a tiny bit about my father's death, a condensed version of how Rob had come to Texas to check up on me and how he had pulled me out of a deep hole.

"He sounds like a good person," she said. "This Rob. It sounds like he rescues people too."

I nodded, to myself, to her. "Sometimes we all need rescuing, I think."

I asked her about her studies, and she walked me up to the point of registering for the PhD she would never finish.

And that was as close as we circled back to the events of the morning. Her clothes came out of the dryer. She dressed in the bathroom, and then we stood in strange shyness by my front door. It was a little like the morning after a one-night stand, two strangers who have seen each other naked. She held out her hand again, shook mine formally.

I held it for longer than the moment indicated.

I held her hand until she looked me in the eyes, curious.

"Please don't kill yourself on the way home," I said again. It felt strange. It seemed only moments ago when I had seized this hand to haul her out of the Seine, onto the bank, back into life, strange and sad as it is.

"All right," she said.

"Thank you," I said.

We shook again.

"Until tonight, then," she said. "*Au revoir*, Calvin Jones."

I let go of her hand. I did not want to. But I knew what happened in *Vertigo* when Jimmy Stewart went into the water to save a troubled woman.

It did not end happily for anyone.

Better if this could just be a story.

"All right," I said. "*Au revoir*, Nadia."

I closed the door behind her, sat down in the chair she had just vacated, and took a sip of her tea. Too sugary—like chai in the Middle East—and immediately I was back in Khalid's dining room, his wife Elena pressing tea and sweets on me.

"Just one," she would say, offering me a shot at everything in their meagre pantry. I knew better than to express more than a polite interest in anything they owned. As was typical of Arab hospitality, if I said I liked something—a fig, a bowl, their dining room table— she would offer it to me as a gift.

"Just Khalid," I would say, always. "That is more than enough."

"I cannot give him to you forever," Elena would tell me, her eyes sparkling brightly. "But you may borrow him."

"I will bring him back," I told her, sipping my tea—too sweet, too hot. I put the cup down. "I promise."

And I always did.

Until, one day, I didn't.

6.

Paris

July 13, 2016
Wednesday

I knew the way to 5, Rue Daunou now more easily, but Rob being Rob, I didn't even emerge from the Metro until our appointed time had passed, and I took more time winding down the main streets to Rue Daunou. This time, I saw the Harry's Bar neon sign easily from a good half a block away, and I stepped through the swinging doors at around 4:20, ready for my first whisky sour in Mr. Hemingway's chair.

"Frederick—" I began, but Rob Granger was already there, already in Hemingway's seat, already flushed.

"*Bonjour*, Monsieur Cal," Frederick said from behind the bar. "Monsieur Rob tells me you owe for his three drinks." His smile seemed to hold a veiled warning. "So far."

"Wow," I said, sliding into the seat next to Rob. "Well. I guess that is the deal. In Bizarro World." I put my hand onto Rob's substantial shoulder, pushed him a little. He wobbled.

"I haven't told the truth about something," he mumbled into the bar. "Haven't told you. Haven't told Brigid. Nobody knows." He took another long swig and put his glass down on the bar with a hearty THUNK.

"I haven't told the truth," he said again, a touch too loud. "Not to anyone. And that's just another way of lying."

I picked up my drink, took a sip, set it down thunk-free. Rob was making plenty of noise for all of us.

"There's something I never told you," he repeated. "Or Brigid. And it's eating me alive."

"You cheated on Brigid," I said, without thinking, without even having to think. Of course. I could almost slap myself on the forehead. I missed the signs, somehow. Only such a straight arrow would be so torn up about doing something so pedestrian, one of the failures endemic to human beings in wartime, forever and always.

He said nothing. He wouldn't look at me.

"Am I right?"

Rob let out a moan that would have been funny, if it hadn't been the sound of purest heartache. It was like someone had distilled a country and western song about lost love into one single note, one long held syllable.

"It happens," I told him.

"Not to me," he said. "Cal, I don't keep secrets. I don't tell lies. I don't do—this."

"The worst lies are the ones we tell ourselves," I said softly. Almost to myself. I had heard Rob say that more than once in Iraq. "When?"

"In country."

"I thought. But why beat yourself up about it now? You've been home—"

He slid his phone over in front of me. A story in the *New York Times*. Dateline: July 12, 2016. Yesterday. The headline: "Bodies of 'Collaborators' Found in Fallujah Mass Grave."

And he slid the story down to a photo of a woman, dark haired, dark eyed.

"I never even knew her name," he said. "Until—this."

I didn't know whether to admire his efficiency or to be appalled. This was not the Rob I knew. Faithful husband. Stacked so high with integrity that there wasn't room in his body for it all. Some of it spilled out into his reporting.

"Tell me," I said. "Tell me everything." I made a show of checking my watch. "It's Wednesday. My day to rescue drowning people."

He looked up at me, confused, and I made a face. "I'm having kind of a weird day. Later. You get to go first."

"Frederick," he called, but there was already a fourth drink in front of him. That was one good bartender.

"Tell me," I repeated.

He took a solid drink. This was going to be an expensive afternoon for me. Or for someone. Drinks at Harry's ran 15 euros a pop.

Rob's lips were tight, his mouth making strange movements. He was trying to think where to start. And knowing Rob, how to tell the story with enough background, but without making himself look better than he felt he deserved. He took a deep breath, let it out, turned to me.

"You remember that car bombing in Fallujah that took out the hospital?"

I took my own deep breath. I remembered a little, although I wasn't there. "You just barely got out of there alive." I had similar close scrapes. All of us did. Waheed and Khalid both had saved me again and again from similar things.

"It was early on, but things had already gone to shit. I know what they said later, but it *was* a car bomb. Irit got footage. All that was left behind was the engine block, smoking in a blast crater. But someone on the edges of the crowd started yelling that an Apache helicopter had fired a missile that took out the market and half the hospital. Even the people who had seen the car blow up started calling out 'Death to America!' And there I was, standing with Irit and with Musawi, my driver then."

"I remember Musawi. How did he get you out?"

He shook his head. Took a drink. Looked down at the bar. After all this time, it still freaked him out. This was not one of those war stories that you told in polite company. "He didn't. We got separated. The chants were louder, all around me: 'Death to America!' 'Allahu Akbar!' Somebody tried to grab me. Someone hit me in the shoulder." He shook his head again, harder, but he couldn't shake the memories. "They were all around me. Not a friendly face anywhere. I turned and ran into an alley. I was panting, panicked, I think. That hadn't happened in a long, long time.

"I took my next left, my next right, slid to a stop to see where to go next. I was in a nicer part of town. There used to be nicer parts of Fallujah." He smiled sadly, and I nodded. I remembered that too.

"All of a sudden, a hand closes on my wrist. Pulls me sideways, out of the street."

"What?" I had a flash of Nadia's wrist, of her hand in mine, as I fished her from the depths, pulled her out of the river.

"A woman. She pulled me through an archway, off the street. A woman in a burqa. All I could see was her hand. Her nails were beautiful. Red red polish. Then her eyes. Then her shoes as we ran. Just peeking out from under her burqa. Red. Expensive. Italian. Stiletto heels. The most beautiful shoes I've ever seen." He laughed. "I can't believe I noticed. Or that I thought that.

"Then she said, 'Come with me,' and she pulled me through a heavy wooden gate, locked it behind us. We ran up two flights of stairs. She closed another door behind us. Locked it."

He shook his head, drained this drink as well. "It turned out everything under that burqa was beautiful." He tapped the glass on the bar, once, twice, a third time. He set it down and turned to me to see what I was thinking. "I still don't understand. What happened next. Why. But—I was so grateful. So grateful to be alive. To feel a human touch. Do you understand?" I nodded slowly. "It wasn't that for a second I stopped loving Brigid. It's that this woman saved me for Brigid, somehow. Saved me for whatever came next." He dropped his head. "Ah, that's just an excuse. We excuse what we should never have done." His forehead hit the bar. "The worst lies are the ones you tell yourself."

I raised his massive head with my fingers under his chin. "She did save you, Rob," I said. "There's no doubt about that. You wouldn't be here without her." And so much for not telling him:

"And you saved me back in Texas. Without her, I'm not here either. Without her—"

I caught myself before telling him about Nadia, but I needn't have worried. Rob was deep in thought. Lost in memory. He looked at me, down at his empty drink, then out through the front window at what we could see of the Rue Daunou.

"Funny thing is—" He shook his head again. "I never saw that woman again. The riot blew over as quick as it blew up. She sneaked me back down into the streets that evening after dark. I called Musawi—he was crazy with worry—and he came and picked me up. When the car pulled up, I turned around to thank her, but she was gone."

"She couldn't be seen with you," I said. "You know that."

He nodded. "Right. She knew that if she was somehow connected to me if would be awful for her. For her family. I understood that. I just never knew if she survived the war. Not until yesterday." He raised a shaking finger to order another drink, looked at his finger, thought better of it. Frederick nodded to me; he too believed Rob had had enough.

Now he just put his massive head back down on his arms, spoke into the bar, spoke his regret. "She died because of me. She saved my life. And I got her killed."

"You don't know that," I said. "You remember those signs in Fallujah. 'Anyone who collaborates with the Americans is a traitor and deserves to die.'"

He nodded.

"You might have been the only American who ever saw her nice lingerie. For some reason, I hope so. But I'd bet good money that wasn't the only time she ever helped an American." I put my hand back on his shoulder. "You didn't kill her, Rob."

He sat with that for a moment. Took another deep breath. Let it out. He was unconvinced. "Maybe so." He raised his head. But he indicated the story on his iPhone, her picture. "I pushed this out of my head for ten years. More. Now I can't pretend I don't know. That it didn't happen." He took a deep breath, let it out. "I can't lie about it anymore."

I looked over at Frederick, for some reason. He was listening without seeming to, and he gave me a slight nod. I nodded back.

"All right," I said. "Then you have to tell her."

"What?" Rob jerked. It's not the usual barroom advice, but I knew Rob, and I knew the only way he could live with himself, could put this to rest, or at least start to.

"You have to tell Brigid. Just exactly the way you told me. Tell her what happened. Tell her the truth. That this woman saved your life. That you didn't intend what happened. It just did."

"I'm a married man. Was a married man when I went to Iraq." He looked up at me, and his face was bitter with self-loathing. "I didn't have to fuck her."

Rob did not say words like that. He was being brutal because he wanted to be brutal to himself. Good people cannot understand their failures.

"You—you were grateful, you said." I sought for the words. "Sometimes only the things that matter most to us matter enough." I set my hands back on the bar, picked up my drink, drained it. I nodded, met his gaze. "Tell her."

He looked terrified, and well he might be. He had a good life, a woman he loved, and this conversation might be the end of all of it, although I hoped and maybe even prayed it would not be.

"You really think I should?" He looked down, back up, and his eyes were fixed on the bottles behind the bar. "Jesus. Jesus fuck."

Frederick leaned in—I mean, he could not pretend he had not heard. "Monsieur Cal," he said. "Is this truly wise? She does not have to know."

I nodded firmly. "I don't know Brigid well," I admitted. I turned to Rob. "But I know you. You said you can't live with yourself. And you. You're—honorable. Chronically late. Yes. Maddeningly late.

But honorable. You, Rob, are a good man." I raised my hands. "You can't do something other than the right thing. And the right thing is to tell your wife the truth, ask her forgiveness, and to take your medicine."

"What will she do?" He still looked terrified.

"Is this the only time—"

"Yes," he spluttered, offended beyond belief. He wouldn't even let me finish my question, and to my great satisfaction, I saw that now he only looked royally pissed off.

This was the Rob I loved.

I nodded. Of course. "You have to tell her the truth."

I caught his eyes, nodded again.

He nodded back. Slowly. Somberly. He had never strayed again. But this one time had to be accounted for.

I got it. We have to make amends. Some time. Somehow.

I let out a deep breath. I couldn't see any other way. "You've got a lot more on the plus side of your ledger. All the times you didn't cheat. That you took out the trash. All the anniversaries you remembered."

It did not comfort him. "She is going to be furious."

I nodded. "Yes. Just as you would be. But you'd listen to her story. You'd weigh all she is to you, all she's ever been, all she's going to be. And I think, on balance, you'd still be grateful to have her, no matter what happened one afternoon on the other side of the world."

"You are rescuing drowning people today," he said, weaving a little before steadying himself upon Mr. Hemingway's stool. "Wait. What does that mean? Drowning people?" He fixed me with his gaze, waited for me to answer.

I looked at Frederick, who was also interested. "I—saw someone jump into the Seine today," I said, weighing what I could say here and what I shouldn't. "Someone I knew." I shrugged. "I went in after her."

Frederick leaned halfway across the bar. "Nadia?" he asked, grasping my forearm.

I nodded, patted his hand until he relaxed his grip. "Yes, Nadia. But she's alive. She's okay." I amended that. "Okay-ish."

Frederick turned, poured himself a full shot glass of something amber, tossed it down, looked across the bartop at me. "She kept talking about her only way out." He was angry with himself, like he somehow could have stopped her. "I am a fool. Such a fool. Always she is talking about going into the river. I thought—I thought maybe she is not serious about this. Just talk." He poured himself a second drink, knocked it back, set the shot glass down with a clack. All of us were going to be tight before very long at this rate. "At least, I did not wish for her to be serious."

"I pulled her out of the river, Frederick. She wasn't badly hurt. And she said she wouldn't try it again. I believe her, although her choices look pretty bleak. They don't seem like choices at all." I shrugged. I had done what I could. "For now, she is among the living. I think she will stay that way."

"That's my lifeguard," Rob said, a little too loud, as he clapped me on the back, a little too hard. "I remember your stories— Hey." He looked at Frederick. "This woman wouldn't happen to be gorgeous, by any chance?"

I too looked at Frederick. He looked at me, wondered how I would respond.

"She is," I whispered, at last. "Lovely." I looked down at the bar, at my drink, at my future. Took a deep breath. Let it out. "And she is getting married on Saturday." I remembered that conversation on the pier, the complications. "Or she's supposed to."

"Huh," Rob said. "Well, she does not appear to be joyful about those impending nuptials."

"No," I snickered, very much against my will. "She most certainly does not."

"It is not Saturday yet," Frederick told me. "And she is not married to this Ali yet." He put his hand on his crisp white apron, right over his heart, his face worked for a moment, and then he decided to say it. "If I had saved such a woman, Monsieur Cal, I could not watch her marry someone else."

He looked at me significantly and I shrugged. Agreed. But.

"What can I do?" I asked the bar.

"Tell her," Rob said, suddenly.

"What?"

"Tell her," he said. "You feel something for this Nadia. I can tell by the way you talk about her."

"I—"

"Tell her the truth," he said. Frederick agreed, his chin going up and down.

"Yes. But. No. I can't—she's—if I—"

Rob hoisted up his hand. I guess maybe when you're cutting through the bullshit in your own life, it inures you to the bullshit in someone else's. "So maybe your heart gets broken. So what? You haven't let that happen to you since we left Iraq. Since your father. Since Khalid died."

"I can't." Nadia was a story. That was all. An interesting story. Maybe a beautiful story.

But she wasn't my story.

She could never be.

"Are you going to see her again?" Rob asked.

I checked my watch again, purely a reflex, although Rob caught it. "Okay. Fuck you. We're having dinner tonight." I caught his eye. "To talk about her story."

"Do not watch her marry this man she does not love," Frederick said leaning back into our conversation. As I said, we were all now a little bit toasty. Or a lot. He shook his head now, two or three times, big arcs of his beard. "Do not do that, I beg of you."

"Tell her," Rob repeated.

"Be like James Bond, Monsieur Cal," Frederick said. Huh. This Frederick remembered every single word said at his bar. He would,

I thought idly, make a hell of a source for some hard-drinking Paris journalist, if I were ever to know such a person.

"James Bond," I said. "Broken?"

He shook his head. "No. Brave. You know this. James Bond is broken by the past, but he goes on. He—perseveres. This is where the bravery is." He pointed his finger right at my heart. "That is what you told Nadia."

Well. I did say that. And at the time, I sort of believed it was true. Rob looked at me. I looked each of them, and decided. Sort of.

"*Inshallah*," I said. It's an Arabic phrase that means "If Allah wills it." Kind of how back in Texas, people would say "God willing and the creeks don't rise." As in Texas, in Iraq what it usually meant was something like maybe, or possibly, or we'll see, or I would like to, but I don't know if that will be possible.

If, in response to your invitation to meet, someone said "*Inshallah*," you might figure that they were planning to do anything but meet you.

"No," Rob said, shaking his head vehemently. He knew what I was saying. "This absolutely has to happen. I'll expect a full report on your conversation tomorrow." Then he had a thought. You could watch as it made its tortured way from his addled brain to his suddenly snapping fingers. "Hey. Invite Nadia to watch the fireworks. At the Cathedral. The Bastille Day fireworks."

"I'm working on Bastille Day. For your network, in case you'd forgotten."

He rolled his eyes. "You're on camera for like four minutes. Either side of that—" He sat up straight, snapped his fingers again. "Your boss says, invite her. This Nadia."

I nodded. "Okay. I'll ask." I turned to the bar, because something had suddenly occurred to me. I looked across the bar top. "With your permission, Frederick. I believe you fell for her before I did."

He smiled sadly. "Good luck, Monsieur. Even if I had rescued her from the Seine, she would not be for me." Then he laughed. "But

I am a bartender. You know what they say. I will probably fall in love with someone else by week's end." His voice was jaunty, although his eyes were sad.

"You need to find someone this week, Frederick," I said. "So you can bring her to Nadia's wedding on Saturday."

"No more of that talk," Rob said, elbowing me, hard. "The truth will set you free." Quite suddenly he got more sober. "And me. All of us, I hope."

Rob climbed slowly down from the stool shortly after. He went downstairs and washed his face in the bathroom, dried his face, hands, hair, tightened his tie. Back upstairs, he turned to me and said, "Say a little prayer for me."

I hated myself, but I couldn't lie. "I'm sorry, Rob. I wish I could."

"I will pray for the both of you," Frederick told me, before turning. "Go with God, Monsieur Rob."

A couple of Japanese tourists pushed through the swinging doors, took a look at Frederick crossing himself with looks of alarm on their faces, and fled, the doors swinging wildly behind them.

"Hmm," Rob said. "Well. Merci, Frederick. Always a pleasure." He turned to me and said, in a clearly audible stage whisper, "Big tip."

I nodded. "Of course. It's going on my expense account. Like dinner tonight."

He arched his eyebrows. "This had better be a good story."

"Oh, there will be. More than one, I suspect, before it's all over." Then I realized something: this whole truth thing might not go well. The right thing was not always the best thing. I called after him. "Rob. Call if you need a place to stay tonight."

"I'll be fine," he said, although he did not appear to be fine. He appeared to be very worried.

He departed for the Metro station, the doors swinging behind him as Frederick went into the kitchen and wrangled food for some customers in the back booths. I stayed on for another drink. There was time before I needed to leave for the restaurant.

Frederick leaned across the bar toward me, lingered for half a moment, and turned his head a little sideways. Then he said, discreetly, "You might wish to shower before you meet Nadia." It was not a suggestion.

"You're right," I said. "My God." I smelled like the Seine. "Just the one drink. And I should dress up, shouldn't I?"

He nodded. "May I say something?" he asked, as he reached for glass and bottle, began making something.

"Of course, Frederick," I said, motioning that he had the floor. "You haven't steered me wrong. Yet."

"In this place," he began, "I sometimes feel like a priest." He indicated himself, his apron, tie, the bottle and glass in his hands. "I offer blessings, I serve communion, I hear confessions. I have heard some of Nadia's."

"Don't tell me anything—" I began, but he shook his head firmly.

"Of course not. A good priest does not dishonor the confessional. But I know this: Something in the past has broken her heart," he said. He shrugged. "I do not know what this is. Or who. But that broken heart makes her more willing to be unhappy. To give up on her dreams. Perhaps even to marry this Ali that she does not love." His face was expressive—you could read the sorrow in his eyes for her. "That sad Nadia does not believe that she will ever love again. She does not believe that happiness is even possible, that dreams can come true. She is afraid." He finished fixing my drink. "Perhaps you are here to help her realize that she is wrong."

He placed the drink in front of me, then leaned against the back bar, shrugged. He had said what he needed to say.

I had been in relationships with women I did not love, had known instinctively what Anna in Selfridge's had said to me in London, that you should not marry where true love isn't present. But maybe I had thought that was all there was ever going to be. I recalled going with Kelly McNair to a weekend party at Lake LBJ in Kingsland, Texas, south and west of Dallas, a few months after we publicly became a couple. Her friend Rebecca owned a house on the lake with lots of balconies and Jet Skis, and Kelly wanted to go out and spend the weekend and drink a lot of champagne cocktails and show me off. I will tell you that people are unaccountably thrilled by meeting personalities on the local news. If they saw my paystub, that thrill would dissipate. I couldn't have paid the bar bill for the weekend, let alone thought about ever buying this second or third home with seven bedrooms and as many baths and three levels of terraces and patios and decks looking out onto the lake.

We were bouncing trough to trough in a speedboat across that lake, then speeding under a highway bridge. Rebecca's boyfriend was driving, fast and a little sloppy, since he was sloppy drunk, and I was lying across the back seat, swimsuit on, shirt off, ready to jump for my life if necessary.

"You two make such a beautiful couple," Rebecca was saying to Kelly, who was nodding.

"I know, right? Look at that face. Look at those abs." She smiled, indicated herself. "Look at these boobs. State of the art."

"I know," Rebecca said. "You have got to set me up with your surgeon." She shouted across at me. "Calvin!" For she was a little toasted as well. She had rented a margarita machine for the back deck, and I had seen her make a steady series of pilgrimages there before we set out. "Calvin!"

"Present," I said.

"When are you going to pop the question to this beautiful lady?"

A whoop came from the front of the boat, Rebecca's boyfriend veered hard to the side to avoid a buoy that somehow he had not noticed until the last moment and then veered back, we sort of all fell into the floor in a heap, and the prospect of impending death rescued me from an answer.

But afterwards, in our room looking out over the water, as I looked at those quite impressive breasts and I suppose she was taking in my not-unimpressive abs—I did my best—I couldn't help speaking what felt like some truth.

"You know that's not love," I said, indicating the two of us with a hand. "Matching body parts. Attractive couples."

"Cal," she snorted. "What does that matter? We look good together. We are good together. We don't expect too much. And the sex is good." She took my hand, put it on one of those breasts.

"The sex is good," I said. And we didn't expect too much. Those things, at least, I could assent to.

Now I looked around Harry's New York Bar on a Paris afternoon.

"The things that break us make it hard to see past them," I murmured, now. "How real happiness might be possible." I didn't mean for Frederick to overhear, but he was nodding.

"I do not know you well, Monsieur. But I see things. I know that you both are afraid that there is no more than what you have seen and felt up to now." He picked up another glass, another bottle, began to pour. "I am only a bartender. But, as I say, I see much from this spot." He indicated the bar, himself. "I see that this hard life is also full of possibility for those who will stop being afraid."

This hard life.

I thought of Khalid, my friend, my lifeline, disappearing in a flash of light. Of my father dying in the midst of his boys, who afterward wept and fired their M-4s toward all the points of the compass in the tiny hope they might inflict some pain on somebody with some connection to that murderous device.

I thought of DPD Officer James Reynolds, who bled out beneath my very fingertips.

And I thought of possibility.

Ten years ago, Rob had sat across from me in Killeen, Texas, and challenged me to go on living, just as this bartender, this whisky priest Frederick was doing now.

"I do not know your story, my friend," he said. "But I do know that now is the time when it could change." He shook his head. "Life does not offer us many such chances."

Maybe only one or two in a lifetime.

I nodded, and I was decided.

"I will try to be brave," I said.

He nodded, then smiled broadly. "Do more than that, Monsieur Cal," he said. "Take a shower. Meet this woman for dinner. Make her happy." He began washing the dirty glassware. There was a lot of it now. Rob and I had not been Frederick's sole customers, although we had been his best. "Maybe the world changes. Here. Now."

"And if not?" I said. "What if this really is as good as it's ever going to be?"

He laughed and indicated the shelves behind him with his head. "Then it is good to know that there is always something to drink at Harry's Bar. And that you know a bartender."

"True that," I said. I got to my feet. It was time to try something new.

Inshallah.

7.

Paris

July 13, 2016
Wednesday

I stood under the water in my tiny shower for a long long time, trying to get a little bit more sober and to get the Seine off me and to wash the stench of my fear down the drain. The water went from hot to warm to lukewarm to cold, and yet I stood while Mumford & Sons played loud in my living room—"And I'll find strength in pain"—one song after another about living with courage and coming out of your cage and facing the ghosts of your past, damn them.

Okay. Okay. I get it. I do not require an entire book full of attempts to get me to eat green eggs and ham. I'm convinced. I will eat them on a boat. And I will eat them with a goat.

And then my phone rang from the bathroom sink: Rock the Casbah. I turned off the water, reached out, checked the caller. Rob.

"Hey," he said. "Are you at dinner?"

"No," I said. "We're meeting at 8:30. Are things okay over there? Did you tell her?" I threw a towel around myself to at least slow down the dripping.

"No. And yes. She is pissed, Cal. She is so angry at me. She's in the bedroom crying. Right now. I can hear her." Then he went into whispers—real whispers, as opposed to drunk stage whispers. "Cal, what if I lose her? I should never have told her. Oh my God. This was a terrible decision."

"Could you live with yourself?" I paused to listen. "If you didn't tell her?"

There was silence on his end.

"Brigid loves you," I said. I could see that the other night, the way she looked at him, the way they finished each other's sentences. "She loves you and she admires you. And yes, she is pissed as hell right now. She was always going to be."

My phone buzzed. *Grand Central Station. Please take a number.*

My Uncle Jack on the other line. I shot him a canned text: "Can I call you back?"

"Stay strong," I said. "Listen to some Mumford and Sons."

"What? What does that even mean? Cal, help me. She's crying like I've never heard her cry before. Like someone died. Like I broke something precious." I could hear the terror and despair in his voice. If he lost this, if he lost her, what would he be?

I didn't even want to think about a world with a hopeless Rob in it. I even thought about saying a prayer.

Then there was a voice in the background—Brigid.

"It's Cal," Rob said. Something I couldn't hear. But with an edge to it. "No. He told me to tell you."

There was a moment, maybe a scuffle. The phone being handed over. Or ripped loose.

"Cal," Brigid wailed. She did sound like she had been crying. I envisioned her eyes red, her face puffy. "Did you know this? Have you always known?"

"No," I said. "I found out today. Just like you did." I took a deep breath. "But I know the same man you know. The one who saved my life when I was trying to step off the planet. The man I will always love and admire."

There was a sniff, then a full-blown sob on the other end.

"Brigid," I went on, "you know Rob better than anyone else. But I know him too. He's my dearest friend. And the most honest man I've ever known. He's got more integrity in his little finger than I have in my whole body." I paused, tried to think about how to put this. "I don't think what happened in Iraq was about betraying you. It was about thanking someone who rescued him."

"You do not have to say thank you with your dick," she wailed, then caught herself. "Forgive me."

Well. There is that.

But.

"Brigid," I said. "Sometimes the only way to say thank you is with the most precious thing you have. That woman saved him for you, and for me, and for the world." I looked at myself in the mirror, dripping, my hair a mess. I needed to be at Fontaine de Mars in mere minutes. But I doubled down: sometimes the hard truth is the only medicine that will heal.

"Do you believe that he loves you and only you?"

There was a small groan from her end of the line.

"Do you believe that Rob is a person who seeks to do what is right?"

Silence.

"Do you know how much courage it took to tell you this thing that he could have kept from you forever?"

Nothing. From the living room, Mumford & Sons sang: "I really fucked it up this time, didn't I, my dear?"

"Brigid," I went on. "I cannot tell you not to be angry. I was surprised when Rob told me today, but I got my head around it. It has not changed the way I think about him. I came across the Atlantic to work for him because he is the finest human being I have ever known. That's all. He still is."

She sobbed. I waited. It slowed. I could hear her trying to stop.

"You are a good friend," she said. "Of course you will defend him."

"Brigid," I said, "it's more than that. Without Rob I would not be on the planet. You know that. And I have to believe that my being here is a good thing, somehow."

"Of course it is," she said.

There was a long pause.

She sniffed. Then she decided.

"He is sleeping on the couch tonight," she said.

"Okay," I said. I could accept that. "Will I see you tomorrow at the Cathedral?"

"Yes," she said. "He said you are going to bring a girl. Your girl. This Nadia."

"Jesus," I said. "He told you that she's my girl?"

"Don't blaspheme. Rob said you need to do this. That you have not loved anyone in too long." I could hear that she still preferred Allison, although I was sure that was low on her current list of issues.

"Do you believe him when he says such things?" I asked.

There was a moment's silence, then a sniff. "Yes," she said. "Of course I do."

"Please put him back on," I said. "I've got to go meet her. This Nadia."

"Cal," he said. I could tell he'd been crying too. "What did you say to her?"

"Just the truth," I said. "Get a comfortable pillow. You may be on the couch for a while."

He laughed. Actually laughed. "You should get going. You're headed to the restaurant, right?"

"Yes," I lied. "You okay?"

"No," he said. "But maybe I will be. Thank you."

"*De nada*," I said. "Or whatever the French version of that might be. I'll see you."

I hung up. Uncle Jack had texted me back: "Call me when you can."

After I brushed my hair and my teeth, I put on deodorant and a spritz or two of Spicebomb, this cologne in a black grenade bottle that Kelly McNair had gotten me for Christmas. Despite the packaging, I liked it. It was bracing. I tugged on a nice pair of khakis, a crisp blue button-down shirt, a striped Repp tie, a black blazer. I slid my feet into some nice black Oxfords I usually wore with a suit. They were polished to a sheen—I could see myself in them.

Then I walked down the stairs and over a few blocks to the restaurant. I checked in with the maître d' and looked around. No Nadia. We still had a few minutes before our reservation time.

"I can seat you now, Monsieur Jones," the maître d' said, "if you wish. I have zis outdoor table for you."

"Very good," I said. Now that I was here, I was suddenly short of breath. I could feel the sweat dripping down my spine. What if she didn't come? What if I was now ready to climb the mountain—and the mountain could not be found?

I was seated in front of the restaurant on the sidewalk. The pedestrian traffic was substantial—lots of people in town for *le 14 juillet*, which Frederick had informed me is what French people call Bastille Day. My waiter checked in with me, and asked in French whether I wanted French or English menus. I hesitated, which was all the information he needed. "I will get zose right out," he said in English. "Would you like anything to drink?"

"Kir Royale," I said, and he went off to put that order in.

I surreptitiously checked my watch. She was late. 8:40.

I looked back up the street behind me, checked the traffic. A sanitation truck was coming down the street. 8:45.

She wasn't coming.

Oh well, I thought. I was willing to try, at least. Maybe that proved something.

"Calvin?" came the soft voice from behind me.

I turned. "Nadia?"

She nodded, put her hand briefly on my shoulder, slid into the seat across from me. She was wearing a navy skirt, a white blouse. She looked like an old-time movie star.

Ingrid Bergman in *Casablanca*. Backlit. Luminous.

Stunning.

Of all the gin joints in all the world . . .

I didn't say it.

She had a small metallic silver clutch that she slid onto her side of the table. "I'm so sorry," she said. She took a deep breath, let it out. "I was sitting in the bar at the Four Seasons. Time got away from me." She looked down at the red-checked table, then across at me. "I don't know why I thought I needed a drink." She smiled.

"Maybe you were nervous," I said. "Or scared, even."

She looked across at me sharply. "Of course I'm scared," she said. "What person jumps into the Seine who isn't scared?"

I picked up a fork, turned it left and right. "I just—" I set it back on the table. "Well." I raised my hands. "Frederick—at Harry's—he told me we were both scared." I shrugged, smiled, ready to move on if this didn't land.

"Frederick? The bartender?" She smiled. "He stands there so quietly."

I shrugged. "But he sees everything."

She shrugged in turn. "I thought about not coming. About just eating at the Four Seasons bar," she said. "Ali can certainly afford it. But my mind rebelled at the prices. Did you know that their Club Sandwich was 86 euros?"

"Holy shit," I said. "Sorry. I do like a good club sandwich. But isn't that, like, $100 American?"

"Exactly," she said. "I could not do it." She sighed. "What is wrong with me? Maybe I'll get used to conspicuous consumption. Maybe I'll eat hundred-dollar sandwiches every day."

Maybe she would. I looked away. All right, then. I felt a gate in my head swing shut with a clang.

Okay. I pulled out my pad, clicked my pen. "So. Let's get started. When was the last time that you saw your father?"

"Hmmm," she said. She pursed her lips. "I think it is many years now. The last time—I was in prep school. At Phillips Exeter. He drove up from New York. He was in the States for a meeting with some American petroleum engineers."

"Did he say anything about what he had planned for your future?"

"Then?" She shook her head. "But I knew. I had friends from Saudi who had been sent to Cornell, Baylor, Vanderbilt. They expected that they would wind up back in Saudi eventually, married to someone very rich. I don't know that they were disturbed by that as I was. Let's just say that they had different goals."

"Could you have told your father that you did not want to marry someone you did not love?"

She shook her head, looked at me gently. "That isn't done in my culture," she said. "I am intelligent, and I have opinions and desires. There are things I hope to accomplish. But in Saudi Arabia, family is everything, and the man is the man. A man decides if you can work, if you can travel. A man makes every important decision. And most of the unimportant ones." She looked into the street, where the garbage truck was collecting trash right next to us, and then back at me. "What about your parents, Calvin? When did you last see your father?"

"Almost ten years," I said.

"Ten years?"

"He died in Fallujah," I said. "On Bastille Day, 2007."

"I'm sorry. He was a soldier, then?"

Oh yes," I said. "To the core."

"Do you miss him?"

I watched the garbage truck from my angle, looked down at the table, across at her. I could not say yes or no to that.

"We left many things unfinished," I said.

"And your mother?"

"Dead before that," I said. "A long time before that. She was lovely. I think."

"Oh, Calvin," she said. "I am sorry for all of that." She looked up from the table and into my eyes. She had beautiful brown eyes.

"Well," I said. "At least they aren't around to try and force me to marry someone. Although my aunt and uncle kindly would like to do that."

"Kindly?"

"It's a true Texan expression," I said. "Instead of 'kind of,' I guess."

"Kindly," she repeated to herself. "I did not learn this at Rice. So your aunt and uncle would kindly like for you to marry the society girlfriend?"

"Maybe," I said. "Kelly McNair. She is beautiful. Perfect. And cold as the grave. I don't know what she thinks or what she wants or what she loves." I sighed. "And I guess she'd say the same about me." I shook my head, shook all the cobwebs loose, turned back to my list of questions. "How long have you known that your father intended to marry you to a wealthy Saudi?"

She looked down at her red nails. "Is all this really what you want to ask me?"

"I thought we were here to talk about your arranged marriage." I indicated my pad. I actually did have questions. "Not mine."

"Is that why you invited me tonight? Why you put on your nice shoes?" She actually smirked a little, her nose twitching. "Why you sprayed yourself with cheap aftershave?"

I put my pen down. I was having a hard time keeping a straight face.

"It's cologne," I said. "And I have it on very good report that it is not cheap."

"Is that why you pulled me out of the water today, Calvin?" she persisted. "Because I was a story? A subject for you to interrogate?"

She looked at me, and I could not deny it. Could not pretend I did not feel something.

Everything.

All right, then.

I clicked my pen. Closed my pad. Put it in my jacket pocket. Crossed my hands on the table in front of me.

"No," I said. "You know that it isn't."

Our waiter turned up at the side of the table, a chalkboard menu in hand. "*Ah, la belle mademoiselle,*" he said.

"*Merci,*" Nadia said, smiling at him.

"May I tell you about our specials?" he asked, and then he proceeded to. He had brought the English board, and we ordered off it. "Does mademoiselle wish a drink before dinner?"

"A drink?" she murmured. She nodded to herself. "*Oui. Un Prosecco, s'il vous plait.*"

"And we'll have a bottle of the house red," I said, "with dinner." He nodded, and went off to put in our orders.

"My mother-in-law almost pulled a knife on me," she said. She looked up at me, and then a small smile began to spread across her face. "When I told her I was going out to dinner with a friend. 'Your days of having friends are over, little girl,' she said. She stood in front of the door, blocking the way out."

"Arab women are tough as hell," I said. I knew all about that.

"I told her she could try to stop me. But I told her that when Ali asked me why his mother was in the hospital with broken bones, I would have to tell him, 'her own clumsiness.'"

"Jesus," I said. "I didn't realize you were a ninja badass."

"I'm not," she said. "But I wanted to come to dinner tonight." She glanced down at the table. "I wanted to see you."

I looked across at her. "Why?"

She looked across the table at me, and her gaze made me tingle.

Our waiter arrived with our drinks and stepped back, waiting expectantly.

"Shall we?" Nadia asked.

We took a look at the menu. Nadia ordered the duck. *Le canard.* I asked for the Wednesday special, *Coq au vin.* We would suspend judgment on dessert, but I suspected chocolate mousse.

The waiter stepped away. Nadia raised her glass, nodded at me.

"*Salud,*" she said.

"*Salud*," I returned. I could not help but say it. "I am glad to see you."

"And I too am glad," she said.

We clinked glasses, drank, set them back on the table. We set for a moment in silence, then she spoke.

"When I was at Stanford," she said, a finger trailing in the bubbles of her glass, "I bought a scooter." She nodded to herself. "It was a radical act."

"Because Saudi women aren't allowed to drive," I said.

She raised her glass, saluted me, drank. "Exactly."

"Fucking sharia," I said.

"Pray let us leave Islam out of this," she said lightly. "I bought the scooter from an engineering student. Ian, at Cal Poly. He was from Brighton, originally. Had come over to study mechanical engineering. Brighton is on the south coast of England. A resort town. I looked it up after we met."

I nodded. I knew vaguely where Brighton was. The shore was rocky, as I recalled. It was a terrible beach.

"When Ian sold me the scooter, he told me he'd teach me to ride. He was good as his word. He used to sit behind me, his fingers on my sides, just on my lowest ribs. He was the only man besides my father who had ever touched me." She spiraled that finger through her Prosecco. "He would ride behind me, hip to hip, shouting into my ear. I'd get off the scooter, vibrating. The feel of his hands still on me."

I nodded.

"I was a sophomore in college," she said. "My suitemates were bright American girls from Michigan, Delaware, Kansas. Their futures were wide open. They were going to meet a man, fall in love, pursue their careers. I wanted all of that. I wanted to make a difference. And I knew that my father intended to marry me to some rich old Saudi sheikh. But for a moment there at Stanford I thought that the future might hold more for me." She drained her Prosecco, nodded to our waiter who wondered if she wanted another. Papa Hemingway would be proud of all of us.

I took a sip of my Kir Royale. "Did you love him? This Ian?"

She deliberated. "Back then? I don't know. Maybe I thought of him as a way out of my dilemma. Maybe that was a part of it." She shrugged. "But I also thought: If he does want me, he will protect me. He will take care of me. I don't have to go home. I can marry someone I choose. I can have a life for myself, not just for my family."

"In Brighton?"

"In Brighton. In California. I did not care."

"Did you love him?" I asked again.

She did not seem to mind. "I slept with him. I thought perhaps we were in love. I thought perhaps we would get married." She made a sour face. "To my very great surprise, I got pregnant."

To my very great surprise I felt my stomach draw tight. I was jealous of Ian from Brighton. If he had showed up at that moment, things would have gone very badly for him.

"I was on the pill. I didn't think that could happen, but it did. When I told him I was going to have a baby, I realized my mistake."

"Mistake?" I asked, my heart falling and soaring all at once.

She took a sip, set her glass back down. "Ian was furious. 'Get rid of it,' he said. 'I have a girl back in Brighton. I'm not going to be tied down to some stupid Muslim bitch who doesn't even know how to take care of herself.'"

And although I was glad he had bowed out, the stupid selfish short-sighted son of a bitch, I could not help but know how badly betrayed Nadia had felt.

Could not help but feel that this had broken her heart.

I had myself gotten a Dear John letter in Iraq, an email from my fianceé back in Texas. The boys in the unit I traveled with commiserated with me. Three of them had gotten Dear John communications that very week. All of us, hearts broken, crying into our contraband alcohol about unfaithful bitches.

All of us dreaming a story that turned out in the end not to be true.

"So you did it?" I asked her. "You had an abortion?"

"I did," she said, her face open and full of heartbreak. "Stupid. I thought maybe when I had done it, when I had gotten rid of my baby, he would come back to me. But he didn't." She laughed, bitterly. "I never saw him again. A few weeks after, something inside me snapped. I can't explain it. I rode that scooter off the road into the San Francisco Bay."

"Like *Vertigo*," I said, my eyes wide.

"Yes," she smiled. "Like in *Vertigo*." Her smile faded. "But that time, no one came to rescue me." She looked across at me. "I told myself that no man would ever make decisions for me again. For the past few years, I even thought that might be possible. But sometimes I think I'm still in the water, flailing, sinking."

The waiter brought back our entrees, set them on the table. He set down her second Prosecco, backed expertly away.

"So that is my story," she said, her palms up. "Or one of them. One of the most important, to be sure." She looked at me pointedly. "Frederick said that we were both scared. What are you scared of? Did you have an Ian?"

I laughed against my will. "I thought so once," I said, pushing my chicken around the plate with a fork. "I was engaged. My fiancée broke up with me when I was in Iraq. I felt like crap for a while. She left me for a sports reporter. Not even a very good one. I heard from a couple of other folks in that newsroom. Turns out they'd been cheating on me the whole time. Even before I left. Once I knew, I actually felt better. It kind of explained a lot that wasn't working." That was bad, but it wasn't the worst. "But no. My heart has only ever really been broken by the men who left me."

"Hmm," she said, cocking her head to one side.

"Not like that," I said. "I am totally rocking the females. But you were asking about heartbreak. Heartbreak is losing the people you love, right? Maybe it's Ian from Brighton, Her Majesty's United Kingdom, even if he turns out to be a world-class shit." I poured myself a glass of the house red. "Or maybe your loss is Master Sergeant Calvin Jones. Who could also be a world-champion." I toasted him. "Or maybe it's an Iraqi interpreter named Khalid who grew to be your closest friend in the world. You know, my father and Khalid died within a few weeks of each other." My smile did not reach my eyes. "I think maybe I went into the bay too."

She inclined her head. "I am sorry, Calvin. I Googled you after you gave me your card. I saw that you covered Iraq for CBS. Guessed that you saw some horrible things. I didn't realize how horrible."

"Bad enough," I affirmed.

"So Master Sergeant Calvin Jones. Your father."

I nodded. "He was." I said. "He did his best. It wasn't—wasn't enough." My lips were in a tight line. "If I ever have children, I will try to do better."

She smiled shyly. "If you have children? Do you want them?"

I nodded. Actually smiled. "The very thought scares me shitless. But yes. I want children. A son. A daughter."

"Me as well," she said quietly.

"You once asked me how I enjoyed the Middle East." I laughed, but there was no humor in it. "I didn't. Iraq broke me. I came back to Texas, just barely holding on. Rob pulled me out of the river. And for ten years, I was okay. Just okay. But. I worked, I found a girlfriend. I lived a little life. No big drama. But at least I didn't die."

"It is good that you didn't die," she nodded. "This girlfriend?" She gave me a significant look.

"I told you," I said, raising a finger. "We look good together. Kelly and me. But I don't know what she loves. What she fears." I chewed on my Coq au Vin, which was very good. I made a happy noise.

She smiled across at me. "Should I be jealous of this Kelly?"

I swallowed. "I don't know," I said. "Should I be jealous of this Ali?"

Her chin dropped. Her shoulders fell.

"I thought perhaps for just a moment," she said, without looking up, "we could just be a boy and a girl at dinner."

"I'm sorry," I said. I reached my hand across the table, laid my fingers atop hers. She pulled them away, put her napkin on the table, pushed her seat back.

"I can't pretend that Ali is not out there somewhere," I told her. "That the clock is not ticking." I motioned out at the night beyond and put my hand on hers again. "But you chose to be here tonight. You could choose other things as well."

"I have not been given a choice," she said angrily. She took a deep breath. "Not the slightest choice." I thought she might get up now and leave.

"You're afraid that nothing will ever get better," I said. "That maybe this hard thing is the most you can ever hope for." Bless you, Frederick.

"Maybe," she shrugged. "What am I supposed to do?"

I looked across at her, this woman I had pulled out of the Seine, this beautiful brilliant woman with her sad brown eyes.

I looked across at her, I saw her, and I decided.

A gate swung open again, clanged against the wall, woke the entire neighborhood.

"*Inshallah*," I muttered to myself, and to whoever might be up there listening.

"Excuse me?" She pulled her hand out from under mine again. "God willing?" Maybe she too knew what that usually meant.

"Nadia," I said. The silence stretched out like ripples in a pond, but I had decided. "Will you come and watch the Bastille Day fireworks with me from the tower of the American Cathedral? It's just down the street from your hotel." She nodded slightly—she knew where it was. "I know you might have to rough up Ali's mother again."

"Fireworks?" she asked, her face blank.

"Yes," I said.

"With you?" she asked.

"Yes," I nodded. "With me."

She looked across the table at me, shaking her head. "Fireworks," she repeated. "Why fireworks?"

"Please, Nadia," I said. "Come out with me tomorrow night. Let's celebrate France. Let's celebrate—" I stopped there.

I reached across the table, my fingers falling atop hers, and this time they did not flee. "Please. Just a boy and a girl."

She looked down at our fingers, mine atop hers, and she too seemed to come to some point of decision.

"*Inshallah*," she said, shrugging.

"No," I said. "Mean it. Please."

She took pity on me. A smile spread across her face, and her hands turned over to give my hands a squeeze before she dropped them, scooted her chair back in, and picked up the menu.

"I love fireworks," she said. Then she handed me the menu. "Let's have dessert."

8.

Paris

———

July 14, 2016
Thursday

I have not told you the truth. Not the whole truth.

I promised you honesty, and there's one significant place where I see that I have fallen woefully short.

I haven't told the whole truth about my father.

I wanted you to love my father, just as I want to love him.

But he was not perfect.

Far from it.

I may, for example, have given the impression that my dad beat my ass that one time when he caught me cheating. But the truth—the whole truth—is that he was a violent man, that whippings were the bare minimum of what he did to me, that he drank hard when he was home, especially after we lost my mom, and that when he drank, he didn't care what he did or who he hurt.

Funny. He didn't drink in country. Maybe that was the one place he ever felt completely at peace.

Because at home in Killeen, after my mom was gone, he drank ten fingers of Jack Daniels or a twelve-pack of Coors every night. And God help you if you crossed his path, drew his attention, pissed him off.

For a long time—too long—I just took it. The open-handed slaps, the fists thudding.

I just took it.

Who knows why? I knew that what he was doing was wrong. I could have told someone. A teacher. Someone on base. There was no part of me that accepted it, no part of me that thought he had the right to treat me like this, no part that ever believed I was somehow in the wrong. But then again, I thought my father was a god. Not the capital-G God. But my father made the world turn, somehow. He was smart and brave and competent. He could make things with his hands, just like he could break things with them. His men looked up to him, followed his orders without a question. He had killed men. Rescued others.

My mother had loved him.

He was larger than life, certainly larger than me.

Somewhere along the way, though, I just got tired of it. When he went on a week-long training mission at Fort Hood, nobody thought anything about his fifteen-year son, left behind at home for seven days. He tried hard not to remind people that he was raising a child. And I was happy for the quiet that week. I got too used to it, maybe. I climbed into my dad's liquor cabinet after school, got down his big liter bottle of Jack Daniels, noted the level, thought I would fill it back up with water the night before he returned.

But they finished the mission a day early because of equipment failure, and I was teenaged drunk on Jack and Coke when he walked in, and took in the scene.

"What the hell are you doing, Cal?" he asked.

I would have thought it was pretty obvious. But for some reason I had to speak.

"Oh," I said. "Are you my father now?"

He set down his duffle, rolled up his sleeves, told me to stand up.

I did.

I pushed my chair back.

I glared.

And I went for him.

Stupid, I know. I didn't have any training in hand to hand. He had training and experience and a man's body. What I had was anger and resentment. And about four and a half Jack and Cokes.

I lurched toward him, threw a hard right he deflected easily with his left hand, threw a left he sidestepped. Then he shook his head, and I knew things were about to go south for me.

Honestly, he was merciful. He took me down onto my back, hard, pinned my arms across my chest, knelt on me. I flinched, ready for the fists that were coming, ready for worse.

My father was trained to kill people.

But there were tears in his eyes. I'd never seen them before, never saw them again.

He shook his head again, hard, like he was shaking something loose from it.

"Don't ever raise your fists to a man if you aren't prepared for the consequences," he told me gruffly.

He got up off my chest. Held out his hand. Pulled me to my feet.

I waited for the pain.

Which didn't come.

He indicated my chair. We sat down together at the table. He took a short glass, poured himself some Jack, neat. Raised it to me. I raised my glass. We clinked.

"To absent friends," he said, rubbing the corners of his eyes. "To those we loved and lost."

"To those we loved and lost," I said. I could assent to that toast.

He never touched me again. I don't know why. Maybe he saw that from that point on he would have to do serious damage to me. Maybe something clicked into place for him that reminded him he was actually my father. I can't say.

All I can say is that I don't know how to bring him to life for you, this man I feared and tried to please and cannot get over.

I want you to love him.

And I want to love him too.

Those were the things I thought as I lay awake, the things that maybe I will always think.

I had not slept well since I arrived in Paris. Not a surprise to me, or, presumably, to anyone who knew me. I had not slept well since Iraq. Since before Iraq, really.

Fitful. Occasional. Light. These were the words that described my sleep.

I hadn't slept on the flight over from Dallas, although I'd done my level best. A whiskey in the DFW airport, another on the plane, wine with dinner. Nothing. Still awake enough to watch *Captain America: Civil War* twice, and to follow the progress of our flight on the seatback screen, watching that tiny little British Airways plane planted over the vast ocean. When we got over the part of the Atlantic that was the deepest and darkest on the map, I started finding it hard to breathe.

This whole thing was impossible. Some ridiculous tube with wings could not possibly fly miles above the surface of a planet.

I felt every shake, every shudder of the plane. We were going down. Of course we were. I only hoped that the impact killed me. I didn't want to drown, to sink into that deep blue darkness forever.

Jesus. I lay in my bed now, sweating in Paris, safe and sound, whatever that means.

Why didn't I think about beautiful Nadia instead of the crash that didn't happen, her smile instead of the water that never filled my lungs?

Well, that's the question, right? Why can't we live into the good in our lives and stop worrying about the things that might never happen?

Maybe because the deep dark seems worse than any possible good we might live into?

I don't know. I didn't solve that problem before my phone was ringing. Rock the Casbah. I had left my ringer on in case Rob needed me. So even though it was 5 a.m. my time, I ended up picking up to talk to my Uncle Jack.

"Nephew," he said. "Are you ducking me?"

"I just answered the phone, old man," I said. "This very moment I am talking to you." I yawned big.

"What was going on that you had to text me that you couldn't talk?"

I had to pause for a second to remember. "Rob," I said. "He had a crisis."

"Rob did?" He sounded floored. As well he might.

"I know," I said. Of all the people who seemed unlikely to endure a crisis of any sort, I would have ranked Rob way up there. "But still."

"Is he okay?"

I took a deep breath, considered, exhaled. "I think he will be," I said.

"Anything you can tell me?"

"Oh no," I said. "But I've got some good news you can take back to Aunt Karen."

"Good news," he said. "Lay it on me."

"Okay," I said. "I met someone."

"Someone."

"A woman."

A long pause. "Praise the Lord," he said at last, although it didn't sound like full-throated praise yet.

"I know. I can hardly believe it myself. It's Lyle Lovett. 'Boy, pick up that fiddle and play that steel guitar, and find yourself a lady, and dance right where you are.'" Wow. Too much. But also, just right. "She's beautiful. And smart. Oh. Also, she's kind of a mess. I'm simultaneously attracted and terrified. Keith Urban. 'It's scary business, your heart and soul is on the line.'"

"How so? How is she a mess, I mean. And no more country songs, if you please. Just the facts."

"Yes, Officer." Right.

So, there were all sorts of ways to be a mess, and I had personal knowledge of many of them. I rolled out of bed, took a seat in the chair next to the window. Best rip that Band-Aid off all at once. "Well. Okay. She tried to kill herself yesterday. I pulled her out of the Seine."

"That river in Paris?"

"The very one."

"Did you just see her go and jump in after her? Or had you had some kind of previous knowledge of her that made that seem like a good idea?"

"We had drinks once," I said, a little defensively. "At Harry's New York Bar."

"Hmm," he grunted. "Drinks." I could hear Aunt Karen asking him something. I'd guess he put a palm over the receiver, said something, shook his head.

"Cal," he said. "You should not be drinkin'."

"I think something is happening here," I told him.

He groaned. "Cal, are you fallin' apart? There's a 12:45 flight from DFW. I checked. It'll cost me $2500 to come today. But I've cleared it with Karen. She says we'll find the money. If you need me to, I will come retrieve you this very instant."

"Wow," I said. "Don't be stupid. I mean, thank you. Thank Karen. But I'm not falling apart. Actually, I think something may be falling together."

"Hmm," he grunted again.

"I haven't loved anybody since Darla. If then."

There was a noise from the background. A disapproving noise. "Jack, do you have me on speaker?"

"I do now," he says. "Your aunt says that woman's name is not to be mentioned in this house." There was another noise and I could just make out Karen's words.

"But why now?" Jack repeated. "Couldn't you find a, I don't know, a nice Christian girl who, you know, didn't just jump into the river?"

"I know. It doesn't make sense, but there it is. And, umm, speaking of nice Christian girls, there's a little more." After the suicide dive into the Seine, these next complications just sort of rolled out more easily. Additional Band-Aids. "Jack, she's a Muslim. From Saudi Arabia." Karen gasped audibly in the background. "Educated in the States, but she's here in Paris because, well, she's supposed to get married to a rich sheikh on Saturday. An arranged marriage, I mean she doesn't actually want to do it."

Now I groaned. Because actually, when you added all that up— and topped it with the Seine—it did feel like a lot. "Okay. She is kind of a hot mess. She's in this no-win situation, and I think she was looking for a way out."

"Which explains why you pulled her out of the river."

"Here's the thing," Jack," I said. "If I'd been thirty seconds later, she'd be dead."

"You have always been a lifeguard," he conceded. "But that doesn't mean you have to fall for the people you save."

"That's not it," I said. "I mean, I managed to get there at that moment. But there's something different—"

"And what happens when this future husband gets wind of you? Jack, them Arabs is dangerous."

"Jack, this guy isn't a terrorist, he's a wealthy businessman. That's—"

I started to say "appalling," but instead I shut down. My uncle and I did not have conversations about racism, or religion, or anything, actually, that mattered. Particularly in front of my aunt. I could tell him about my work or my workouts, but not about my inner life, negligible as that might be.

"Nephew," he began.

"I am all right, Jack," I told him. "I'm strong."

"Are you sleeping?"

I snorted. Why not ask if I'd discovered gold in the toilet?

"You said you had drinks with this girl. Are you drinking again? A lot?"

"Yes. I am drinking. Everyone drinks here. Maybe I have had a little too much." Aunt Karen humphed another Baptist disapproval in the background, as though I needed it.

"Jack," he moaned. "You were doin' so good."

"I'm not drinking like that," I said. Not yet.

"Are you runnin'?"

"Every morning."

"How is the job?"

"We're about to find out," I said. "I've got a live broadcast in a few hours. Bastille Day Parade. But Jack: I am fine. Believe me. More than fine. It feels like I'm figuring some things out."

He covered the receiver. I could hear his voice, but not his words, as he and Aunt Karen conferred.

When he came back on: "Are you sure you don't need me to come and get you?"

"I think you've done more than enough by sending Kelly over here."

"Oh," he said. "Yeah. I forgot about that. She's callin' me back in the morning. What should I tell her?"

"Everything. Nothing. I couldn't care less."

"Karen is lookin' across the kitchen table at me with concern. She wonders if you've lost yourself. And so do I." A pregnant pause. "Does this have anything to do with your dad? With the day comin' up?"

Damn. Because here we are on the anniversary of his death. Nine years. "I'd kindly forgotten about that," I said quietly.

"No, you haven't," he said.

True that. My. How many years was this going to hurt?

"Jack," I said. "Tell me something. Was my father ever—happy? When my mom was alive?"

He did not pretend he did not know what I was asking, even though, as I said, we did not have such talks. "I believe he was. Once."

"And after she died—"

There was silence across the Atlantic.

"Jack?"

"I believe he lost himself," Jack said.

I nodded. Since we were this deep in, I took a deep breath and decided to ask that one more thing. "Jack," I said. "After she died. Did you know what he was doing to me? That he was hurting me?"

I heard my aunt sob.

"No," he said. "Not then. I wish I had. He told me. Later. He could not look at me. Could not." He paused for a moment, and I could almost see him wipe his eyes. "I have never seen such shame in a man. And I have known some bad men, nephew."

"He was so angry," I said. "When he came home. Every night. I just figured it was something I had done. For a while, anyway. Then it was clear. Nothing I did deserved that."

There was another long silence. I raised the phone to see if we were still connected. "Uncle Jack?"

Nothing.

"Are you okay?"

"I am still standin'," he said gruffly. I heard a noise, could imagine Karen coming around the table to hug him. "Son, I have to say, I am worried. We are worried. None of this makes sense. This girl. This talk about your dad. It feels like you are in a bad space and a million miles from home."

"Fair enough," I said. "I have made a huge leap, and it appears that I haven't hit ground yet. But here's the thing. I am 35 years old now, Jack. I have got to play with the hand I got dealt. The past, and this present. And Aunt Karen, you always told me that things happen for a reason. Why did I meet this girl? Why did I show up on the bridge right before she went over? Wouldn't you say God has a plan?"

Of course she would say that. Even if I wouldn't.

I got up, strode over to my window, pulled back the blind on the lightening Paris sky. "Listen, I am grateful for you. For both of you. But this seems to be my life. Warts and all."

"Warts." He snorted. "If you can call this Iraqi woman marryin' some ayatollah . . ."

"She's Saudi, Jack," I said. "And maybe she won't get married. I don't want her to. Jesus—"

"Don't blaspheme," he reminded me.

"Sorry," I said. "Jack, I'll call you later. I'm going for my run."

"Don't rescue any more women," he warned. "There's only so many hours in the day."

I laughed. I actually got that. But you have to help the people in front of you. Sometimes, maybe, if you're lucky, they rescue you in the process. "Hug Karen for me."

"That I will do," he said, and he hung up.

They were worried, and I got it. Mine was not a history that inspired confidence, and this thing? Like if I brought my fiancée home to Christmas dinner and told everyone that we met in AA. Although, I considered, I had met my actual fiancée while we were both in J-School at the University of Texas, and it might have been better if we had met in rehab. We'd at least have had something honest in common.

I put on my shorts, a t-shirt, my running shoes, and slipped quietly down the stairs. To my great surprise, Fantine was not outside and scrubbing the sidewalks or something when I slipped out of the building. I pulled out my phone, dialed up Imagine Dragons, great bass and drums, mixed far forward, just where I needed the help, and set out at a good brisk pace as I ran up the Avenue de la Bourdonnais toward the Seine. I ran past the Musée du Quai Branly, the strange wet tufted textures of its outer wall covered with living plants and mosses, the black asphalt of the sidewalk wet with the dripping water, and then on toward the Pont de l'Alma.

Something was prickling in the arch of my left foot in that way a tiny thing has of making itself known in a larger-than-life way. The running shoes I liked were New Balance, and they ran a little small, which meant I could wear only very thin socks with them. Something seemed to have slipped into my shoe, maybe a tiny piece of gravel or some road debris. I tried to tune it out—often you have a clothes or equipment malfunction when you first set out on a run and can somehow ignore it. I ran across the bridge, past the spot where Nadia and I had gone into the Seine—would I ever not remember this spot in that way?—made my left onto the Avenue de New York, and huffed down the stairs to the docks, but if anything, the every-stride pain in my shoe got worse. I ran past the stairs in the stone wall where I had pulled Nadia out of the river onto dry ground—a homeless guy, probably the usual one, was bathing in the river at the base of those steps—and pulled up lame about 50 yards onward. An alcove full of trash stank just to my right, and I put as much distance between me and it as I could before plopping down on the edge of the dock and taking off my shoe.

I didn't see anything inside, but I shook it out, rubbed the outside of my sock, and put my shoe back on. I tied the laces tightly and stood up. I tested my weight on that left foot. Nothing. No sharp pain. Okay then.

I set off down the pier. Now the footing was those rough cobblestones, uneven, requiring all my attention, and the smell of garbage was replaced by the bitter smell of piss and vomit from people who had come down here last night to do their business against the wall.

Oh, Paris, how I love you.

I hopped stone to stone to stone, centering my toes on each to avoid my foot going sideways in the gap. That was a good way to tear up your knees, as I knew only too well.

In Baghdad, I used to run in the Green Zone—every night after the sun set, since it was too hot to even imagine running in daylight.

To be more precise, I ran along the Tigris River from the Green Zone outside into the Danger Zone, past Iraqi Army goons and barbed wire, into a ruined city marked with gunfire and bombed-out vehicles, burning tires and hungry stray dogs and hungry Iraqi kids. Some of them—dogs and kids—ran with me. The kids knew no English—usually just "George Bush" or "GI!" or "Chocolate!" And I didn't know enough of any language yet to say much to them in return. But they ran with me—barefoot or in their ruined sandals—sometimes for a mile, or two, laughing, cheering.

It made me smile and it broke my heart.

I was young and thought I was invincible, but I most certainly was not. Like everybody else who went to Iraq, I ended up damaged. Funny—I didn't get blown up by insurgents, or shot up by poorly trained Iraqi security forces mistaking me for an insurgent. No, I stumbled on a stretch of blasted-up pavement, tore up my knee, and face-planted. The little girl—I think it was a girl jabbering alongside me that evening—ran back to the Iraqi Army outpost, and twenty minutes later, I was on a Bradley heading home to the Green Zone. I told them to find the girl and give her something. If I'd lain out there all night, I don't think there would have been much of me left to repair the next morning. But I never knew if they did, and I didn't see her again. Iraq never worked that way.

The network pulled some strings and got me on a plane out the next morning. It was the Maimed Express back to Andrews AFB, me and a bunch of badly wounded or mostly dead soldiers, and this confusion would be important later, but at the time, it was just the best way back to the States, there being no commercial flights into or out of Baghdad. That plane torqued up into the sky, corkscrewed, it felt like, to avoid the risk of insurgent SAMs, and I remember almost sliding out of my seat.

At Andrews, a producer from the network met me, assessed my condition and mostly wondered if I was going to sue, then seeing that I was just banged up and hobbled, that my condition was transitory and not life-threatening, sent me back to Texas, where an orthopedic surgeon repaired my knee.

My Uncle Jack and Aunt Karen came down from Dallas to Killeen, and they were waiting in the hospital room when I came out. It wasn't a serious surgery, but they'd actually given me a recovery room to wait out the anesthesia, and I didn't mind. It was the quietest place I'd been in a long time, and I was pleasantly high and not ready to face the world outside.

It was at that exact moment that my ex-fiancée Darla stormed in the door to my room, a hand over her face, as though she wanted to be ready to shield her vision from some horrible sight, from me maimed or in pieces.

She looked around, took in the landscape. No friendly faces in the room. She stepped toward my bed.

"Cal," she said, still a little frantic. "Cal, it's me, Darla. I came as soon as I heard."

I may have nodded. I don't remember. I was pretty loopy.

"You showed up on the casualty lists at the station. We heard you were badly wounded."

"Jesus, woman," I said, finally believing in her existence, her presence in my hospital room.

"Don't blaspheme," my uncle and aunt said, at the same time, in stereo.

I shook my head to try and clear the cobwebs, but all I could think about was her Dear John letter, and I fear I did not react well to her presence.

"You are as stupid as you are faithless," I said.

She jumped like I'd tased her.

"Cal," my aunt said, although I'm sure she was thinking the same damn words. "Do the Christian thing."

"Take the high road," my uncle urged.

"He's on a lot of pain meds," he told her.

They had also previously liked Darla. For all the good that did any of us.

"I do not intend to take the high road," I told the room. I was still more than a little woozy, but I was also supremely offended. "I could take the highest road. I could drive my badass BMW down an autobahn in the Alps. If they have them. In the Alps. And this one"—I indicated Darla with my right hand—"would still have been sleeping with Barry from Sports the whole time we were together."

"Cal," my aunt cautioned.

"Really?" my uncle asked me.

"He's not even a good sportscaster," I moaned. And for the first time, I felt some real emotion. Fuck. To be left for a schmuck who didn't even know his craft. I could feel my shoulders sink. I turned to her. "Anyway, what kind of person breaks up with a guy who's ten thousand miles away?"

It's actually 7391. But sometimes overstatement is your friend.

"I know you must hate me," Darla said. I did not interrupt to overturn that assessment. "And you've got good reason. I mean, there you are, reporting the news from Iraq and serving our country. And then you got wounded." She sniffed a little, just to try it out. My God, what did I ever see in her? University of Texas J-School, you did me wrong. "I just wanted to see if you were okay." She reached into her pocket. "And if you were going to live, I needed to give you this. It has kindly been weighing on my conscience."

She reached out her left hand, a tiny diamond ring pinched between forefinger and thumb. It was my mom's wedding ring, the ring my dad put on her finger in 1979. We took it off her finger when she was killed by a drunk driver in Killeen in 1992, just after my dad had come home from Desert Storm. When I told him I was going to propose to Darla, he encouraged me to give her Mom's ring.

"Thank you," I said softly, rolling it around in the palm of my hand and almost dropping it. "Whoop!" I set it on the bedside table. "Well. I hope you and Jody will be very happy together."

"Jo—? His name is Barry, Cal," she said with a look of concern, thinking that maybe I'd been wounded in my brain. I hadn't. In Country, I learned, a Dear John letter always meant your beloved was leaving you for Jody, some civilian prick who was making time with your girl and making good money in the private sector while you were keeping their lying selves safe at night.

"In the unit I serve with," I said, not knowing why I felt I had to tell her this, "a staff sergeant got divorce papers last week, tucked away in a CARE package from home. They were stuffed in the box between a package of Twizzlers and a case of Copenhagen. He read them. Tore up his room, yelling, screaming. After that, he got real quiet. When we went out on patrol that evening, he stepped out into enemy fire instead of taking cover."

"Jesus," Uncle Jack breathed.

"Don't blaspheme," Karen told him.

"Darla, this is a shitty thing to do to anyone," I began, but then I stopped myself. It was done. There had to be something better than this faithless woman, our almost-accidental relationship. I had thought we were brought together by fate. But clearly it was just proximity.

I turned to her, fixed her with my gaze. "I hope you and Jody will never have to be in a place where all anyone thinks about is coming home," I said. "Where that's all that's keeping you going. Home." I let out a sigh. "Jesus. It's a horrible thing to have your legs cut out from under you." Worse than knee surgery, that's for damn sure.

"I'm sorry," she whispered. Tears were running down her cheeks. I'm not sure what she'd imagined was going to happen when she came. I'd guess this wasn't it. But honestly, she must have known that if I was even slightly conscious, things were probably not going to go well for her.

Which meant it took guts to walk in here. More than I gave her credit for. More than I had ever given her credit for.

All right.

I was done.

I held up the ring. The tiny diamond was a third of a carat, worth next to nothing. My dad bought it on an installment plan at Zales. They were dirt-poor when he joined this man's army. But it had been on my mom's finger from the moment my dad asked her to marry him to the afternoon a one-ton GMC pickup truck t-boned her on her way to get groceries at the HEB in Killeen.

"Thank you, Darla," I said. "For bringing this. It means a lot."

She nodded, wiped her eyes.

Aunt Karen beamed. I was capable of doing the right thing, after all.

Somehow I looked back up at Darla and said something like "I hope you and Barry will be very happy."

She blushed red. At least she had the decency to do that, on her way out the door.

They weren't, of course. Happy, let alone very. The newsroom isn't conducive to that. People cheat on each other with alarming frequency. It's just the business. So Barry was cheating on Darla with the weekend weather girl, maybe even at the very instant that Darla was standing in my hospital room. After she found out, she left him for a local anchor at another network. After that—news drips back, as it always does, we are a tiny band of news warriors—I heard they went out to Las Vegas, and had three kids, that Darla does the occasional weekend anchor gig and her husband opens car dealerships and cuts ribbons for casinos. Big fish in a surprisingly small pond, and he's probably cheating on her, again, ever, even as I write these words.

I guess I feel more sorry for her than I realized. Once, I thought Darla was going to be my world. Now I'm not sure I'd even recognize her.

Life moves on, and so do we.

I jogged up the stairs from the pier, ready to cross back over the Seine, and saw that New York Avenue was blocked off, for the

Bastille Day parade, I supposed. The city was quieter, at least around here. In a few hours, there would be a huge military promenade down the Champs-Élysées with a zillion people watching. Tanks and trucks and helicopters.

At the top of the stairs, I paused for a second, bent over, puffing. I took my phone out to go back a few songs when it vibrated in my hand.

Kelly.

Uncle Jack, I could just kill you.

I pressed the button on my headphones. "I'm running," I panted.

"Of course you are, darling," Kelly said. "But you can't get away."

I snickered. Couldn't help it. She is funny. "I did mean to call you," I said. "And to tell you: Don't come to Paris."

"I knew you would say that," she said. "I already bought tickets. I'm arriving Saturday night. I'm booked into the Ritz."

"I told you not to do that," I said, straightening up.

"You'll change your mind," she said.

"I met someone," I said.

"Hmm," she said. She either tried to sound—or was—supremely unconcerned. "Yes, Jack told me that you rescued somebody."

"Kelly," I started, and she cut me off.

"Go on and have your little rescue fling," she said.

"It's not a fling," I said.

"Oh, Cal," she said. "You are as predictable as the sunrise. Tell me: Did you buy me lingerie in London?"

My mouth dropped open and I think I must have stuttered a few untranslatable syllables. "Um. Wow. Kelly, I can't see what possible difference—"

"Did you buy me some lingerie?" she persisted.

"Well, yes," I muttered, remembering Anna and Selfridges Department Store and the moment that had somehow led me inexorably into the story I was now living. "I did, I guess."

I could hear her smile. "All right, then. I'll try it on for you Monday."

She hung up as I was saying "No." Honestly, woman.

"Kelly," I started to text. Then I stopped. She too was predictable as the sunrise. She was going to come to Paris. I could see her or not see her, but she'd probably already scheduled a spa day, laid out her shopping itinerary. I could get on board with it or hide out, and it probably wouldn't change her plans either way.

I settled for texting "Have a nice flight." And then I checked the time and took off across the bridge at a good clip.

I had to get ready for work.

The Bastille Day parade waited for no man. No, nor woman neither.

When the tanks started rolling into the city, I had to be ready.

9.

Paris

July 14, 2016
Thursday

Every species of military and paramilitary person in France had marched for hours down the Avenue des Champs-Élysées in an unending stream. Tanks and troop carriers and fire fighters and garbage workers had rumbled past the review stand at the Place de la Concorde, and fighter jets had just rocketed overhead rocking tricolored smoke.

"The American Cathedral is a block or so away from the Four Seasons," Rob reminded me after my live feed, as the last planes had soared over the Louvre and Notre Dame emitting blue, white, and red smoke, and I was comparing notes with Ahmed, my cameraman. "Where your Nadia is staying."

"That's on George Sank?"

"Oui," he said. "I think Brigid is mad at you for bringing another woman to watch fireworks. She had high hopes for you and Allison."

"Brigid is upset right now about other women in general," I said. Whoa. I thought for a moment that he might hit me, but he made a rueful face.

"Please don't say things like that out loud." He looked around to see if Ahmed or anyone else had heard.

"Allison is perfectly lovely," I said, trying to calm him down. "I think we are going to be good friends."

"She is," he said. "Lovely, I mean."

I fell in line next to him as we walked back toward the sound truck. "My Uncle Jack thinks I am crazy for falling for Nadia. There are all these complications. The religion thing. The culture thing. The impending marriage thing. Oh. And the jumping into the Seine."

"Those are a lot of complications," he conceded.

"So, I'll meet her at the Four Seasons," I said, pushing past all of it. "We'll maybe have a drink there, then come down and meet you at the Cathedral."

"I'll be working the grill," he said. "Along with Father Cam. Oh, I forget to tell you about Cam. You'll have a lot to talk about. He was a military chaplain. At Fort Hood from 2004. Then he went to Iraq in 2006."

"Wow," I said. "It's weird we never crossed paths." I had met a few chaplains. They always showed up at the worst moments, which had to be a hard self-identity. Nobody needed a chaplain until somebody in their unit bought it, or they got a Dear John letter, text, or email, or they had a crisis of faith, or they just realized that they were going batshit crazy.

"Why would it be weird?" Rob asked. "We never had that much to do with chaplains."

True. As little as I could, as a person of no faith. But since the chaplains were your conduits to the tragedy, they were often connected to the story. I had met a few, and they came in discernable varieties. Full-on soul saver. Gung-ho warrior for God. Small-town pastor trying to keep his own sanity. I wondered what kind this Father Cam was. "Cam. Short for Cameron?"

"Oh, he's a real live Episcopalian. Cameron Something Gaines the Fourth. Filthy-rich back as far as they have ancestral records. The Mayflower. Or whatever."

I imagined this Father Cameron, and in my mind, he looked, at the very least, well-preserved, that look that money can give you. He could be 20, or a pampered 50 with a little work done and some

Botox. "I'll bet there were some unhappy stockbrokers in his family the day Cameron enlisted."

"That is cruel stereotyping," he said, then he snorted. "And I would guess that the Camerons have always hired someone else to manage their money."

I barked an appreciative little laugh. "What time should we get to the Cathedral?"

"The only set in stone for you is the live feed late. Come when you want. We'll have burgers and chicken and veggie kebabs and plenty of champagne. The grateful network is expensing everything tonight."

"Well done, grateful network." And I got to the crux of my concern for the evening. Strangely it wasn't that I was meeting a beautiful woman at the Four Seasons, where she was staying with her future mother-in-law. "So, this tower. The wall on the observation deck. How high?"

"Waist high," he said, holding a hand in front of him, then seeing the panic on my face, revised it upward to something in front of his chest. "Don't worry about the wall. The spiral staircase up is the worst part."

"Oh, how I hate you at this moment," I said.

"Think of it as an opportunity, Cal," he said. "Growing up on the plains left you vertically challenged. You can vanquish a childhood fear."

"Be ready to step in if I can't do it," I said. He started to make a joke, then he saw that I was genuinely terrified.

It's good to know what genuinely terrifies you, right? I mean, I have seen people blown apart, I have seen wild dogs lick human blood off the asphalt, I have held men as they died. But nothing—nothing—scares me more than heights. The flight over, with that terrible moment when I realized we were above the deepest part of the ocean—that was just the inside-the-plane version. But when I've been up in a minaret or on the side of a mountain or you name it—I've been so scared that I literally couldn't move. My knees buckled under me.

So I don't know what that means, that I've been more scared by looking down from a high place than in firefights where mortars were falling or bullets flying or when I was chased by insurgents intent on maybe cutting my head off on live TV. I mean, all that should petrify you.

It is a scary freaking world.

But Rob looked at me, and saw that deep down I was still that Texas boy who hated to climb things.

"If you need me," he said, "I'll be ready. I'll take my cook's apron off before we go up."

"I hate you with the heat of a thousand suns," I returned.

"Right," he said. "Forgive me for saying that heights should be low on the list of either of our problems at the current moment."

Which was also true, I realized as I walked past the hostess into Le Bar at the Four Seasons, feeling woefully underdressed in khakis, polo shirt, and a decent sportscoat. It was 6:30, but perhaps because of the July 14 holiday, the bar was full.

I didn't see Nadia, but I found a low table with some empty couches and took a seat.

A couple followed me in—he a muscular brute with an angular jaw attired in a tuxedo—she with drawn-on eyebrows and wearing shiny something. Silk? Taffeta? I don't even know. They settled at the sofa across from me. She was speaking animatedly, nay violently, in a language I didn't recognize—maybe Slavic or Russian—and he was nodding without looking at her. He pulled out his phone, checked something, nodded, put it away.

Nadia stepped into the bar, looked across the room, saw me, and a smile spread wide across her face. Jesus, I thought. I'd jump into the river all over again just to see that smile.

She was wearing a diagonal striped silk dress, gray and white. It fell to her knees. She had on a gray head scarf, but it could have been either the head covering of a faithful Muslim or a simple fashion accessory. She looked lovely. Like summer.

"The girls of summer," I murmured.

"The Don Henley song?" she asked, sitting down next to me.

"Those are boys," I admitted. "But sure. That may have been what I was talking about."

"I saw an Eagles concert in Houston," she said. "Before all of them died. They played that song. 'My love will still be strong, after the boys of summer are gone.'"

"Yes," I admitted. "That is the one."

"Would you like a drink?" She took a look at the menu. Across from us, the model was taking her date (boyfriend/husband/ bodyguard?) to task for something, and he just kept checking his phone, like her words didn't matter in the slightest.

I took a look over at the bar, which was a work of art. They had Bulleit, as I had suspected they would. "Maybe a little something," I said. Then I took another look. The big man sitting at the bar—dark suit, salt and pepper hair, his back to us after taking a look in our direction—he was familiar. You got an instinct for such things In Country.

"That man was at La Fontaine last night," I said. "Table for one, also on the street. He sat down after you joined me."

"What man?" she asked. And that was fair enough. He had gotten his drink and now was walking to the far end of the room, away from us.

Maybe my instincts were off.

"Nothing," I said. The cocktail waitress stopped at our table. The model across from us wanted Cristal Rosé. He shook his head. "A bottle of the 2006," he told the waitress in heavily accented English. "None of this pink stuff."

"An Old Fashioned with Bulleit," I told her, when she turned her attention to us.

"Two," Nadia said. Off my look, she responded, "I've never had an Old Fashioned. Who knows when I'll have another chance?"

"Nadia," I said.

"I know," she said. "And yet. If this is my last night out, I want to try your drink. The first time we met, Frederick made you drink Mr. Hemingway's drink. Correct?"

Shrug. "He did indeed," I said.

"All right then," she said. "Let's drink yours." She touched my arm. "I hope for your sake it's good."

"Me too," I said. I had seen the prices, and this was another substantial debit against my paycheck.

When the drinks returned, they were perfect. I reached for my wallet, but the young female waitress was looking at Nadia.

"1204," she said, already writing it down.

"*Oui*," Nadia said. "*Certainement*."

"I was going to get these," I told her.

She waved it away. "Ali won't even notice. It is small change. Which," she said gently, "I think is more than I could say for my friend and his journalist's paycheck."

I sighed. "It's not prodigious," I said. "If what you're looking for is economic security—"

"Stop," she said. "You have other compelling gifts."

"You have no idea," I said. I meant it to be funny. But she blushed.

"I put on this scarf to make Wahida happy," she said, touching it with her hand. "I thought perhaps we were going to have a fistfight. 'I have told Ali that you are unworthy of him,' she told me. 'At least show some modesty tonight among the Frenchmen.'"

"I doubt that anything you do makes Wahida happy," I acknowledged. "But you do look beautiful. Jesus."

She blushed again. She lifted her Old Fashioned. "Shall we?"

"Yes, we shall," I said. I cast about for a toast. Not to absent friends. That staff sergeant who went and got himself killed after he got his divorce papers. Grogan. Many was the night when we had opened contraband whiskey and he had toasted his men, raised a glass to all of us, for all of us.

"May the saddest day of your future," I said slowly, willing his past words into place, "be no worse than the happiest day of your past."

We toasted. We drank. She sputtered a little. It was stronger than she was used to.

"It's okay," I told her. "You don't have to finish it."

"*Au contraire*," she said. She took another sip, nodded to herself. "It is fine."

She knocked it down, looking a little flushed. I hoped she wouldn't throw up from the tower. Ah. The tower.

"There's something I have to tell you," I said. "Before we go to the Cathedral."

"You have a cowgirl at home," she said, immediately.

"Umm, no, actually," I said. "I mean, I told you I was dating that woman. That we were going nowhere. First, she's not a cowgirl. Yee-haw. And second, that's not what I wanted to say."

"Nowhere," Nadia said. "What might somewhere look like?"

"Like this," I said. I indicated the room, the drinks, us. "This. I think. I hope."

"Like the Four Seasons, Paris?" A wry smile danced on her lips.

"Don't make me say it," I said. "This is already—"

"Okay," she said. "I won't make you say it. What was your big secret then, if it isn't about your cowgirl or your strong feelings about me?"

"Note to self," I said. "Old Fashioned equals truth serum for Nadia."

She shrugged. Smiled again. "Apparently so."

"I know you've seen me as a capable and perhaps even somewhat slightly desirable human being up until now," I said. "But my Kryptonite is about to be brought into play."

"Kryptonite?" She looked confused, like I was talking about alien abduction.

"You know. Superman's secret weakness."

Eye roll. "I know what Kryptonite is. Everyone knows what Kryptonite is."

Okay. Here goes. "I'm not sure I can make it up the cathedral tower tonight," I said. "I'm really really really afraid of heights."

"Really," she said. "Three times worth?"

"Yes. Like, deathly afraid."

"This is your Kryptonite?"

"Yes."

She looked away for a second, as though she was trying to get her head around it. "I thought it would be commitment. Or intimacy. Or something like. For most men—"

"Okay, also a little bit those," I said. "But I'm not flat-out terrified of commitment. What I'm really afraid of is that I won't be able to make it up those stairs. That I'll screw up the live feed."

I drained my Old Fashioned, set it down gently, raised my hands, palms up. What could I say?

We fear what we fear.

The couple across from us had vanished, to where I couldn't say, their bottle of Cristal still half full on the table in front of us.

Nadia and I saw this at the same time—and looked at each other.

"I'm not proud," I said, indicating the bottle with a tilt of my head. "Maybe just a taste."

Nadia looked around. Nobody seemed to be watching. She reached across to the table and poured a bit in each of our glasses. "You know," she whispered, "before this was the champagne of the supermodels and rappers, it was created for the Czar."

"I didn't know that," I said. What I don't know about champagne, about bars in four-star hotels, about the lifestyles of the rich and famous, could fill a big-assed yacht. So, a large yacht. I didn't know exactly what a large yacht would look like. Any yacht was a big one to me.

She raised her glass, twinkled at me, and toasted: "May your fears be overwhelmed by your hopes."

Yes. That was a good toast. "Amen," I said. We drank. Damn, that was good. Maybe we should just hang out in Le Bar finishing up expensive drinks left over by the filthy rich. Could that be a job with benefits?

Or, I supposed, we could go watch fireworks shot off the Eiffel Tower.

"*Mademoiselle?*"

"*Oui,*" she said.

"*Ma belle fille,*" I said.

She blushed. "Your beautiful girl?"

I nodded. "For this evening, yes? Shall we go to a church and speak to some Americans and eat some hamburgers and climb a tall tower?" I shuddered involuntarily. Not about the hamburgers, of course.

"Oh, I believe we shall," she said, acting as though I hadn't just put my worst fear on display.

I offered her my arm and she took it. We walked out of Le Bar, past the crazy gorgeous multi-colored hydrangeas in the lobby, and out onto the sidewalk on George V, where crowds of people loitered across the street hoping for someone famous to come out, phones and cameras up for pictures.

And lowered at the sight of us. We were a disappointment, I guess. While I didn't hear an audible groan from the crowd, it was clear that no one was going to be fetching our Ferrari.

We walked down George V in the direction of the Seine, crossed at the light, and then stopped in front of the American Cathedral. Its black wrought-iron gate stood open, and a security guard waited to look us over and check us in. "We're here for the Bastille Day party—" I began, but he waved a wand over each of us and then indicated the courtyard with a tilt of his head. He was already scanning up and down the street again for the next potential menace. My trained eyes registered: the American Cathedral was a soft target with double value, American and Christian. No wonder they had a front-gate presence.

Through the small black wrought-iron gate ahead was the Dean's Garden. It was floored with stone and surrounded by more hydrangeas and other plants in beds. Already a small crowd was milling about inside there, and smoke was rising from two grills. Rob was working one of them, sweating from the heat rising from his coals. On his grill were steaks, sausages, hamburgers, and chicken breasts, and although I said hello, he could barely look up. I understood. The grill makes its demands.

Allison stepped forward, and if she was in any way dismayed by my showing up with another beautiful woman, she did not betray it. She simply looked genuinely happy to see me. That was nice.

"Hello," Allison said, taking my hand and directing me to someone next to her. "May I? Clarice, this is our friend Calvin Jones. Cal, Dean Clarice Washington, the priest in charge of the Cathedral."

The Dean of the Cathedral was a tall, lovely African-American woman in her late fifties or early sixties. "Cal," she said. "I have been looking forward to welcoming you."

"Thank you," I said. "Thanks so much for hosting this. And this," I said, raising a hand to indicate her, "is my friend Nadia Al-Dosari. From Saudi Arabia and the Great State of Texas."

"Nadia," Clarice bowed slightly. "*Salaam Alaikum*. And Howdy."

"Peace be upon you," Nadia returned, smiling, inclining her head. "Thank you so much for inviting us."

Us?

I got a little shiver from that, somehow.

A good little shiver.

"Please come in and make yourselves at home," Allison said. "There's wine, beer, and champagne over at that table. Chips, veggies, and artichoke dip at that one." She smiled to herself. "I made the artichoke dip. We'll be ready to start eating for real when the food comes off the grill."

Clarice pulled me aside. "Rob told me that you were with him in Iraq," she said. "Would you mind saying hello to my Canon Pastor?" She indicated the tall man at the second grill, dressed in a red, white, and blue Hawaiian shirt. "I think the two of you might have some things in common. He had some life-changing experiences over there." Her face was neutral. Life-changing can be good, or bad, or both, all at the exact same time.

"Of course," I said. "I was hoping to meet Cameron." And Nadia was now talking to Allison and a few others—and it looked as though it was genuinely safe for her to be in that group—so I stepped over to meet him.

"Father Cam?"

He looked up—or rather down, for he was a good three or four inches taller than me, patrician, a thick head of hair gone majestically gray. "Yes?"

I touched his shoulder, for we could not shake hands. He had a grill mitt on one hand, barbecue tongs in the other. "I'm Calvin Jones. Rob told me you were at Fort Hood, and then in Iraq?"

"Oh, yes, hi," he said. "It's so good to meet you." The accent was Boston. Back Bay, not Southie. "I've been looking forward to your coming. I followed you back when you were at CBS. Really good work. It helped me get my feet under for me for what was coming. I wanted to thank you."

"You're welcome," I said. "Thanks so much for saying so. It seems like a long long time ago."

"I know," he said. "Except it isn't, is it? Sometimes I wake up at night and think I hear somebody yelling 'Where's the fucking chaplain?'"

"True that," I said.

He turned over some veggie skewers. "When'd you get in?"

"Monday," I said. "Is that right?" Rob nodded over at me from his grill. "No, wait. Sunday."

"It'll be a madhouse tonight," he said apologetically. "Lots of things to char." He smiled. "But maybe we could talk soon. Lunch?"

"Sure," I said.

"Rob said you were bringing a friend." He nodded over toward Nadia, who was engaged in passionate conversation with a group of people over in the corner of the garden, among them the Dean and a tall handsome Black man who looked like he was chiseled from ebony.

"It's complicated," I said.

He laughed. "It always is. She's welcome. Both of you are."

"Thanks," I said. "I'll catch up to you in a bit." I wandered over to Nadia, who was listening to the tall Black man speak in French I could not completely follow, nodding, then laughing.

"Perhaps we are simply doomed to fall for Christians," I heard Nadia say in French, and they laughed some more.

"Hey," I said, sidling up to her. She smiled up at me.

"I was just talking to Nkwele," she said, taking my arm. "He's an envoy at the Embassy of Cameroon."

"Cameroon? I was just talking to Cameron."

"And we were just laughing about that. Nkwele and the Dean are dating. So she works with Cameron during the day and goes out with Cameroon at night."

"That is pretty funny. My God, he must be seven feet tall."

"Six seven," Clarice, the Dean, said. "Plenty tall. Umm." She stopped talking. I could not tell from her pigment if she was blushing, but she gave every other sign of it.

"*Bonsoir*," I said to Nkwele. I shook his hand with some trepidation, but his hands, monstrously large, were also surprisingly gentle.

"He does not speak much English," Nadia said. "But he was telling me what it is like to date a Christian."

"I would dearly love to know what he said."

She looked shyly down for a moment before looking back up at me. "He said it could be a very good thing."

"*Une bonne chose*," Nkwele agreed. And again, Clarice, if she wasn't blushing, was doing everything but.

"I'll hope to hear more," I said. "This might be information I need."

"Come and get a drink," Clarice said. "I have to make a toast."

I poured champagne into a plastic cup, passed it to Nadia, poured another for myself. Everyone was grabbing something. "Rob?" I asked.

"I'm set," he said, raising a can of beer.

"*Mesdames et messieurs*," Clarice said, raising her glass of wine. "To France and the French, to our home, adopted or actual, *bonne fête du 14 juillet!*"

"*Bonne fête*," someone said.

"Hear hear," said some Brits.

We drank.

"Let's eat!" Clarice directed, and people formed queues, started filling their plates.

Nadia eased in close to me, not touching, exactly, but clearly beside me. I turned to smile at her. She was at home in this setting, making conversation, speaking in Arabic and French and English. It was stunning. Dizzying. She could be the greatest cocktail party hostess ever.

"Nkwele told me that there are 279 languages spoken in Cameroon," Nadia said. She looked at him for confirmation and he nodded. "He speaks French, Arabic, and his tribal language."

"Wow," I said. "Tell him I speak a little Arabic. Ask him to say something."

She asked him if he would speak some Arabic with me, forgiving me for my poor command of the tongue.

"Hey," I said. "I understood that."

Nkwele looked at me, his grin a thing of beauty, and asked, "What do you want to hear me say, little man?"

"My Arabic is better than my French," I told him, in Arabic.

"Then neither of them is very good," he observed, truthfully.

Nadia laughed, then drifted over toward the grill to see what was there.

I laughed too, but I was serious soon enough. "I have a question." I looked at Nadia, who seemed to be occupied in conversation with Allison, Clarice, and Brigid as they filled their plates. "How is it to love someone from another faith? Is this a difficulty?"

He bit his lip, nodding. "Many people ask me this. 'Nkwele,' they say. 'You are a child of Mohammed. How can you love this woman— this woman!—who serves the Christian God?'" He looked across at Clarice, and his fierce expression softened. "And I say: Have you seen her?"

"Ah," I said. "And when you pray Fajr, do you think somehow she is excluded from who you are? Nadia is a praying person, and I am not. But I honor that desire."

He considered. "Your Nadia and I were just talking. Religion divides us. Too much, I think. Do I believe I have all the answers? I do not. Does she think she has all the answers? She does not. The same with Clarice, even though she wears a collar and serves the Christian God. Our answers are satisfying to each of us. And, as you say, we must honor the other's answers. Honor the other." He spread his huge hands out in front of him. "That is, I think, enough."

I put my hand on my heart. "I thank you. Peace be upon you."

He smiled, echoed my gesture, then put his huge hand on my shoulder like a blessing. "And you, little man. Good luck."

I moved back into Nadia's circle, where now she was talking about Texas with Allison and Brigid as they took a seat to eat.

"Don't let her fool you: Houston is not Texas," I said. "It's Los Angeles. Or something."

"We had Whataburger," she said.

"Well," I said. "That's a thing, actually." I looked down at her plate, woefully empty except for salad. "Can I get you something to eat?"

She smiled at me. "I am very happy at the moment. Do you want something?"

"I want to honor the hard work that Cam and Rob have done. So some sort of smoked meat."

"Can I have a bit of yours?"

I smiled at her. "*Oui,*" I said. "*Certainement.*"

I took a plate over to Rob, whose head was wreathed in smoke. He looked like some sort of Greek oracle.

"Offer me some wisdom," I said.

"A hamburger?" he asked, looking at my expectant hamburger bun.

"Yes, that too. How are things at your house?"

He looked across at Brigid, who was laughing with Allison, Nadia, and Clarice. "They will be okay. Not tonight. And not tomorrow. But they will be okay again someday. I think."

"That's good," I said. I nodded to myself. "That's really good." He placed a patty on my bun.

"You want another?" he asked. "Nadia said she'd wait on you."

"Jack thinks that I am insane," I told him. "And I sometimes wonder. I haven't felt like this since—" There was not actually an end to that sentence. Darla? Ha. Kelly? Beautiful, spoiled, funny. But I didn't love her. "I know we're talking about hamburgers. But at this moment I feel like I'm smack dab in the middle of a Springsteen song."

"Which one?" he asked. "Because that's the question. 'Glory Days'? 'Born in the USA'?"

"Sadly, no," I said. "That would be manageable. No. 'Jungleland,' maybe. 'Candy's Room.'" I gulped. "'Thunder Road.'" Wow. I caught my breath. "The night's busted open, these two lanes'll take us anywhere."

"Wow," he repeated. "'Thunder Road.' No wonder Jack thinks you're crazy," he said. "There's no way anything can live up to that."

"I know," I said. "But every time I look at her, Clarence Clemons starts playing a saxophone solo."

"The Big Man," Rob said. "Of blessed memory." He crossed himself. With his spatula hand.

"Precisely," I said. I jumped. "Rob, I've played it safe for so long, I don't know what to do now that the Big Man is playing. Because if he stops—"

I shrugged. That was it, wasn't it?

"What are you going to do?" He looked across at those smart, beautiful women, laughing, their heads thrown back.

"I'm going to see what happens. 'She has men who give her anything she wants, but they don't see that what she wants is me.'" That's "Candy's Room," by the way.

"Okay, Boss. I'm going to give you another hamburger. Cooked to Medium, because I remember that's what you like."

"Okay," I said. "That's a good start."

Uncle Jack thought I was crazy, and he knew me well, had known me my whole life, had been a father to me for a decade. At my dad's funeral, he had helped me sober up, had pushed me into a corner after I changed into my suit and told me I had to say something in honor of my father.

"What, exactly," I wondered aloud to him, "would I say? 'Here's to my father, who didn't quite manage to beat me to death.' 'Goodbye Dad, I'm sorry you lost the only person you ever gave a shit about.' 'Good news, Dad: Jack Daniels sent flowers.'"

I could feel my fists clench.

"Cal," my uncle said, putting his hands on my shoulders. I shook free.

"How come," I asked, "all the Jones men are drunks?"

"Cal," he repeated, and again he put his hands on my shoulders. I pushed his hands off me, involuntarily raised my fists.

And Jack looked at me with tears in his eyes, actual tears, hands raised in front of himself, shaking his head.

"Don't ever raise your fist to another man if you aren't prepared for the consequences," he said in a whisper.

I dropped my hands. My mouth dropped open. "My father said that to me. How did you—"

"His father said it to him," Jack said. "He said it to both of his sons." He shook his head again. "He was a violent man, your grandfather. A violent drunk. I've tried my whole life to get out from under that shadow. To be sober. Peaceful."

My uncle went to meetings. I knew he hadn't had a drink for years. And for a man in a potentially violent profession, I knew that he prided himself on keeping his gun holstered.

"Grampa John was—"

Jack nodded. "A horror. I'm sorry, but it's true. It's not an excuse for your father. But you should hear this: that was all he knew."

"I didn't—I didn't realize. I'm sorry."

Jack took me in his arms. I put my head on his shoulder. "We are all trying to improve on what we were taught," he said. "To do better. And today, it's your turn. Bury the man you hated. Mourn the one you loved."

"I don't how know to do that," I said.

"Find a time when he made you smile," he said. "And tell us about it."

I thought about it. I thought about that day I hitched a ride out to Anbar Province, about my father introducing me to his men, to the shopkeepers, probably to some insurgents. "We didn't see eye to eye about much," I told Jack, realizing for the first time how true that was. "My father and I. But I admired him. Maybe even loved him."

"Yeah," Jack said. "So did I."

Jack was right. I went out in front of that crowd and found some things to say about my father that weren't cruel and weren't lies. I buried what was left of him and tried to move on.

And clearly I was not doing that very well, even now, the moving on part. My anger with him, with the people who killed him, with everyone who had ever let me down or left me flat was still burning a hole in me.

Jack thought I was crazy. But he also believed I was capable of better. Of doing the right thing. Of improving on what I was taught.

So he thought I was crazy to fall for Nadia?

I walked back across the courtyard, with my answer for him ready, because I knew that there was no way to argue it:

Have you seen her?

10.

Paris

July 14, 2016
Thursday

Nadia and I sat in the Dean's Garden, smiling, eating, sipping our bubbly. On my left, the American ambassador and his wife were telling some stories about when Obama came to town. On my right, a journalist from the *New York Times* and the director of the American Library in Paris were talking about Putin, and Allison was engaging them with animation, her head bobbing. Down at the end of our table, Nkwele had reached across the table and taken Dean Clarice's hand into his own enormous hands and was laughing at some remark she had made, laughter that seemed to shake the foundations of the world.

I reached across the table myself, to where Nadia sat, chewing the last of the second hamburger Rob had given us and nodding at whatever Allison was saying. I reached for her hand—and stopped. There on her left hand was an iceberg, a fiery diamond that only a billionaire could have bought.

I couldn't believe I hadn't noticed it before.

"You're wearing your engagement ring," I said to her.

Her eyes dropped to her hand, then back up to my face. "Yes," she said. "To get out of the suite tonight. Well, I guess I could have put it in my purse when I got on the elevator. But I'm afraid to take it off. If I lose it, my family could never—"

"I can see that," I said, my voice deliberately light. "How big is that? Like, three, four carats?"

Her face colored. "Nine," she said. "Nine point four, I am told. Colorless. Flawless." She shook her head. "Wahida says it is perfect. Too perfect for me." She lowered her head. "If she only knew."

My face colored too as heat rose up my neck. I thought about my mother's third-carat diamond rolling in my palm in the hospital in Texas. I thought about having slipped it onto Darla's hand in a Wendy's one night. More hamburgers.

I thought about what sort of ring I could afford to slip onto someone's hand now. A lot more like my mother's than like this.

"How much?" I asked.

The ambassador's wife, Karen, caught our gaze and looked up at me, a little dazzled. "Calvin," she said. "My God, that's a gorgeous ring."

"I didn't buy it," I said quickly, before realizing that this would leave things more confused than they had been. "Borrowed," I said. "Just for the evening."

"Somebody must trust you very much," she said.

"You have no idea," I said. I pulled my hand back, leaned back in my chair. Karen responded to a question from her husband—yes, more bubbly, please—and I pushed back from the table, followed the ambassador toward the champagne.

That was a J Lo engagement ring, a Kardashian ring, an Elizabeth Taylor from Richard Burton sort of ring. We were talking about the kind of crazy money I had never even imagined seeing, let alone standing next to. What could I offer this woman? Me with the smallest bathroom in continental Europe, my tapped-out bank account, my three nice suits, my ruined pair of running shoes.

I smelled her first, then felt her hand in the small of my back. I turned stiffly to see her holding the ring in the palm of her hand.

Holding it out to me.

"Put it in your pocket," she said. "Someone does trust you very much."

"No," I said. "And anyway, it's your ring. He gave it to you. You should wear it."

"It is *one* of my rings," she said. "My bedroom at the Four Seasons is decked out with my trousseau. Dear God. Isn't that what you call it? Other rings, earrings, bracelets. My father, of course, received the Mahr. The dowry."

"I think a trousseau is clothes and linens," I said. I covered a marriage show at the Dallas Convention Center once.

"I have hidden nothing from you, Calvin," she said. "I do not love Ali. I have never even met him. All I know of this man is his outrageous wealth. He gave my father $500,000 for the Mahr. That is obscene, with so many people starving. But I know my father needed it, and I did not object." She looked at me. "You think perhaps I should have?"

I shook my head, thought about swatting her outstretched hand away, then wondered what the rest of the evening would look like if we ended up hunting for her nine-carat ring in the hydrangeas of the Dean's Garden. "Here," I said, holding out my right hand. "I'll give it back to you when we get back to the hotel and you can wear it home."

"You are angry at me," she said. "You look at this ring and you think it has bought me." She looked at me reproachfully. "Calvin, I have not been bought. It has only bought my father. My mind is still free. I have not decided. Not yet."

I tried to get my head around that. "Nadia," I said, turning to look out the front gate to the street beyond, to the crowds pouring down the Avenue George V for the fireworks at the Tour Eiffel, "I look at that ring and I can't help but think about everything that I can *never* give you. And then I start to think that I am an idiot for even imagining—"

"Hello," Brigid said. She was holding out two plastic cups full of champagne, then she saw me accepting the ring from Nadia. "Customarily the ring is given from the man to the woman."

"Customarily the man has bought a ring," I said, more curtly than I intended. "And the woman awaits it." I looked at Brigid's finger, saw that she was wearing her ring. A good sign. I pocketed Nadia's, burying it deep in my right front pants pocket, next to some vital parts. Nothing was going to happen to it there if I could possibly help it.

Nadia was looking down at the large paving stones of the garden. "I have offended him," she said to Brigid.

"No," I said to them both. "I am not offended." I checked my watch—it was getting late. We needed to get set up on the observation deck. "Sadly, I have no time to be offended." I looked around for Ahmed, for Rob, both of whom nodded at me.

"I'll see you up there," I told them both, indicating the heights, the tower rising above us with my craning neck. I patted my pocket and looked at Nadia. "I will take very good care of this."

"I do not care, Calvin," she said, but I had turned, ready to try to follow Rob up into the tower.

"Spiral stairs," he told me, like a coach before the big game. "Like in a castle." We went behind the reception desk, Ahmed trailing me with his camera bag. He was a short, squat muscular man who looked as if he might have been one of the professional wrestlers of my youth—possibly one of the bad guys, a foil for Hulk Hogan.

Rob pushed the thick wooden door in with a creak, and the stone stairs spiraled up and up. "All right," he said. "Here we go."

He led the way. I followed. It was a blessing, really, that I couldn't see how high we were climbing, circle after circle after circle. The stairs had tiny arrow slit windows, but I intentionally looked straight in front of me as my right hand traced the stone central post higher, higher. We passed one banded wooden door—an apartment, Rob said—and went up another flight to the top of the stairs and another door.

"All right," he said. "Next stage."

"There's more," I said. How could that even be possible?

He gave me a mirthless smile and pushed the door open. Another apartment, with one distinguishing figure—a wrought-iron spiral staircase winding up to a trapdoor in the ceiling.

"Let's go," he said. He went up to the ceiling, pushed the door open, and then above us I could see stairs going up and up by the light filtering in somehow from outside.

"Go ahead," I said to Ahmed. "I'll bring up the rear."

He shrugged, shouldered the bag, and climbed through the ceiling.

"Jesus," I said, poking my head through for a better look. What was up next was the bell section of the bell tower. The old bells were on the floor, and outside light was coming in through what looked like louvers. I could see, dimly, that it was a long way up. 100 feet? More?

And you could see through the iron stairs, up and down, both ways. And the railings, for that matter.

My legs began to shudder beneath me.

"Come on," I told them. "Come on."

I took a step onto the staircase and started spiraling up again. Most of me was shaking by the time I was twenty feet up. I closed my eyes, held one hand on the railing, used the other to pull myself up. I heard voices from below, then closer.

"Is this it?" someone was asking beneath me, and I thought I heard James, the American ambassador, answer in the affirmative.

"Come on," I told myself. "Come on." Shame and terror were fighting for supremacy. I chanced a look up—I didn't dare look down—and opened my eyes. I was close. A few more circuits and I could see the outline of the door leading outside.

I was close. I eased myself up, step by step. Rob had done this. Ahmed had done it. I could do it too.

"You're almost there," Rob called, just above me. "Almost up." I gained the wrought-iron landing, maybe the most welcome way-station I had ever known, and looked out through the door at the city beyond—or more precisely, at the roofs and towers of Paris, for we were high, high above the city.

The limestone railing beyond came up to my waist. Maybe. I poked my head through the door, saw the two-foot or less passageway between wall and railing, and saw that we were on the opposite side of the Eiffel Tower, where we needed to be to shoot the fireworks.

"Come on," Rob said, beckoning me out.

"Absolutely not," I said.

"Come on," he said. He squeezed through a little alcove and called back to me. "Just right through here. It's a great shot."

"Nope," I said. My hands held white-knuckled to the door frame. I couldn't go out. And I couldn't go in. I was stuck. I would remain here for the rest of my days. I would die on this landing.

Voices approached from below. Two dozen people had been at the party, but maybe not all of them were coming up.

Perhaps Nadia was staying below. I brushed at my pocket, at the substantial heft of her engagement ring. It would serve everyone right if I didn't survive this.

Nkwele squeezed past me. "Pardon, little man," he said in French, with Clarice just behind him.

"Isn't it an amazing view?" she asked, and did not wait for my reply. She and Nkwele went left, in the opposite direction, and squeezed through the alcove at the other corner.

The ambassador and his wife came next, and followed them on around.

"Where is Ahmed?" I called through the door.

Rob poked his head around. "He's set up and waiting for you."

I edged through the door, saw the rooftops of Paris over the railing, staggered backward onto the landing, almost lost my balance and went backward down the stairs in a heap.

"I can't do it, Rob," I called. "I'm sorry. But I can't."

"It's a one-minute read, Cal," he said. "Seriously. Intro and outro. That's all. We'll have you back down the stairs in three minutes."

I chanced a look down into the city. Oh, such a mistake. I had to sit down on the top step. My legs could not be trusted.

"Jesus," I said. I wanted to weep.

"Do not blaspheme," came the still small voice beside me as Nadia made her way up the last few stairs, both her own hands white-knuckled on the rail.

"I didn't think you were coming," I said.

"Nor did I," she said. "We share this Kryptonite, Calvin." Her head was rigid, eyes now looking directly into mine and nowhere else.

"Oh my God," I said. "Nadia. Take my hand."

Her right hand shot forward and I grabbed it. We stood at the door, opening out onto the observation deck.

"I thought the wall would be higher," she said.

"I know," I said. "It's a travesty."

"Cal," Rob called from the corner. "I need you now."

"I can't do it," I said. I turned to Nadia. "I'm so sorry," I said to her in Arabic. "You shouldn't have come. I shouldn't have come."

"But here we are," she said. "And you have a job to do." She indicated the door with her head.

"I can't," I said.

She stepped through the doorway, put both hands against the railing in front of her, nodded, took a deep breath, and slid right one step.

"Yes, you can," she told me.

Well. Who could deny such a woman? I followed. Two hands against the railing, my back hard against the inner limestone wall, moving slowly, slowly, eyes looking straight out, most assuredly not down.

"Don't be so afraid, Calvin Coolidge," Khalid would have said.

Don't be so afraid.

And yet I was.

I was.

We reached the alcove, Nadia letting me squeeze around first and through it. I could see the Tour Eiffel across the river. It would have been beautiful indeed to anyone who didn't fear this was the last thing he would ever see.

"Ahmed is set up there at the corner," Rob said. "All you have to do is slide over to him so he can get the Tower behind you."

"And put my back to the open air and stand up straight and tall," I said. "Oh my sweet Jesus."

That's all. Don't worry about toppling to the pavement with a zillion-dollar bauble in your pocket. Or anything else.

But to my credit, I slid. I made myself as skinny as I have ever been, and I hugged the inner wall of the tower, and looking only at Ahmed, I willed myself the distance.

But when it came time to turn around, take my hands off the railing, pick up my mic?

I shook my head. Nope.

Nope.

It could not be done.

And then I saw Nadia, creeping across just as I had, pressing against the wall, a look of terror on her face, her eyes fixed unblinking at me.

She stopped next to me, against me, actually. Then she pried my hand loose from the railing and took it in hers. "Turn around," she said.

I am entirely too old to cry over something like this. But that's what I wanted to do.

"I can't," I said.

"Look at me," she said. "Just look at me."

I looked at her, and scared as she was, she was also determined. It reminded me of the look she had worn when she went off the bridge.

"Please do not jump," I told her.

"Calvin," she said, "I have realized something. If we let fear stop us from living, we are already dead." It sounded as if she was speaking as much to herself as to me. "The Blessed Qur'an says that for those who believe, 'on them shall be no fear, neither shall they grieve.'"

"That sounds wonderful," I said. "I wish—"

"Cal," Rob said. The Tower had gone dark. Things were getting ready to blow up.

The fireworks were about to start.

"Calvin, I will believe for you," Nadia said, squeezing hard. "Until the time you can believe for yourself."

"Cal," Rob said again, a growing panic in his voice. Ahmed had his fingers raised and was counting down. "We have got to get the start of the fireworks for the live feed, man. We've got to. I'm begging you."

"I will stand with you until you are done," Nadia told me. She nodded once to herself, once to me, squeezed my hand. "And after."

"And then we will get down the stairs together?" I asked.

I looked to her, to Ahmed, to Cal.

"Whatever is next is next." She looked at Ahmed, who was running out of fingers. "But now is now."

I lifted my mic in my left hand and turned toward Ahmed. Nadia held my right hand, tightly, out of shot.

I took a deep breath.

And I stood tall.

"This is Calvin Jones, reporting from the tower of the American Cathedral in Paris," I said. A firework boomed behind me, and I tried not to flinch. Nadia squeezed my hand. "Behind me, as you can see, the July 14 fireworks display is being fired off the Eiffel Tower." And I actually turned my head, got a look at greens and reds and sparkling silver fireworks arcing through the air.

It was beautiful.

"Today, the people of France celebrate what some call Bastille Day," I went on, feeling Nadia's hand in mine, feeling like I could do this forever if I had to, "and what the French call *La Fête Nationale*.

This isn't a French Fourth of July, as some people think, but it does mark the beginnings of the French movement toward independence, the storming of the Bastille Prison on July 14, 1789. Every year it is commemorated by parades, parties, and fireworks across France, as you can see. And this is one of the best views in all of Paris. We hope you'll enjoy it as much as we do."

Ahmed turned, focused on the glittering lights for a moment, then counted down from three with his fingers, and we were back in.

"This is Cal Jones for News Europe, wishing you *un joyeux Quatorze Juillet* and a very good evening."

And we were out.

I handed Ahmed my mic.

I turned quickly and pressed my back firmly against the tower wall.

"Let us out," I begged Rob, and he scurried to clear the alcove and set us free.

How we got down the stairs, how we walked out into the streets, the fireworks still going off across the river—none of that matters much.

What mattered was that Nadia never once let go of my hand.

We walked down onto the crowded pier, past the spot where I had pulled her out of the water, walked along the Seine well down past the Tower, the moonlight flickering on the water, walked until the fireworks had stopped and the crowds began to disperse, walked all the way down to the Pont de Grenelle and began to cross the bridge there.

We could not at first stop laughing, which I guess makes sense, considering both of us felt we had somehow narrowly escaped extinction, but at last, we began to calm a bit, and to look down at our hands, still connected, and that sobered us.

My phone had begun to buzz in my pocket shortly after the fireworks stopped.

"Should you get that?" she asked me, now swinging our hands a little like sixteen-year-olds on a date.

I shook my head. "It's Rob," I said. "I'm sure he wants to chew me out, or to congratulate me, or to apologize, or something. I don't need to hear any of those things at this particular moment."

"What do you need to hear?" she asked.

"Well," I said. "Maybe why you climbed up that tower even though I was kind of an ass to you. Oh my God," I remembered, patting my pants pocket with my free hand. Yes. The iceberg was still there.

She smiled. "I saw how frightened you were," she said. "And I thought, 'He has already been punished enough.'"

"But you didn't have to come after me." And I stopped us there in the middle of the Pont de Grenelle bridge, where we could get a good look at the faux Statue of Liberty at the western end of the Île aux Cygnes, the Island of Swans, a long, narrow manmade isle in the middle of the Seine. It was just beneath us. "Seriously. Why did you?"

She shrugged. "I thought you might need me."

I let go her hand. "I do need you," I said.

And then I leaned in and kissed her.

It was not a monumental kiss, just a short one on the lips. The fireworks were finished. No tour boats blasted their horns in celebration. I pulled back to make sure I hadn't just done a bad thing, but she was smiling.

"I'm sorry," I said. "I'll take you home."

"I don't want to go back to the hotel," she said, and she took my hand again and pulled me back to her. "Just so you know: I don't want to sleep with you. I am confused enough without involving my body. But I do want to know: why does an American boy jump off a bridge to save a drowning woman?"

"You don't want to go home?" I asked.

"I want to go to your home," she said. And she leaned in and planted one on me.

I believe there were actual fireworks with that second kiss.

And the next thing I knew, I was lying in bed, looking down at a sleeping Nadia with something dangerously like love in my heart.

Rob used to tell me about the early days in Baghdad, after Saddam fell and we had nothing to put in his place. How soldiers in Bradleys and Humvees would sit, still, their hands on their weapons, safeties on, as looters cleared out ministry after ministry, hauled off everything that had any potential value. He told me about how they sat outside the ministry of the interior or some such place watching people load air conditioners and filing cabinets and desk lamps into trucks. And then they stole the trucks.

"Shouldn't we stop this?" one soldier asked his LT.

"How?" he asked. "This is their damn country. If they want to tear it all to shit, what can we do?"

These were our lives, to tear to shit if we chose.

Or maybe to rebuild something from the ruins.

So, anyway, I was lying partly awake, mulling that over in my head for some reason, my hand on Nadia's hip, her head on my shoulder, when the doorbell started ringing. I remembered that scene in *The Sun Also Rises*, where Jake is already in bed and Brett talks his disapproving landlady into letting her come upstairs.

"Jesus," I said. I scooped up my phone, because I guessed whoever it was might be calling too—this would be a great time for Uncle Jack to arrive. Or Kelly McNair.

"Jesus," I said again.

But when I looked at my phone, I knew it wasn't Kelly, and it wasn't Jack, and it wasn't anyone else but my boss.

Because I saw all these banners, news alert after news alert on my phone, all of them saying something like "Terror Attack in Nice."

And message after message from Rob lighting up my phone.

"Oh, Jesus," I said.

It was Rob, of course, downstairs at my gate and then moments later, at my front door. I had just enough time to send Nadia fleeing into the bathroom to put all her clothes on, and to pull on my pants. There wasn't much of a way to keep secrets in my little apartment.

"You have got to answer your phone," he growled, every inch my boss, as I opened the front door and admitted him. "I've been calling for hours. There was an attack in Nice. Maybe a hundred dead. Son of a bitch used a cargo truck," he mopped his forehead, panted. "Ran people down for blocks and blocks. I've got you and Ahmed on the first flight out. Then I want you back in the studio by 6 o'clock tomorrow night." He plopped himself into my one good chair, which sighed audibly. "What the hell have you been doing?"

Then he heard water running in the bathroom, saw Nadia's shoes in the corner, and he blinked a couple of times. "Nothing happened," I said.

He shook his head. "Oh, I think something did." And he mouthed to me, Nadia?

I nodded.

"I am so sorry, Nadia," he called. "*Je suis désolé.*"

"*Ne vous inquiétez pas,*" she said. Don't worry.

"Do you really need me?" I asked. "And I'm not just asking because—" and I indicated the bathroom with my head.

"Of course I do," he said. "I'm not just sending you out into a storm to tell people not to come out in the storm." That pet peeve of all newspeople. "We need our own footage, and we need your take on what we're seeing."

I nodded. Of course, he was right. That was the job. "Okay," I said. "What time is my flight?"

"6:40 on Air France," he said. "Your return is at 12:10. Ahmed has the details. A driver will pick you up here at 5 a.m."

"Okay," I said. "Listen, Rob, I didn't know anything about it. I'm sorry."

"It's godawful," he said. He checked his watch. "But that gives you a few more hours. I'd take advantage of them." He nodded toward the bathroom.

"Yeah," I said. "Nothing charges my libido like the death of innocents."

I showed him to the door.

"This is it," he said, working into his pep talk. "This is why I brought you here."

"That and my sparkling personality," I said. I nodded. I put a hand on his arm. "Don't worry. I've got this."

He nodded back, turned, and I closed the door behind him.

"Can I come out?" Nadia called, the bathroom door cracked just slightly. "Or, rather, how should I come out?"

"I liked what you were wearing while ago," I said. Which was not much.

"Sadly," she said, coming back into the living area, "that look is so last night." She had pulled on her dress, and now was searching for her shoes. She saw my look—which I'm sure was disappointment on the scale of learning that Santa was actually my parents—and laughed sadly.

I reached out, touched that beautiful face. "Do you have to go?"

She took a deep breath. "I think I may have sown the whirlwind," she said. "Is that how you say it?"

"I believe so. Let me focus my question. Do you have to go back?"

She had one shoe in her hand now, and she looked across the room at me. "Calvin, do you believe people can escape the consequences of their actions?"

"No," I said. I shook my head firmly. "But—"

That was a big but. I couldn't finish the sentence. Nadia jumped in. "Perhaps she will believe that I was out late walking, or that I made new friends at the fireworks, or that I went dancing at some fire station." She shook her head. "But all of this will get back to Ali."

"Maybe," I said. "I could come with you. Stand beside you." I felt the weight of her ring in my pocket, pulled it out, offered it to her.

She crossed the room, one shoe on, took it from me, and kissed me on the cheek. "You already have," she said.

"I mean—"

She shushed me, kissed me on the mouth. "Meet me at Harry's tomorrow afternoon when you get back." She kissed my ear. "We'll talk there. I'll tell you what I know. You tell me what you've seen."

"Okay," I said. "I'll walk you home." I started getting dressed.

"To the hotel," she corrected.

"Yes," I said.

"Ali's hotel," she said.

"Yes," I said.

"This is home," she said, gesturing around the room as though I needed to be reminded. And perhaps I did. "Whatever happens, whatever I may have to do or say, please don't ever doubt that I chose this place, this moment. I know you, Calvin."

"Yes," I said. She did, in a way no one ever had.

For the first time, Paris felt like home to me as well, like I belonged to it and it to me, and despite everything I did not and could not know about the future, I could not help but smile.

11.

Nice

——

July 15, 2016
Friday

At 9 a.m., I was in the city of Nice walking the Promenade des Anglais, the long avenue adjoining the Mediterranean Sea. It was mostly deserted except for news trucks, and police still working it as a crime scene, and sad ragged bits of human debris—bloodstains, baby carriages, clothes, shoes, and brand-new memorials of flower, ribbon, and paper. I was following the trail of the 19-ton cargo truck one Mohamed Lahouaiej-Bouhlel had driven through a crowd the night before, the city on my left, the seawall, beach, and sparkling sea to my right. A team of four French soldiers in camo, assault rifles at the ready, walked in front of us down the wide promenade, a classic case of locking the gate after the cow has decamped.

We had gone first to the hospital in hopes of getting some comments from wounded or their families. The Pasteur Hospital, where many of the victims had been taken, was a madhouse, the emergency room stacked to the ceilings, and you could hear people crying, both back in the emergency bays and in the waiting room, where some of the less badly injured still waited to be seen.

I walked up to a number of people, asking them in French, Arabic, and finally, English, if they could tell me anything about the attack. Most of them didn't even look at me. One looked at me, made an obscene gesture, and turned away. But a couple were willing to say something on background, an old man and a young woman. They were both very clear that they did not want to be on television. Both were French, both visiting Nice for the holiday, both had brought their families to enjoy the fireworks, and now one or more of the people they loved were fighting for their lives in the bays behind us.

The stories they told me were about chaos in the dark, people running and screaming, a white truck weaving back and forth, cutting people down like a scythe. The young woman's husband had pushed her to safety, lifted her up over a fence or retaining wall of some kind. He had been hit before he could follow. His pelvis and four ribs were shattered.

"It is funny," she told me, in French. "At first, I could not stop weeping. Now I cannot seem to remember how."

The old man told me he had been separated from his family in the press and knocked over the seawall onto the rocky beach. His face was scraped and bruised from his fall, but when I asked if he needed medical attention, he looked at me as though I were crazy. "My son and grandson," he said. "They are hurt. I am not hurt." He indicated himself, shook his head. He could not be hurt. Not when those he loved were so much more badly injured.

It was a relief to be away from there now, to be outside in the sunshine, a long way from that chaos in the dark. Even though it was early morning, the light was intense and it was already warm, but the breeze was cooling. I walked underneath palm trees as I weaved back and forth, looking at the story from all directions. Ahmed followed me patiently, camera rig on his shoulder. I had asked him to get shots of a few of the spontaneous memorials, and we'd shoot the site where the driver was killed, maybe talk to somebody in authority or an eyewitness if we could find one willing to talk. But just now we were walking down the Promenade des Anglais, trying to figure how it happened, trying to imagine what it must have been like as a man driving a cargo truck plowed into an unsuspecting crowd with the intent of murdering as many as he could.

"What do you see?" I asked Ahmed. "What do we know?"

He shrugged. With his head, he indicated some tire marks. "They said he steered back and forth trying to hit people as they ran. Targeted them." He made a disgusted face, for that, and for what he was about to say. "They say that he ate pork, and slept with men and women."

Early reports were that the suspected perpetrator had been recently radicalized after a checkered past. He was married and divorced. Drank and did drugs. What Ahmed was saying was that he was not a good Muslim, or maybe not a Muslim at all.

But all the same, a local paper, the *Nice-Matin*, had a witness who reported hearing him call out "*Allahu Akbar.*"

This Lahouaiej-Bouhlel didn't run down hundreds of people with a cargo truck just for grins and giggles.

I grew up Southern Baptist, and my most notable memory of religion, before I departed it, was the First Baptist Church of Killeen, Texas. Lots of Fort Hood families, of course, generally more when someone they loved was deployed in harm's way. Since 2009, that place has been a looming gymnasium of a church, but the experience I remember is a little more intimate, a wall of contemporary stained glass, hymns instead of a worship band. And lots and lots of hellfire and brimstone.

Sunday after Sunday, whether my dad was deployed overseas or grudgingly in the pew beside us, my mom and I listened to Dr. Frank Harkness tell us about the grudging love of God and the brooding anger of God, about how we were all one halting breath away from eternity, about how those who did not love this capricious God with all our hearts, souls, and pocketbooks were going to burn in hell for all eternity.

I have since come to understand—even before I met Episcopalians in Paris—that Dr. Harkness was not representative of the Christian faith. That not all Christians shared his belief in an angry God, that not all Christians lacked a pastoral response to those who were frightened for their loved ones, who weren't sure how they were going to make their bills, who saw the world as a violent and dangerous place.

But I also know that Dr. Frank Harkness did what he did, said what he said—and what he didn't say—because he called himself a Christian.

He didn't shame those who fell short because he was required to by his fellow Elks.

He didn't set out to frighten little kids just because he had a Y chromosome.

One person may not represent a faith, but the faith still has to reckon with that one person, and with others like him.

And while I knew gentle and generous Muslims, while my life had been saved many times by a Muslim, while I, had in fact, fallen hard for a Muslim, there was also this. The Muslims who killed innocents in Paris in a night club and a soccer stadium and a restaurant. Who slit the throat of a French priest. Who attacked a Jewish grocery store.

And who did it because of their faith, not despite it.

"Those plazas we saw in the Old Town, the architecture. This city doesn't look French," I told Ahmed. "It looks, I don't know, Italian, I guess."

"Nice was Italian until 1860," he said. "We are, I guess, only a few of your miles from Italy now."

"Hmm," I said. There was so much I didn't know about France.

"You have been to Italy?"

"Yes," I said. The previous summer I had been on a family vacation with the McNair family to Rome and Venice. I had left the theme t-shirt and goodie bag behind in Texas.

Dennis McNair was a typical Dallas oilman. He wore a gray Stetson. I don't know how big. Do they make a 50-gallon hat? He was the classic "All Hat, No Cattle," sort of person, and his wife, Camille, had had work done until her face was rigid, immobile. What she thought or felt behind that Kabuki mask I could not have told you.

But the two of them were kind enough to me. I was, after all, a local celebrity who might someday contribute good-looking grandchildren. So together the four of us stayed in big suites in nice hotels, and walked through St. Mark's in Venice, and saw that fountain in Rome that you throw coins into.

I tossed in a bunch of euros and wished for someone to love. I'm not sure that was Kelly's intent when she handed them to me, but there you go.

"Oh yes," I told him now. "I have been to Italy."

Ahmed was a news junkie, which is a good thing to be in the news business. He had been consulting his phone constantly, checking Twitter since we landed at the airport, was still reading things from his feed and the interwebs as we walked the promenade.

"Bono was trapped in a restaurant a few blocks off the Promenade," he said. "La Petite Maison."

"Bono?" I asked. My worlds were colliding.

"Oui," he said. "Also Alain Ducasse." Off my blank look: "The chef." And my continued blank look. He shook his head. "The most famous chef in the world," he sighed. I was hopeless. He scrolled down.

And then he looked over at me. "There are American victims," he said. "I am sorry, Calvin."

"What does it say?" I said. I stopped walking. Below me on the beach, debris and abandoned clothing offered additional evidence that people had run for their lives just last night.

"From Texas," he said. "Oh." He looked at me, stricken. "You are from Texas, yes?"

I nodded. "Names?"

He shook his head. "Not yet. But a father and a son. Here in Nice from a place called Westlake, it says. Westlake?" He turned to me for confirmation.

"It's outside Austin," I said. "Not too far from where I grew up. We played them in football." Drew Brees and some of the world's great quarterbacks came from Westlake. The Chaparrals won the 5A State title with Drew Brees under center in 1996. Maybe this dead boy dreamed of being a quarterback. And because of some murderous Muslim with a hankering for Paradise and virgins, he would never get the chance.

"How can you stand it?" I asked Ahmed, my stomach tightening with rage, heat rising into my face. "When they take your faith and twist it to do things like this?"

He looked down. His face too was flushed. I thought at first that maybe he would hit me. We did not know each other well yet, although if we did not break up over this, eventually we would know each other inside and out. A reporter and photographer are like a husband and wife. They know the best and worst of each other, cover for each other's mistakes, make each other look better. A photog cuts together their footage so that they tell a story that looks as though they dreamed it together.

"The same way you do," he said at last. "When America blows up some family trying to kill a terrorist. It is not your intent. We are better than our worst actions. Our worst actors." He took a deep breath. "And, Allah be praised, we do more good in the world than bad. Just like, I think, your USA."

I nodded. Good response. I relaxed just a bit. I had been leaning forward, my shoulders drawn tight.

My phone rang then, and Ahmed could not hide his pleasure that my ringtone was "Rock the Casbah." I snuck a look. Uncle Jack. I held up a finger to Ahmed and answered.

"What is it, old man?" I said.

"I just saw the news. Are you okay? Is that anywhere near you?"

I took a deep breath. "It is right where I am," I said. "I am this moment standing on the promenade the perpetrator drove last night."

"Huhn. What are you doin' there?"

"This is my beat, Uncle Jack. Terror in Europe."

"I was afraid of that," he said. He clearly spent a second framing this: "How are you?"

I shook my head, my teeth set. "I am furious, Jack. This is bringing up a hell of a lot of bad stuff for me."

"I was afraid of that," he repeated.

"I am walking down this street. It is supposed to be one of the most beautiful avenues in the world, I hear, and all the same, it feels like Fallujah," I said, which surprised me until I said it out loud. "Like the whole world is dangerous. Like you could lose everything you care about at any moment."

"Son," he said quietly, "you have got to let that go."

"Animals," I spat. "No human would do this."

Would kill Khalid.

Would kill my father.

"They aren't all animals," Jack said. "Them Muslims. You know that, son, even now. Your driver. Khalid. He was a good 'un."

I couldn't answer. I felt doubled-over with pain.

I felt like I was surrounded by a ring of fire.

"And that girl of yours," Jack said. "Nadia. She's a sweet somethin', right? I've never seen you fall so far so fast in my whole life." He was shaking his head. I could see it from here. "You jumped off a bridge for her."

"Right," I said. "That sweet Muslim girl of mine. Her future husband probably funded this attack."

"Jack," he said, reproachfully. He was appalled. The tables had turned. And he was right; I was appalled at myself. Ahmed was trying hard not to hear, but could not help himself. I was broadcasting my prejudice to the entire promenade. To the world.

"I'm working," I said. "It helps. And I will be okay. But I am not okay. Not at the present moment. I am far from okay."

"I worry for you, Cal," he said, and it if I hadn't known better, I would have thought he was crying. My aunt was saying something in the background, and I could see Jack shaking his big shaggy head, No, No, I've got to say this.

"I think maybe you should come home," he said. "I think maybe bein' there, doin' this work, is goin' to be bad for you."

"I can't," I said. "I gave my word, Jack. I gave my word to my friend that I would do this." And now I could see him nodding, even against his will. That was sacred.

"Jack," I said, hoping that saying all this out loud would be magical somehow. "I will get this right. Or I will lose my shit. And either way, you will be the first to know about it."

"Right," he said gruffly. "Okay. Call me if you need me." Aunt Karen said something. "We love you."

"I know," I said. I hung up, put my phone away, couldn't help smiling even in my extremity.

"I'm sorry," I told Ahmed. "I don't know—I don't mean to be—" I stopped. What was I being? Prejudiced? Shell-shocked?

He put a hand on my shoulder. "I am affected as well," he said. "I do not understand how such things can happen. How anyone can justify them."

I felt like he was forgiving me, even though I hadn't even had the presence of mind to ask for forgiveness yet.

"Thank you," I said. I did not deserve that forgiveness, that grace.

I was still so full of hate and anger from the past that I couldn't deal with the present.

We started walking again. The trail of destruction was over a mile long, and I expected we'd want to do a remote from the place where the truck had stopped. I'd seen some photos of it, a big white Renault truck, its windscreen starred with bullets.

The Promenade was quiet as death. The soldiers had gotten a good lead on us, but they continued marching, thoughtfully, heads twisting back and forth, as though something dangerous might still emerge.

"I too have never known someone who would do a thing like this," Ahmed went on as we walked. "The most dangerous person I have ever known would not have killed women. Children. This—" He shook his head. He could not get his head around it either, and that was saying something.

I knew that Ahmed had seen some things.

Ahmed was from Egypt. His brother, he told me, had been in an Egyptian prison ever since Mubarak stepped down. The Muslim Brotherhood didn't like his brother, Ahmed said, and the generals didn't like him either. So he was screwed. Ahmed sent money home to his brother's wife and children. Hoped for things to get better. But they hadn't, and probably never would. He hadn't seen his brother for over five years, wasn't one hundred per cent sure he was even still alive, and he didn't dare go back to Egypt himself to lobby for his release for fear of sharing whatever fate it was.

Like me, he knew a lot about dangerous men, about violence, about people using religion to do harm instead of to heal.

But still, neither one of us had seen anything like this.

Across from the domed Hotel Negresco, the grande dame of Nice hotels, where the driver had first exchanged gunfire with the police, we found a witness who was willing to talk on air. She was an old French woman, and she was laying flowers on the pavement. From a couple of blocks away, we had seen her kneeling awkwardly and maybe painfully to put down her flowers and pray, and by the time we drew near to her she was crossing herself and slowly getting to her feet.

"Madame," I said, in my best French, "did you see the attack?"

"*Oui*," she said.

I asked her permission to film, and she pursed her lips, nodded. She was close to tears, but I could see that she wanted to talk. Sometimes telling your story is the only thing that can keep you upright.

"We were watching the fireworks," she said. "Thousands of us. Tens of thousands. Laughing, clapping." I nodded. I had been watching fireworks myself, and it had been pretty amazing.

"When did you know something was wrong?"

"I looked at my watch," she said. "I used to be a nurse. It was always important to note when something happened." She smiled ruefully. "It was just after 10:30, just after the fireworks concluded. We heard people screaming, then people running, jumping off the seawall, a surge of people like a wave onto the shore. And then we saw the white truck behind them. I saw a man throw a child onto the beach before he was crushed." Tears filled her eyes. "I saw a mother and her baby struck down right here. A Muslim woman in a scarf. What kind of animal would do such a thing?"

I wanted to reach out to her, but of course I could not. I was on camera. I could hear the voice of my Dallas producer as gunfire rang out: "Don't you dare stop broadcasting."

"Did you run?"

She shook her head. "I was not in his path, thanks be to God," she said, crossing herself. "In a moment, he was gone, running down new victims." She indicated further down the promenade with her head, the end of the spree. When she looked back at us, she was a nurse again. "He was gone, and the wounded were left. We did what we could for them. Some of them we carried to the hotel," she said, indicating the Hotel Negresco across the street. "Some of them were dead."

"Are you from Nice?"

"*Oui*," she said. "They say so was this driver." She used a French curse word and spat.

"Born in Tunisia," I said. As though that mattered. "In France for ten years now, they say."

"So he was one of us."

I shrugged.

"How could one of us do this horrible thing?" I shook my head. I didn't know if she meant someone from Nice, or a member of the human race.

"Why do you think he did it?" I asked.

She shook her head. "This was the act of a crazy man," she said. "No reason can explain it."

I thanked her for her time, for talking to us. Ahmed nodded as she walked away. It was good TV.

We walked on a bit and stopped at last on the Promenade across from the Palais de la Méditerranée, where the white truck still sat, although it was screened off from view. I approached one of the guarding gendarmes, who would not go on camera, but confirmed for me that the driver was killed in an exchange of gunfire with police at that spot.

"What else do you know?" I asked him. He looked like a baby, like he wasn't old enough to shave, let alone enforce the law.

He shrugged. "Not a thing," he said. "I just came on shift. Just another crazy Muslim who wants to blow up the whole world." He spat.

"Thanks," I said, turning away. I shook my head at Ahmed. Nothing on the record.

"Let's get some kind of panoramic shot," I suggested to him as we walked to the stairs going down into a beach club. "Back up the promenade. Or maybe something down on the beach. The stuff people abandoned as they fled."

"The manager of the beach club here talked to the media," he said, consulting his phone. "Hundreds of people jumped or fell off the sea wall, ten feet down into his restaurant. Broken arms and legs."

"They ran," I said. "Maybe they kept running even with broken legs."

We took the stairs down into the abandoned club, walked past scattered beach chairs and out onto the beach. It was all rocks and pebbles. I picked my way through the trash and remnants of last night's panic to the shoreline, where I stopped, balanced on the steep bank of the beach where it dropped to the surf.

A wave came in. A flash of color caught my eye and I looked down. A tiny Minnie Mouse tennis shoe, pink, flowered, washed in, then out with a clatter of fleeing pebbles, then back in, almost onto my shoes.

The pebbles shifted beneath me, my feet went out from under me, and I fell heavily, not much more than a 180-pound sack of flesh.

"Calvin," Ahmed said. He reached out a hand, put it on my shoulder. "Calvin?"

I was still staring down at that shoe, caught up in its cycle of arrival and departure.

I did not feel him shake me. I was not there anymore.

Khalid had seven children, from 13 years old to two. I sometimes forgot how important his kids were to him, how much he loved them, how he feared for them in the charnel house that Iraq had become, and then I would see him offering money or food to a street urchin as we walked through Fallujah and I would remember.

He talked about his children often, three daughters, four sons. Unlike some Arab men, he loved his daughters fiercely, as much as the boys if not more. He talked about their futures, about how out of this garbage heap something beautiful was someday going to blossom.

Maybe that was why his antenna were out when he saw the ragged little girl hunched over in the marketplace that day. She was scared. Anyone could see that. What she was doing, to whom she belonged—none of that was clear.

But she was scared, and Khalid saw that instantly, and he stepped forward before I could do anything.

He was across the plaza and at her side in an instant.

I heard him asking her if he could help, if she needed money or food.

She raised her hand, her index finger lifted. She wanted help, I believe, and Khalid could have done something, somehow, if only there had been time.

Because then she exploded. Was detonated, maybe, is a more proper way to describe what happened.

I was lucky, if you can call it that. I was knocked on my ass, horizontal, my ears bleeding. Some metal pierced my sleeve, but I wasn't myself struck by any of the flying debris, by any of the body parts and splintered bone scattered across the square. Twenty-some people closer than me to the marketplace were shredded, turned into red ghosts, barely identifiable as formerly human. I counted them as I got to my feet, moved toward the blast site.

You don't stop being a newsman just because your friend has been blown up.

For he was. Blown up.

Khalid was destroyed.

There were no pieces of him left large enough to identify.

At ground zero, I found only a shoe, a tiny unlaced sneaker standing up, a foot still in it, the ankle bone white and obscene in the sunlight, although I heard that they later found the little girl's head on a pile of debris a hundred feet away. This often happened with suicide bombers or those wearing explosives, that their heads were among the few surviving artifacts. Often their faces bore a surprised expression.

"Calvin," Ahmed was saying to me now on the beach in Nice, calling my name again and again, his voice rising in pitch and volume. He was shaking me, violently, actually, which was probably a good thing. You don't dread a thing for a decade and come back easily from reliving it.

"I'm okay," I lied. The shoe was still rolling in and out on the surf. I turned away from it, let him pull me to my feet. "I'm okay. Let's do this."

He looked dubiously at me. I was pretty sure that other camera people were going to get an earful about this when we got back, if not Rob himself. Things got around. But I was okay for now. Look at me.

I am strong. I am invincible. I am woman.

I took a deep breath, stood up straight. "Let's do it. Let's get the standup."

We went back, off the beach, up the stairs, Ahmed framing the shot with the empty promenade behind me, the palm trees, the ocean.

He counted down, and we were shooting.

"At 10:30 last night," I said, after I introduced myself and tagged the network, "just after 'Prom Party,' the fireworks commemorating the celebration of Bastille Day, a heavy white cargo truck drove onto the heavily congested Promenade des Anglais here in Nice, and for 17 minutes and over the distance of a mile, the driver intentionally ran down pedestrians, killing or injuring over 500 people before he was himself killed in a shootout with local police.

"The driver of the truck, a Tunisian resident of Nice named Mohamed Lahouaiej-Bouhlel, has been connected to the Islamic State, and French president François Hollande has called this attack another instance of Islamic terrorism in this country. Regardless of how and why this attack happened, today the people of Nice—and people around the world—struggle to understand how faith could lead someone to such depravity. So do I."

I went on in that vein for three minutes total. It was a good report, although it would be clear to anyone watching to the end that I was emotionally invested. Sometimes that's off-putting when you just want the facts. But sometimes personal feelings are a positive thing. *If you'd been here,* my report was saying, *if you'd seen what I've seen, you would be shaken too.*

Ahmed didn't say one way or another what he thought. He wasn't paid to have an opinion, although I knew him well enough already to know that he did have them. "I called a cab," was all he said. "We will catch the next flight back."

"Good enough," I said. It wouldn't take us long to edit. I had been putting the story together in my head all day as we shot, and now that we had the wrap-around, I could see almost exactly how I wanted to cut it.

I was done. Thank God.

Because now I could think of life, and life didn't want to be stuffed in a back corner any longer.

I texted Nadia to tell her I could meet her at Harry's around 3, if she could get out. I had thought about her a lot on the way down, and now that the work was done, I was thinking about her again, wondering how her return had been, wondering how she was feeling, wondering if she was thinking about me as I was thinking about her.

I was a little giddy, I realized. And that scared me. I hadn't been even slightly giddy about anything for a long time. Giddy had never worked out very well for me. And particularly not when paired with fragile.

"Don't be so afraid, Calvin Coolidge," Khalid used to say. I know he thought that was good advice. But it turned out that there was plenty in this world to be afraid of. Love, hate, all of it could be turned into hurt.

Sticking your neck out could get you reduced to nothing.

"Calvin," Ahmed was saying, again. There was an Uber ready for us, and there I stood, thinking, remembering, none of it changing a thing.

"I'm good," I said. "I'm good." I climbed into the car. We set off for the airport. I took some notes for the 6 o'clock broadcast.

The totals for Nice: Over 80 dead, including the perpetrator. Over 400 wounded. Thousands of people emotionally shattered. Thousands more grieving. Who knows how many more shaken by the events. A whole city. A whole country. The president had declared three days of national mourning.

This was too much for me. Too many emotions.

Too much pain.

"I think I may have made a mistake," I told the cab as we drove.

"What?" Ahmed said.

"I think I may have been better suited to weather remotes and city council," I said.

"I don't know what that means," Ahmed said.

I shook myself. "Of course you don't," I said. "It's nothing. Some past life stuff."

My phone pinged. "I'll see you there," Nadia said. "Leash in hand."

Nothing about how she had been for the past 12 hours. Nothing about the future. But against my better judgment, I smiled.

"I can't wait to see you," I texted back. "Order me a whisky sour." And I gave her a string of heart emojis like a Vegas slot machine.

I was giddy, I realized.

Oh boy.

Oh boy.

12.

Paris

July 15, 2016
Friday

I fell asleep on the short flight back to Paris Orly, which turned out not to be such a great thing. Because even though I had gotten almost no sleep the night before, I would maybe have preferred the exhaustion to the terror. I was still having the dream, you see, only now it seemed to be shifting, mutating in front of my eyes, the giant footsteps exploding closer and closer, yes, the horrible white light, yes, but now Khalid was only the first person to disappear.

Next, the white light took my father.

A baby, so small he looked more like a sonogram than a human being.

Officer Roberts.

And Nadia.

The light kept flashing.

People kept disappearing.

And I was losing any semblance of calm. I was screaming. I was screaming at the top of my lungs.

Until I was shaken awake.

"Calvin," Ahmed was saying, as always. He was holding my shoulder, and people around us were looking at me with a substantial degree of alarm. "Calvin!"

He turned around to the other passengers, and to a male flight attendant with short spiky dark hair who was standing just close enough to my aisle seat to be safely out of arm's reach. "See," Ahmed said, a big calming smile on his face, as though he were talking to children. "It is okay. He was dreaming. A bad dream." He shook me again, as if to prove his point. "See. Everything is okay."

They nodded, the old woman across the aisle from me and the flight attendant turned back to what they were doing, although the flight attendant lingered, watching for a moment, until I looked up at him, met his eyes, nodded.

"*Bien,*" I said.

"*Certainement,*" he said, bowing a little before turning and making his way back up the aisle to the front of the plane. I half-expected an announcement over the intercom: "There is nothing to be worried over. *C'est bien.*"

Back at the studio I edited my Nice report, which they wanted to push out live as soon as it was finished, and as I worked, I started giving some thought to what I would say at 6 o'clock. To go big or go calm. Right now I wanted to go big: to say that this was another horrific example of radical Muslim terrorism. That the pendulum had swung to the far reaches of what our lives could encompass. That in this act we were once again facing the worst of human reality, the very tippy-top depravity of which humans were capable.

Rob poked his head into my editing bay at one point.

"Hey," he said. He was eating an apple, and I suddenly realized that I hadn't eaten all day. That I was, in fact, starving.

"What?" I asked. I actually had a pencil in my mouth. That's a real thing. People still do it. "I'm working here."

"How are you holding up?" he asked, taking another bite.

"Nice was pretty awful," I said. "But it always is." I knew that he would get that. Rob had seen his own suicide bomber heads, their eyebrows vaulted in astonishment.

"I heard that you were having nightmares."

Ahmed. Well, I didn't expect it to stay hidden. There are few secrets in a newsroom.

"Of course I am," I said. "Why should that have changed?"

He raised his hands, palms high. "I'm just checking in," he said. "Is there anything you need?"

"No," I said. "Not at the present moment."

"Come for an apéro this evening?" He looked meaningfully at me. I could see that he was wondering if he had done a smart thing in inviting me to France.

"Of course," I said. I was beginning to wonder the same thing myself. "I'm meeting Nadia at Harry's in a bit. But I—or we—will come by. What time?"

"After the broadcast," he said.

"Okay," I said. "Of course. Hey. How are things at home?"

"Tense," he said. "It'll be a good thing, actually, to have some buffers."

"Is Brigid still mad?"

He took another bite. "Oh yes. Angry and everything else."

"Well, if one of those things is gratitude that you're still alive, then I think things will work out."

"See you around seven?"

"Sure," I said.

"Great," he said. "And Cal. Thank you. For Nice and whatever comes next."

I nodded. That was true. This work was hard and real and valuable. It had to be done, and I was good at it. Maybe it would work out.

"You're welcome," I said.

"I hope you don't regret it," he said.

I nodded and turned back to my editing. "Yeah. See you soon."

Harry's New York Bar was quiet, the mid-afternoon lull before, I suspected, the Friday evening busy. A French family sat in a booth in back—two stylish parents in their thirties, three kids. They were looking over the menus Frederick had proffered as though there were significant lunch choices to be made. Salad or grilled cheese, I wanted to say to them. That's all we're really talking about.

God, I was starving.

I waved to Frederick, walked back and took a booth underneath banners for Virginia, Villanova, Vanderbilt, Northern Arizona University, Michigan, Sweet Briar College.

"Monsieur Cal," he said, coming over. "Are you perhaps meeting someone?" His need was so transparent that I could not help myself.

"Nadia should be on the way," I said.

"What—" he began, then caught himself. "Do you know what she intends to do yet?"

I shook my head. "I have no knowledge," I said. "Nothing. Only hope."

He looked down. Looked up, nodded to himself. "I just—" And again he caught himself. Totally a professional. "What would you like to drink?"

"Gin and tonic," I said. "Double. Tall. And I'm going to need to eat something."

Frederick left me a menu. He went away to put my drink together, and I sat, staring at the entrance, the swinging doors leading out to the Rue Daunou.

How many broken people had walked through those doors over the years?

How often had Mr. Hemingway come through those doors not knowing what he was doing, what was going to happen next, why he was even here?

That was important, I thought. I was not the only person wondering what would happen next. It's so easy to lock ourselves into our own perceptions, our own needs. We can forget that our brokenness is not unique or even particularly interesting.

Brokenness.

My father was flown back to Dover Air Base in Delaware in pieces. The casket was sealed, as it should have been. There was no more of my father to show the world than there had been of Khalid. No photographers or cameramen had been allowed at the facility because of Bush administration policies, which, amazingly, worked for the news organizations as well. Our ratings declined when we broadcast images of the honored dead. People didn't actually want to watch news reports from Iraq and Afghanistan, didn't want to read or hear about the real cost of the war to the one per cent of Americans actually fighting it.

They turned to other parts of the paper, flipped over to other channels whenever we started talking about the honored dead. It was too much.

Which I got. I didn't want to be there either.

In Iraq, I was embedded with a unit trying to root out IED's like the one that had killed my father. The night before he died, we got word of some locals who were crawling like worms toward the roadway we were traveling. Our LT told his men to paint them with lasers. If that didn't dissuade them from whatever devious actions they were taking, he told them, "Light them up."

By which, of course, he meant, blast them back to the Stone Age.

The miscreants ran. Somehow, they eluded our men, and disappeared back into the city. Sometimes it seemed like everyone in Iraq was the enemy.

The IED they left behind was disarmed, turned into scrap metal. No one was killed or maimed.

We celebrated with near-lethal energy drinks, played dominos with the locals.

And then the call came through. "Cal," the LT said, "your dad got hit." And all of them—these nineteen-year-old privates from Georgia and Oregon and Nebraska and New Hampshire—looked at me, and held out their hands, and expressed their sorrow.

There was no point in going to Fallujah. There was nothing to see there. Or, rather, there was plenty to see there, but nothing identifiable of my father. So I caught the flight that would take me to Dover.

Rob checked in with me before I boarded.

"Do you need me?" he asked, as though FOX would turn him loose just because the war had now claimed a life that mattered to him.

"I've got this," I said. Which I didn't. And trusted him to know.

"Are you sure?"

"No," I told him. "I am a hell of a long way from sure. But this is where I am. I've got to go bury my father, God damn him."

I hung up. I stood on the tarmac for a solid ten minutes, wondering what came next, before I pulled myself together, marched up the stairs, took a seat on a cargo plane headed back to the States.

The next time I saw Rob was in my kitchen in Killeen, Texas, when he held up a light against the darkness and demonstrated that he'd rather risk getting the shit kicked out of him than watch me disappear beneath the water.

Those were bad times, and I was feeling them again. You don't lose the feeling. You just shove it back into a closet, and hope that it won't claw its way out.

And yet, it seems to force open the closet door with an avalanche of feeling, knock you down, cover you head to foot.

That's how it felt as I took a deep breath, seeking some clarity.

And that was the moment when Nadia walked in the front door.

Frederick came out from behind the bar, where he was putting the finishing touches on my double tall gin and tonic, and he embraced her. She saw me in the corner, and her face lit up.

I got to my feet, met her in the middle of the room, threw my arms around her.

"Thank God," I said, "thank God." Which is not how I greet most of my dates.

I pulled her into my shoulder, smelled her musky smell, kissed her beautiful lips once, twice, three times.

"Allah be praised," she said in return, at last pulling away so that she could look at me. "How are you, Calvin?"

I shook my head, struggled to get something out. "Nice was pretty terrible." She could see it in my eyes.

"I've been following," she said. "I watched your first report."

"Is that already out?"

She nodded. "I saw it on the web. You looked shaken."

"I am shaken," I said. "I've been shaken. And stirred."

I looked at her. She was stunning.

And she was also one of them.

"I know," she said. "This has been a hard week for both of us. Do you have a drink coming?"

I smiled a little. "Is Frederick Frederick?"

She smiled back, spared some glow in his direction. "Of course he is."

"Mademoiselle," he responded, as he carried my towering gin and tonic to the table. "What can I get you?"

"Would peace of mind be too much to ask for?" She smiled to defuse that question, but it was, nonetheless, a real question. I was not the only one wrestling with the past, present, future.

"I think I may have a bottle of that stashed behind the bar," he smiled. He nodded at us both, and hurried to the kitchen to fetch the French family their Croque-Monsieurs and Madames.

And Nadia slid into the booth next to me, took my hand, kissed it.

Her lips burned like flame. I rubbed my hand, cupped her face, her strong chin, put my fingers on her lips.

"I missed you," she said. She took a handful of peanuts from the bowl, tossed them into her mouth, smiled at me.

"Were you in trouble when you got home?"

"*Certainement*," she said. "She did not believe I had been to any party at a firehouse. It was not," she admitted, "my strongest alibi."

"Are they following you? Remember last night in the bar—"

"I think yes," she said. "That tall man you saw in the bar. With the salt and pepper hair. I think he may have followed us back to the suite from your apartment."

"Were you afraid then?"

She shook her head.

"Are you afraid now?"

She shook her head again. "All this will lead where it leads," she said. "And so far, it has lead to this. To us. Sitting here."

"Nadia," Frederick said, a towel over his forearm, his eyes trained on her face. He asked again, "What can I bring you?"

"A French 75," she smiled, laying her fingers on his forearm. "And thank you, Frederick," she said. "I am grateful for you."

He bowed, a surprisingly graceful move from a large bearded bartender. "You are welcome," he said. And he smiled. "I am glad you are here."

"This could be the last time," she said quietly, after Frederick had retired to the bar.

"Really?" I said, landing on a synthetic lightness I did not feel. "I was sort of planning that you and I might be popping in here for the rest of our lives."

"For myself," she said, touching her chest, "I can imagine no greater joy. But I have more to think about than my own happiness. There's my family. I owe them a duty. There is much more beyond that."

I let out a sigh.

"Ali," I murmured. "Is he in town yet?"

"He arrives late tonight," she said. "But now we know that he has been following my actions for a while." She held up her leash, shook it, her head sadly. "Pathetic excuse of an excuse."

"So, that guy in the Four Seasons bar?"

She nodded. "I would guess now that Ali has had me followed since I arrived. He would perhaps say for my safety, although it scarcely feels like that. All my walks. All my dinners." She indicated the swinging doors of the bar by inclining her head. "I think that man with the salt and pepper hair is outside just now on the Rue Daunou."

I slid out from the booth, my teeth clenched. "I'll go out there and—"

"That will change nothing," she said, taking my hand and urging me to sit back down. "Last night, Wahida told me that she knew everything. I'm sorry, Cal. I hate that you are caught up in this."

"Okay," I said. "So she knows. And Ali knows. That will make it easier, right? To tell him?" I looked at her, and the look of pregnant expectation on my face was probably laughable.

She took my hand. "We'll see," she said. "We'll see where this leads us."

"What do you mean?" I asked. I untangled my fingers from hers.

"I have more to think about than my own happiness," she repeated.

I think maybe I had forgotten that, but it pushed me wrong. I was thinking only about my own happiness after so much unhappiness, and she felt essential in that equation.

I had found joy for the first time in a long time, maybe ever.

I did not see how I could get to happiness without her.

"So what are you thinking?" I asked, crossing my arms. "That in 24 hours, you could be marrying another man?"

"Calvin," she said quietly, "I have to choose whether to marry a man I've never met or to be out on the streets of Paris with no job and no money, whether I will rescue my family from poverty or ruin them, whether I might be happy with you or unhappy with you, whether I might someday be happy or unhappy with someone else."

"Why wouldn't you be happy with me?" I asked, too quickly, jumping past every single one of those other alternatives.

"Cal," she said, "sometimes there are no perfect choices. Sometimes no matter what you decide, something is still lost. And in this matter, I have no perfect choice. No matter what I do, someone will be hurt. You, my family, myself. What matters, perhaps, is which choice will help the most people."

I don't know why I chose to be offended by that. It was noble. She was noble. But maybe because now I was doing the hard work of realizing that I really wanted her to choose me, was leaning hard into that choice for myself, I couldn't see why she wouldn't want that too.

Maybe because I couldn't stand the thought that I might be the one who ended up getting hurt.

She saw it. "Please, Cal," she said, touching my face. "Right now I just want to be here with you. A boy and a girl, oui? To talk to you. To touch you." She turned my face toward her. I had been looking down at the table. "You've had a horrible day. What are you feeling?"

She reached for me, and God forgive me, I shifted away from her touch.

"Every time I open the door to my heart the tiniest crack," I said, "something comes along and burns it to ashes."

She sat up straight. "Don't treat me like someone who has choices," she said. "If our hearts were the only things—"

"You do have choices, Nadia," I said. "We all make choices. We live and die with them." I looked at the opposite wall, at a picture of Papa Hemingway kicking a can down a road in Idaho. He looked so full of life. But within weeks or months of that photo he had put a shotgun in his mouth.

Sometimes we choose oblivion. I don't know why.

On that day that my father was buried in Killeen—when the pieces of my father were buried, I should say—a number of his soldiers got up to talk about him. People who had served with him for thirty years spoke of his humor and his courage. And when they were done, everyone turned to me, his son, to close out the festivities, to zip the bag shut.

And as you have seen, I did not know what I could say about the man who had been absent for so much of my life, about the man who had suffered the loss of his wife and lashed out in pain, about the man who had chosen danger and ultimately death over the son who survived.

I'm sure that my aunt and uncle were watching with some suspense. I was myself kindly interested in what I was going to end up saying, whether the better part of me or the most damaged part would show up.

"There are only pieces of my father in that coffin," I ultimately said, standing at the graveside. It was a hot Texas morning late in July—although not as hot as Fallujah—and already I could feel the sweat breaking out on my brow. "I don't mean to be offensive. It's just the plain truth. And there are only pieces of my father here today. I've heard things about him I never knew before. And I knew him my whole life."

I looked around at the mourners. Some of them met my gaze. Some looked at the ground. This wasn't easy for any of us.

"My father was a man of slogans," I said. "Words you could find on a t-shirt, maybe. But they were good words. Duty. Honor. Courage. Responsibility." I paused, seeing that maybe my best self meant to show up after all. "And love. Not like I always understood it. He didn't really display love, although I think in his own way he did love me. But it's like they say in the Bible, no man has greater love than to offer his life for his friends. That love was exclusive. He could never love me the way he loved those he cared for most. Who cared for him. His real family. His boys. But he loved you with all his heart. I hope you know that."

I sat down then. There was nothing more I could say. I didn't know where I could go after that, but most likely it was to some place where I made an ass of myself, looked like an ingrate, clearly didn't understand what it means to serve alongside those who have sworn to give their lives, if need be, for the rest of us.

All I did realize was this, something clicking shut in my brain: If you really love somebody, you don't forsake them.

If you really love somebody, you don't leave them alone and broken.

"My father died on Bastille Day nine years ago," I said. "Did I tell you that?"

"Calvin," she said. She wanted me to say more, but I was a long way away, behind a wall, and she looked at me, trying to figure out where I was, why.

"You seem so different, Cal," she said quietly, reaching out to me again. I let her put a hand on my arm, felt her fingers caress my bicep. "What is happening? Talk to me."

I wondered if my father had ever thought about this exchange consciously, his men for his son at home. And if so, why he had made that choice.

"For over a mile," I said, looking down at my clenched fists, "a Muslim extremist drove a cargo truck down a crowded pedestrian byway in Nice, crushing women and old people and children in the name of Allah." My teeth were also clenched. Perhaps my very heart was clenched. These words were not communication. They were intended to wound, and they found their mark.

"Surely," she said, her hand falling from my arm, "you know this murdering bastard does not represent my faith."

I did not—could not—look up. I had chosen. "This driver did not invoke the name of Bruce Springsteen as he drove. He did not call on Barack Obama or Hermione Granger." There was an edge to my voice that I did not want there, but I did not see how to call it back, did not know why I had gone down this particular byway, did not even understand why I was so angry. For I was angry. Furious. Beyond control.

"'God is great!' witnesses reported him shouting as he plowed through the crowd. *He* clearly believed he was running down the innocent on behalf of Allah."

Nadia brought her hand up to her face. I could not tell if she was angry or sad, but it was clear that she was powerfully affected. She shook her head, her face screened by her fingers.

She shook her head.

Frederick brought Nadia's drink over, set it down, could see that something was happening at our table. He looked from me to her and back to me and backed warily away.

Nadia's face was colored, and her fists now clenched too, but she still wanted to think the best of me, so she still tried to speak as to a rational being.

"I read that a third of his victims were Muslim." She looked up at me, although I did not meet her eyes. "You yourself talked to a woman who witnessed the death of a Muslim woman and her child. There is nothing in the Blessed Koran about killing women and children. Calvin, this attacker was an animal." I looked up now, and her eyes were blazing. "How dare you make these comparisons? He does not represent my faith. I reject this man, and any attempt to equate his acts with Islam. These are crimes against humanity. All of humanity."

"Oh, sure," I said, raising a finger. "This bad man doesn't represent you." I raised my thumb. "That bad man doesn't represent you. But the bombs keep exploding, don't they? The smoke keeps rising. People keep dying. Don't they?"

I saw the white light, saw those I loved disappearing into it.

Nadia dropped her hand from her face. She looked at me, and she smiled, and her smile was not harsh, but sad. Like she had seen into the heart of something.

"I too wish things could be different, Calvin," she said. "I wish I had bought that scooter from you. I wish we were riding together under the Golden Gate Bridge with no one but ourselves and our future to consider. I wish that I were marrying you tomorrow night. But maybe none of those things were ever possible." She blinked rapidly, three or four times, shook her head, coming to her own realizations. "Life is the art of what is possible, and only that. Everything else is illusion."

I too wished those things for us. I wished I had known Nadia when she was an undergrad first trying to figure out the world.

I wished I had offered her my mother's one-third carat diamond ring as a tiny token of the love I bore her.

I wished I had offered her my heart before it was so badly mangled, before that door seemed again to be closed and padlocked.

"Yes," I sighed. "Everything else is illusion." I shifted slightly away from her so that we were no longer touching.

So, this was it. Whatever we had hoped, whatever we had imagined, this was the end of our story. And I was at fault as much as the circumstances. Nadia did not wish to be in this place, choosing between unforeseeable alternatives, but I was choosing to make that choice a simple one.

I was choosing to drive her away.

I lowered my head, and closed my eyes, and so it was that I did not see Nadia get up from her seat, did not see her as she made for the exit, although I heard her steps, slow, sad, heard the swinging door open and close, heard her weeping until I did not.

When I opened my eyes, she was gone.

I was sitting in the booth at Harry's, college pennants over my head, a French family nearby, but I was alone.

Until Frederick stomped over to me, indicated Nadia's hardly-troubled French 75 with an emphatic flick of his hand, and demanded, "What is wrong with you, Monsieur Cal?"

"Wrong with me? Frederick, I just came from a terrorist attack—"

"You just drove away a darling girl, a girl who loves you." He smoothed down his white apron, which had gapped at his chest as he leaned over me, stopped and collected himself because I'm sure it is bad business for a bartender to yell at his customers. "Why are you so angry, Monsieur Cal? Who are you so angry at? Because I can assure you it is not Nadia. That girl has never done anything but desire your happiness."

"Does she?" I said. "What if she marries this Ali? Where is my happiness then?"

He shook his head like a lion, mane flung everywhere. "Do you imagine I will be happy if she marries this rich Saudi? No! I will be heart-broke! But if she does, it will be because it is the right thing to do. The only thing she can do. She is a smart girl. A good girl. She must make the very best choice, for her, for her family, for the world. Can you not see this? Can you not see anything beyond your own desire? Your own pain?"

"Nice speech," I said. I picked up Nadia's glass, drained her French 75 in four big gulps, set it down with a clatter. "Can any of us?"

"You may imagine that you are angry at that girl," he repeated, sitting down quietly across from me. "Or frightened by what her decision might mean for you. I understand that. But I am watching you. I am always watching. Your anger is deeper and so much longer lasting than this moment, than this attack. You are angry about something else, and Nadia is caught in the crossfire." He looked at me inquisitively. "Crossfire, yes?"

"Yes," I said. "That is right. Crossfire. All of that is right." I dropped my head onto the table with a thunk. It hurt. It should hurt. "Oh, sweet baby Jesus. What have I done?"

Frederick stood up, picked up Nadia's glass, wiped the table under it, draped the towel back over his arm. "You have hurt the woman you love."

"The woman we love," I muttered, looking up at him accusingly.

He looked sideways at me, and I hung my aching head. I was better than that. He went on. "Perhaps neither of you have said the word, but you know I am right. And now you must correct it. You are not angry with her. You must apologize. You must fix what is broken."

"I am a self-centered idiot," I said.

"Yes," he said. "And so. You must apologize."

I pulled out my phone and started to text her, but I put it away. It was too late. This could not be fixed by a text, perhaps could not be fixed by anything I could possibly say.

"The check, please, Frederick," I said.

"Oui, Monsieur Cal," he said.

I slammed my fists against the table, alarming the French family who were now eating their French sandwiches.

"Oh, this life," I said. Now my hands hurt.

Frederick looked at me, but he nodded sympathetically. "Oui, Monsieur Cal," he said, and he passed over the bill.

13.

Paris

July 15, 2016
Friday

When you make a mistake as a journalist, you issue an apology and offer a correction. It's important to set things rights, to remake yourself in the eyes of those watching as a person worthy of trust.

Your allegiance is not to yourself, but to the truth.

It's a good lesson for life, I thought, as I walked to the Metro station. Too often we are caught up in our way of seeing, so sure of our way of being that we don't make room for the possible. The truth is what we make it, not what it is.

And today, the truth was that I was overwhelmed by hatred and destruction, and was placing the blame squarely on Islam, when Nadia and others were assuring me that the blame was on individual human beings who chose violence and death.

We didn't blow up the whole WASP Christian populace when a white supremacist blew up a government building in OKC, did we?

Why was I doing this?

I walked down stairs and stairs, boarded a rattling Métropolitain train, stood at a pole, ignoring a panhandling busker singing Edith Piaf directly into my face.

I needed some perspective. Some wisdom. Who else would get what I was going through?

And then it came to me: Father Cameron.

Of course, part of me was appalled. A priest? Really?

But no, I thought.

When things go to shit, you ask: Where is the fucking chaplain?

I checked the stops quickly, got off at Concorde, gave the male Piaf a couple of euros on my way out. In some perverse way, he had helped me make a decision. I changed to the Yellow train, and got off at George V. When I came upstairs onto the Champs Elysees, I called the Cathedral, and actually got Father Cameron on the line.

"I didn't think you'd be there," I said, after greeting him, reminding him who I was.

"Friday is normally my Sabbath," he admitted. "But this Sunday is the national Day of Mourning, and the Cathedral is going to be packed. We have a lot of prep to do."

"I'm just back from Nice," I told him. "Reporting on the attack. I'm—" I couldn't say exactly what I was. But something about how I couldn't say what I was let Cameron know all he needed to know. After a short silence, he spoke.

"Can you come by?"

"I'm five minutes out," I told him.

"Great," he said. "Good. I'll meet you at the front gate and we'll find a place to talk."

I crossed the Champs, looking back up the hill to the Arc de Triomphe, to the people pausing in the middle of the street to take selfies with the Arc. On the corner, a line of people waiting to get into the Louis Vuitton flagship stretched down George V. The tower of the American Cathedral soared over the trees. I could scarcely believe I'd stood up there of my own free will. And of course, I hadn't. It had taken the material intervention of Nadia to get me up there. It made me wonder what else she might be capable of helping me do.

Three blocks down I passed the Four Seasons, where Nadia was hidden on some upper floor, where another crowd lined the street waiting for someone famous to come out. Kardashians or J Lo. Bono, maybe. The American Cathedral was the next block down, and at the black wrought-iron gates Father Cameron waited—in another Hawaiian shirt, this one with a white clerical collar affixed.

He shook my hand, firmly. "Cal."

"Father. Nice shirt."

"I know. And call me Cam, if you can." He pulled me in through the gates. An ancient woman sat behind the glass at the front desk, and when he waved at her, her face lit up like she had encountered Yves Montand or something. "Madame Le Clerc, Monsieur Jones." I waved, and I did not score anything like that reaction. Cameron was an Episcopal rock star.

With an unobtrusive hand on my arm, he steered me to the right, past the Dean's Garden, past the cloisters, into what turned out to be the church itself. "My office is packed," he explained. "I think the nave is our best option. Allan, the organist, is practicing. I hope you don't mind. He's quite good. And a fucking mess. But there you go. That's organists for you."

We walked into the nave, and I saw the towering organ pipes above me to the right. Then I turned and saw all the way down to the altar. It was gorgeous. I felt immediately at peace, which was a strange thing to say about church, where I had rarely felt at peace in my life.

"It's—" I shook my head. Again, I was struggling for words. State flags hung above, to either side: Arizona, Oklahoma, Rhode Island. The high altar on the far shore from us was golden, a painting of Christ on the cross flanked by two panels, and the ceiling was cross-vaulted and seemed almost out of sight. It was not the largest cathedral I'd ever seen, but it was exquisite.

"I know," he said, watching me. "I get that feeling every time I walk in here. This church was consecrated in 1886. John B. Morgan—cousin of J. P. Morgan—was the rector who built this place. I'm sure that didn't hurt with the fund-raising. George Edmund Street, maybe the greatest architect of the Gothic Revival style, designed it. My favorite bit is the chapel off to the left. The altarpiece is a triptych from the early fifteenth century by a painter called the Master of Roussillon. We don't even know how much the painting is worth. It's uninsurable."

I snorted. "Is that a word? Uninsurable?"

"Of course it is. Like when we were in country, right?"

I smiled, nodded. "Exactly." Aetna or whoever thought I was a goner from the moment I arrived, but they had to try and fix a figure to that risk.

The organist was playing something slow and haunting, but it didn't keep us from hearing each other. "Fauré," Cameron said after listening for a moment. "Probably an introit."

"I'll take your word for it," I said.

"Cal, you should come be with us Sunday," he said. "It'd probably be good for you."

"I'll take your word for it."

"Not much of a churchgoer," he intuited. He looked sharply at me, then directed me into a pew.

We took seats on the left side of the aisle, him just in front of me and turning to address me, me behind him and leaning in to make sure he could hear me.

"My church history militates against it. Churchgoing, I mean." I remembered Dr. Frank Harkness, First Baptist Killeen, remembered feeling beaten and battered after every service there, as though I could not be worth less, remembered how on the way home from church I tugged off my clip-on tie, discovered I could breathe again.

"Maybe so. But these doors are open to you, Cal," he said. "Always. This is a house of prayer for all people."

"Even people who don't think they can pray?"

He reached across and patted my shoulder. "Maybe especially those people."

Allan finished the piece he'd been practicing, started something new, something with lots of splashy arpeggios and two-handed independence. Bach, maybe.

"Definitely closing service stuff," Cameron said. "That's where he gets to show off. People stand and applaud. Organists love that."

We both smiled. It was clear he was waiting. I was stalling, though. Father Cameron nodded to say I could tell him why I was there, but I found I couldn't, quite.

Not yet.

"I was in Nice this morning," I began, by way of explanation, the beginning of something. "But really I was back in Fallujah. A cargo truck instead of bullets and bombs. But still." I had flashes of car bombs, of IEDs and flaming cars, of suicide bombers with looks of surprise on what remained of their faces.

Of Khalid disappearing in a flash of light.

Of Khalid's wife, when I came to bring her the news.

Cam nodded again. "What exactly are you wrestling with? Can you name it?"

I let out a deep breath.

Love. Hate. Fear. Anger. Regret. Where to start?

No. There was only one place, the place where everything intersected.

The one thing that mattered.

"I think I've fallen in love with Nadia."

"The woman you brought here last night?"

I nodded.

"And that's a good thing?"

"No," I said. "It's awful. I can't separate her from all of this. The love from the devastation. From the history."

"I saw the way she looked at you," he said. "I think she returns your feelings. The positive ones, I mean. And she talked to me about going up the tower after you left with Rob. She was, excuse my French, scared shitless. But she climbed it. For you."

Wow. Could I feel worse? "I came back from Nice," I said. "And I met her for a drink. And I could not think about anything but the killing, the damage and the hatred."

He let out a deep breath. "Cal," he said, "let me tell you a secret." He pursed his lips, tried to figure out how to say this. "I loved those men and women who got killed and mangled," he said. "We built relationships at Fort Hood. And when we got over there, and they started dying, it was a whole lot worse than the first season of *Game of Thrones*."

"Where people die who you didn't expect to die," I said, trying to fill in the gaps.

"Exactly," he said. "I know you don't know me, but trust me when I say that I don't exactly come from a family familiar with military service. With death. We served in presidential cabinets. Not this kind of stuff. Nothing where you could lose your leg or your life or your sanity."

"Your mom must have been proud." My mom would have been.

"That's one way to put it," he said, and his tone was bitter. "We don't disinherit people in my family," he sighed. "That would be counterproductive. But we can make our disapproval obvious." He waved that off. "But we're not here to talk about the Gaines family."

Allan was backtracking now at the organ—apparently he was unhappy with his first take on something, although I hadn't heard a single mistake.

"I am so angry," I said. "I don't want to be. Nadia is the best thing that's happened to me since—ever." I shook my head, hard. "Why would I beat her up about her faith? She's a genuinely good person. Not a terrorist. I know that."

"Oh," Cam said. "Oh. I see what you're saying." He tapped his chin a couple of times, his eyes focused elsewhere. "And I get it," he said. "When I was in country, my biggest challenge was not to get eaten up by hatred. Whenever we lost a man or woman I loved, whenever people started calling for the fucking chaplain, my first impulse was to ask 'What is wrong with these people? How can they do things like this?' And of course, we did our share of horrifying things over there. Families who were collateral damage.

Grandmothers lying in three pieces in Ramadi courtyards. But that was us. Not *them*."

I nodded slowly. It was making sense. "It's easier to hate them."

"Yes," he said. "And so bad for us, even if it seems good in the moment. If you can somehow manage to hate this Nadia, then you cannot be hurt by her. You think." Something came to him. "Cormac McCarthy, the American novelist, wrote that when you hate someone, that person builds a home in your heart. From then on, they are guests that you can't seem to get rid of. No matter what you do."

"Dr. King said something like that," I remembered. "Hate cannot drive out hate."

"Right," Cameron said. "Only love can accomplish that."

I dropped my head to the top of the pew, bounced it, not gently, off it once or thrice. "I am so in the wrong here."

"That's the thing," he said. "Can you consciously accept that Nadia is not a person who would blow people up after you've watched so many people get blown up?"

"I can," I said. "If I get the chance, I will tell her."

"Well," he said. "There's the challenge." He looked to see if I was at a place where we were done, or if there was more that needed to be said.

I was done. I knew where I was in the wrong. Everywhere. And I thought I knew what I needed to do to start making things right, if they could ever be made so.

"Okay," he said. "Call me if you need me." He gave me his cell number, and I shook his hand. Again, firm shake. You knew he was there.

"Should I watch your broadcast tonight?" he asked.

I nodded. "I think maybe so. I'm in a better place, anyway. And I will reach out to Nadia and let her know how sorry I am."

We stood up. Allan was doing some elaborate run that I would love to have heard all of, but my broadcast was looming.

"Thank you," I said. "I'll see you."

"I hope so," Cameron said. "I'll be praying for you. For both of you."

And I walked out of the music and the beauty and back into the streets of Paris.

It was a short walk down George V and across the Seine to the studio. I checked in through security, went up in the elevator, sat back down in my cubie to look at the report I'd put together earlier. It was angry, or worse—damaged. I seemed at my wit's end, even to myself. I could and should not go on the air and say such things.

Maybe only I saw that I was broken. I was pretty good at hiding things behind my eyes, even though I knew what I was feeling.

But I don't think you could hear the report I'd planned and not recoil at the confusion, at the fury.

Ahmed was in the bullpen when I arrived. He was laughing and shooting the shit with some of the other cameramen. When he saw me come in, he raised a hand, excused himself, and followed me back to my cubie.

"That was a hard morning," he said.

"Yes, it was," I said. "What's new?"

"Oh," he said. "The usual. The attack is claimed by the Islamic State, even though their Mohamed does not much resemble our Mohamed, Grace be upon him."

I paused for a moment, and then asked, "Ahmed, could a good Muslim have done this?"

He looked at me sorrowfully, as though he could somehow see my afternoon laid bare before his eyes. "No good Muslim would kill the innocent, Calvin."

"What am I going to say tonight?"

"Why are you asking me?" he said.

"Because—" I started, and stopped.

Because I am coming to this story consumed with my own loss and heartbreak.

Because I cannot stop seeing this story through the prism of my own experience.

Because I have observed Islam both as a force for good and a force of terrifying evil.

"Because," I finally told him, "there is always more to the story than just my story."

He put a hand on my shoulder. "Tell the people what we saw and heard, Calvin," he said. "Tell them who was at fault. Tell them about the heroes. Tell them about the courage and sacrifice. That is the story here. Not this evil supposedly done in Allah's name."

I nodded. "I could have used you earlier," I said.

"Well, I am here now," he said. "I can see that this is hard for you. Our own stories complicate things, I think."

I shrugged. "We cannot escape the stories we were living before we walked into the stories we tell."

"No," he said. "But the story is never only about us. About this, you are right."

He patted my shoulder again, this man whose brother rotted in an Egyptian jail, if, indeed, he was even still alive. "Break a leg?"

"Yes," I said. "That is what we say. I will most certainly break a leg."

I revised my remarks in light of my greater sanity, my broken heart, my new hope. The images from Nice could not and would not change—they were images of horror and violence, images that spoke for themselves no matter what I might say. But I was called to give some context to them, to explain them, and maybe to help people come to some new meanings about them. That was why Rob had brought me here, why I had agreed to come.

Something bigger than me and my anger, something more meaningful than my pain needed to go out on the air tonight.

Before I stepped on set, I texted Nadia. "Please watch my broadcast tonight. And please forgive me. I was so wrong, and I can do better. You make me want to do better."

I went into the studio. François, the evening anchor, was already live. When I walked in, he was introducing the Nice story which of course led everything. I sat down, put on my ear piece, straightened my tie. Just in time.

"We're joined in studio by our terrorism correspondent Calvin Jones," François said, and as he looked sideways down the desk, they switched cameras and suddenly I was live.

I nodded to François, to the audience, and I looked at the teleprompter. "At 10:30 last night," I began, "a Tunisian resident of Nice named Mohamed Lahouaiej-Bouhlel steered a white cargo truck onto the heavily congested Promenade des Anglais in Nice after the fireworks celebrating 14 July. For 17 minutes and for over a mile, he ran down pedestrians, killing or injuring over 500 people before he was shot and killed by the local police."

I looked down at my papers, took a deep breath, and launched into what I had to say. "Monsieur Lahouaiej-Bouhlel claimed an affiliation with the Islamic State, and witnesses heard him calling out '*Allahu akbar*' as he proceeded in his attack. While the investigation continues, it does appear that this is a terror attack driven by hateful ideologies."

I looked into the camera. Took another breath. Please hear me. "But a Muslim friend reminded me today that this attack, this person, does not represent true Islam. Because I covered suicide attacks in Iraq, I tend to move immediately to a place of anger and outrage against the faith." Rob was in the control booth, and his eyes grew wide.

"But to immediately condemn an entire group of people because of the actions of a few, or one, is anathema in any free society. Certainly many Christians of my acquaintance would negatively color the opinions of the world if they were taken as representative of the faith. And in Iraq and since, I have met many Muslims who condemn violence against innocents."

I looked meaningfully at Rob in the booth, and hoped he would trust me to do the right thing—and not cut me off midsentence.

"My initial reaction, like perhaps some of you, was to go to a dark place. A place of anger and resentment. A place of hatred. But a friend, a Christian priest, reminded me today that hate is never the proper response to hate. 'An eye for an eye leaves everyone blind,' Gandhi said. And Dr. Martin Luther King Jr. said that what was called for in this life was radical love. Love in the face of hatred. Love as the alternative to hatred."

I looked into the camera. Looked directly out at Nadia. "An American father and son from my native Texas were killed in this attack, and I am heartbroken by that. So too were French men and women, of all races, all religions and none. Muslim grandparents and parents and children were run down by this supposed Muslim attacker. Innocents, all of them.

"At the end of the day, we have to be better than this broken soul. What he did was horrible. But our response must be better. We must be better. 500 and more lives were shattered by this attack. But if we allow ourselves to continue to be shattered, if we answer like for like, then he has won. His hatred is stronger than our love, his anarchy stronger than our community.

"I don't think I can stand to live in a world where that can be true.

"Thankfully," I said. "I don't have to. Within minutes of the attack, the term #opendoor was trending on Twitter." I nodded at Ahmed, who had found this. "A single madman drove into a crowd of innocents. An entire city opened their doors to the victims, to the frightened, the stranded, the struggling. The people of Nice looked at those in need, and they didn't see strangers. They saw neighbors.

"So yes, Nice is in mourning, as is France, as are people of good will everywhere. But the terrible actions of one man remind us that the human spirit still loves, still welcomes, still hopes.

"And I think I can go on a little longer, realizing that hope is stronger than hate.

"This is Calvin Jones, reporting for News Europe. Back to you, François."

I slumped back in my chair as François thanked me and moved on to the next story. When the director nodded to me, I took my earbud out, slid back silently in my chair, and walked off set.

Rob met me offstage. He nodded, let out a deep breath which maybe he had held the whole time I was speaking. "Good," he said. "A little more personal than I'd imagined. But good. Solid."

I gave him a small smile. "This is all personal for me," I said. "As you knew when you brought me here."

He nodded again. "I know. Hang close. You want to come with me back to the house?"

"Sure," I said. "Apéro?"

"Yes. Is Nadia coming?"

"No," I said. "I don't think so." I wanted to check my phone. Maybe the broadcast would change some things. My apology, delivered on air.

But there was nothing.

After the broadcast, I walked Rob over to his place. He was mostly quiet on the way, and it was left to me to ask questions.

"Do you want me to do some follow-up tomorrow? Man on the street stuff for the days of mourning?"

"What? Oh, sure, yeah. Of course. Get some sense of how people are feeling."

"I was thinking I might also get something from Father Cam."

"Hmmm."

"You know. Find out how we might deal with this grief in a healthy way."

"Oh. Right."

"He had some really good advice for me. I went to talk to him today, and he was solid."

"Hmmm."

Rob was clearly far from here. I was surprised he was managing to stay on the sidewalk. I fell in alongside him, patted him on the shoulder to get his attention.

"Rob. How are things with Brigid?"

He shrugged. "Is it that obvious?"

I laughed. "I've had to pull you out of the street like three times. Now you owe me your life."

He nodded, sighed. "We're committed to the long term," he said. "I know that. But the short term is going to be hard as hell."

"Are you sorry you told her?"

He shook his head. "No. You were right. I couldn't go without telling her. But I had to face some hard things about myself to get to that point."

We crossed the street. "You are entirely too hard on yourself, Rob."

He looked across at me when we'd gained the safety of the other side and held out a hand. "Pot, meet kettle."

"Good friends have a lot in common," I said, shaking. "We'll toast to that, somewhere down the line."

"Ah," he said. "Down the line. Further on down the road."

I nodded.

We walked in silence for a bit as we came onto Rob's street.

"Anything from Nadia yet?" he asked as we approached his front door.

I shook my head. "No. And maybe there never will be. Maybe I broke everything we had. God knows it was hard enough. We were reaching across a ton of boundaries. And I was—God, help me, I was awful."

He stopped me at the front door before he entered the code. "It's not Saturday night yet," he said.

"Okay," I said. "True enough." I had a sudden vision of Nadia standing in Rob's apartment, thanking me for my segment, stepping into my arms.

Brigid opened the door for us as we walked up to it. She swept me into her arms, hugged me hard, then turned to Rob. "Darling," she said. No hug was offered.

"Darling," he said in response. They smiled sadly at each other.

"Hello, Rob," Allison called from the living room. "Can I make you a drink?"

"Hello, Allison," I said. "And yes. I would love something."

"I can try an Old Fashioned," she said. "With Bulleit, correct?"

"You paid attention," I said, stepping across the room to her and giving her the French double-kiss, *la bise*. I saw that she had a tall gin and tonic with a slice of lemon already poured, and that on the table we had pâté and brie and some bread. A fine apéro.

"How was your day?" she asked, handing me my drink. With extra bitters, I noted.

I looked down at my drink, back up at her. I took a sip. I told the truth. "I flew into Nice this morning. It sparked some . . . very bad things for me. And this afternoon, I blamed Nadia for resembling the man who had done it all. On the whole, this was not my best, most enlightened day. No." I hung my head. "I am ashamed."

"You did a beautiful broadcast just now," Brigid offered. "You should watch it on the web," she told Allison.

"Well, I had a come-to-Jesus talk with Father Cam after I blasted Nadia," I told the room. Allison looked at me with some confusion. I'd guess Anglicans—or cultural Anglicans—do not come to Jesus. "He asked me to name what I was feeling. I couldn't. But he could tell that my anger and my hatred were poisonous. Why else would I say such things to Nadia? Who never did anything to hurt me except wrestle with a decision that should never have been given her?" I put my head in my hands. I did not know if you could ruin an apéro, but I felt that this might be the way to proceed.

There was a hand on my shoulder. Rob, I thought, but it was too light. It was Allison's voice that followed that touch. "Since we were at dinner the other night," she said, "there is something I have wanted to say to this group. Perhaps this will be of some help. I hope so."

She waited for me to look up at her, which, at last, I did.

"You told us a story the other night," she said, taking a big gulp of her gin and tonic. "And I saw myself in it."

"Really?" I asked.

"Oh yes," she said. "Your best friend in college. Daniel? David. He was me."

"Really?" I asked. "David was you?" I looked confused, I'm sure.

"He was," she said. "I fell in love with one of my dormmates at Oxford." She turned to Brigid and Rob, her eyes wide, and said, "Because I am drawn to women, you see."

Now their eyes were wide.

Then she reached out a hand to me, touched my forearm. "I was in that place of confessing my love to the person who had been my best friend. And discovering that she did not feel what I did."

"I am so sorry," I said. "That must have been awful."

"It was," she said. "I was hurt. And I was angry. I had gone so far out there with my feelings. I had told the absolute truth, and I thought there should be some reward for that." She shook her head. "But there was not."

She turned away to the window, looked out at the tower. Just as I thought she was finished talking, she went on, speaking out into the night.

"So I thought maybe I could hate her instead of loving her. That is a natural reaction when someone has hurt you. I lashed out at her. I told terrible stories about her. But it did not help."

"No," I said, coming up behind her. "I can see now that it wouldn't."

"She did not ask me to love her," Allison said, and tears were glistening in her eyes. "But I could not forgive her for not loving me."

Brigid reached out to her, her own eyes glistening.

"For years. Years!" She shook her head sadly, disbelieving. "I was filled with rage. I could not forgive her. Even though that was what was most needed."

"I think it's about forgiveness," I murmured. Don Henley, again, "The Heart of the Matter."

Rob nodded. He knew the song. And that was also his greatest hope at this present moment, I supposed.

"Forgiveness," Brigid repeated into the night, and now she was openly weeping.

"Wow," I said. Did I start all this? But no. This is the human condition. We are hurt, we are broken, and we have to decide how we are going to proceed from there.

Speaking of which, I checked my phone surreptitiously.

Nothing.

"I could use a drink," Rob said, moving over to the bar. Allison and Brigid were embracing. I walked over to the window, looked out and up at the Tour Eiffel. Here I was, in France, with a group of sobbing Parisians. This was now my reality, strange as it seemed.

Allison stepped over to me now. "Cal? How are you?"

"It seems that perhaps I should be asking you that question."

She smiled. "You are sweet."

I laughed. "I can be," I said. "But, sadly, often I am not."

"I hope that things can be mended with Nadia," she said. "She is lovely."

"Yes," I said, a catch in my voice. "She is indeed."

Brigid had gone over to help Rob make his drink, and now they were locked in an embrace, and she was still weeping. And despite that, I felt hope for them.

"I would like to be your friend," I said to Allison.

She looked at me for a moment, blinked once, nodded.

"I would like that as well," she said. We got out our phones and traded numbers right there, tried not to look across the room at Rob and Brigid, who were having a moment not necessarily meant to be shared by us. "Call me if you need me."

"And you," I said. "I was—" No. Not yet. "Thank you for your story."

Rob and Brigid walked over to us, both of them wiping their eyes. "I'm sorry," Brigid said, and Allison and I raised our hands. No need. This is a hard life. Do what you have to.

I think it's about forgiveness.

We finished our apéro, then Brigid asked if we'd like to stay for dinner. I looked at Allison, who gave me a slight but clear "no" with her head. And she was right—they needed to be together. Needed to be alone, together.

So we walked out, Allison and I, her leaning in to me as though we were close friends, which I thought we might actually someday be. In the tiny elevator, she turned her head—all she could turn—and asked, "Would you like to have dinner?"

"I'm not sure I'd be such good company," I said. "I am a trifle preoccupied." I've noticed that when I'm with British people, I start speaking more British. Precise. Formal.

"Check your mobile," she said. "And if you haven't yet heard anything, come with me. It is better to have somebody than nobody."

I squeezed her shoulder—all I could reach—because that was God's truth.

When we got out, I checked—a voicemail from Jack, probably asking how I was doing—and that was it.

"I am yours," I said.

She took my arm. "Let's go to Philippe Excoffier," she said. "I've actually got a reservation for two. I just didn't know who the other would be."

"That's faith," I said.

"Maybe so," she said.

We walked, talking, down the Rue Saint-Dominique, past Nicolas and Café Constant, crowded with diners, and turned onto the Rue de L'Exposition at La Fontaine de Mars. It was an alley, really, just a residential street, and I was surprised when we arrived at this tiny restaurant on the right side of the street, hidden behind scooters and garbage bins.

"This is it?" I asked.

She took my arm and ushered me in. "Don't judge, American boy."

Why does everyone call me that?

She greeted the hostess and waiter, and they embraced her. Two kisses, one for each cheek. They ushered us to a table for two. I let her have the booth side and I took the chair. No sooner were we seated than Philippe himself came out of the kitchen to speak with her.

"Mademoiselle," he said, taking her hand and kissing it. Then he looked to me with some curiosity. Like, who is this dude?

"Philippe," she said. "May I introduce my friend, Calvin Jones. He is an American journalist. He works with Rob."

Ah, that got me some love. "*Monsieur*," he said, with a bow. "*Bienvenue.*"

"*Merci*," I said. "*C'est un bel endroit.*" This is a beautiful place.

He bowed to me, beamed. "*Merci. J'en suis fier.*" I am proud of it.

"For you," he told Allison, "I have your favorite. The ravioli foie gras." That lit up her face as well.

"Merci, Philippe," she said. The waiter, who we realized had been standing patiently by, asked for our drink orders. Allison wanted a French 75. I concurred. That sounded just precisely right.

Phillipe went back to the kitchen. Our drinks came. Allison and I toasted each other. She offered familiar words: "May the saddest day of your future," she said, "be no worse than the happiest day of your past."

"Thank you," I said. We drank. Good French 75. Cognac, not gin, for its base. I approved.

We ordered. I got the poached oysters as a starter, duck breast for my main, and we ordered a soufflé with Grand Marnier to share for dessert.

And then things got a bit quiet. Because, let's face it, we didn't really know each other much, and some big bad doors had been banged open this evening, some big hurts exposed to the open air.

Well. I guess there are some things that must be said in any case.

"So," I began. "I think that Brigid and Rob thought we were going to be a couple. You and me, I mean."

"Of course they did," she said. "Two such good-looking people as ourselves. Why wouldn't we mate?"

I started laughing. I couldn't help myself. "Brigid got mad at me for meeting Nadia. She had everything planned out. She thought."

"They want us to be happy," she said. "Even if they don't know anything about us." She could not help but joining me in laughter.

I raised a hand. Just to clarify that I wasn't laughing because the idea was ridiculous. "You are a lovely person," I said. "If I hadn't fallen for Nadia—"

"And if I were not a lesbian," she interjected.

"And that," I admitted. "I'd be all over you."

"Thank you," she said, then made a face. "I think." She took a drink, looked across the table at me, reached her hand across the table and put it on mine for a moment. The subject changed. The evening shifted. She removed her hand, looked down, looked back up. "What has happened between them? Brigid and Rob? Just in the past few days, something between them has shifted. For the worse, I think. That scene tonight—"

I shook my head. "I'm afraid I can't tell you," I said.

"Oh," she said. "That bad." She pursed her lips, formed her next sentence. "Will they be all right?"

I sat with that for a moment. I thought of the Rob I knew, the lifesaver, the man of integrity, the man who loved his wife so much he was willing to risk losing her rather than lie to her.

I thought of Brigid, who took care of people.

"Yes," I said. "Yes, I think they will."

She let out a long-held breath. "Thanks be to God." She looked across at me, and then up at the cosmos. "And will we, perhaps, someday be all right? Will we know love? Will we forgive and be forgiven?"

"Jesus," I said. I was a little surprised when nobody said "Don't blaspheme." "On down the road, do you mean?"

She shrugged. "I suppose."

I looked across the table at her, at her avid attention to my answer, and at last, I nodded. "Maybe," I said. "I don't know where we're going or what we're doing. I don't know what Vladimir Putin has in store for the West. What Islamic militants will do to Paris next time they attack. But maybe we will be."

She ran her finger around the lip of her glass. "I wonder, what would that look like?"

The waiter poured us more sparkling water, the bubbles climbing up the glass, and I nodded my thanks and held it up. "This, maybe. Happiness? Contentment? Joy?"

She raised her French 75, drank, looked at the amber effervescence inside. "I'd like joy, I believe. I am content now. Maybe even happy. I love my work. I have friends. But I have no one to share my life with." She flushed red. "I'm sorry," she said. "I did not mean to be so personal."

"It's okay," I said. "I think we can talk to each other. Tell each other the truth."

"Very well," she said. "Then I can say that I want you to be happy. To know joy. With Nadia, God willing."

"*Inshallah*," I agreed. "But I am starting to realize that so much is not up to me. That maybe it never was."

I checked my phone. Nothing.

Nothing.

Our starters arrived, and they looked glorious.

"Let's eat," Allison Evans said to me, a light in the darkness.

And so we ate. My oysters were, indeed, glorious. "Oh my," I think I said after the first bite.

"I know," she said. "Philippe." As though that said it all. She offered me a scallop, which I gladly took. Buttery, tender.

"Oh my," I said again.

Something she had said stuck with me. Because it seemed to be the heart of the matter. Our starters were cleared away. We ordered another round of drinks. And I looked down at the table, too afraid even to meet Allison's gaze. "Forgive and be forgiven," I said.

"Yes," she said gently.

"What does that look like?" I asked. "Feel like? I think I might be able to forgive. But I don't know how to be forgiven." I took a deep breath. Let it out. "I have so much red in my ledger." Black Widow is always a reliable go-to.

"*Avengers Assemble*," she said. "Yes, I know the movie." In the UK, the film was renamed to distinguish it from the old *Avengers* TV show. "How is this possible, that you need to be forgiven? You were a journalist. You didn't torture prisoners. You didn't kill people."

"Did I not?"

"Tell me," she said. "You are carrying something too big for one person alone."

"So people have said." I took a deep breath, shrugged. "Okay."

And I told her about Khalid. I told her about the times he saved my life, about the stories he had opened for me, about the days he was my rock, about how after my father was killed, Khalid's sunny steady presence helped preserve my sanity.

"He was my friend," I said. "My best friend. And I got him killed."

I told her about how he died, about the blast, about going home to his wife Elena to tell her face to face. The least I owed her surely.

All those times I sat in their kitchen enjoying tea and sweets, all the laughter, all of that was gone. We sat at an empty table as Elena wept, wept as though she herself would die, as the weeping children pressed into her lap, a succession of downy ducklings wondering where their father was.

At last, the tears stopped for a moment, and she looked across the table at me, as she had many times. But this time, her look was pure hatred, and I thought her gaze would reduce me to ashes.

"You have killed him, Calvin," she said.

"No," I said. It was though the oxygen had been sucked out of the room. I gasped for air.

"Yes," she said. "He did not have to die."

"Please," I said. I was begging.

She got up from the table. She turned away from me without another word, swept up the stairs and out of sight.

I sat there, watching Khalid running toward that little girl.

Watching him disappear in the white light.

"So you cannot forgive yourself," Allison said, back in Paris, many years and many miles later. "Even though you know he chose this."

"I cannot," I said. "If we had not come to Iraq. If I had not come—"

Our entrees arrived just then, and even the wonder of them could not rescue me.

Allison regarded her foie gras ravioli, then regarded me. "Nothing I can say will fix this," she said, and she shook her head sadly. "Fix you."

"No," I said, and this was actually kind of funny. "Why is that?"

"We are two of a kind, I think," she said. "My head is full of such rubbish about myself. Everyone who looks at me sees a better me than I do." She looked at me. "When I look at you, Calvin, I see someone who is gentle, and generous, and broken. Who wants to do better. To be better. But there is so much to escape. To transcend. However you wish to put it." She raised her hands, palms up. "This is what I see."

"You're not wrong," I said. "I take responsibility for things I don't even know about."

She indicated my duck. "Still it would be—in my theological understanding of the word—a sin not to eat that."

I smiled. "You're not wrong," I said again.

I lifted my fork.

I took a bite.

And it was very good.

14.

Paris

———

July 15, 2016
Friday

I walked Allison back to her apartment in the 15th, a long heart-pounding jaunt up the Trocadero steps and past. We had a nightcap at her place, port, and as I strode back across the river to my apartment on the rue Edmond Valentin, I was in some ways in a better place. Yet in some ways, still in the worst place of my life.

As I walked, the streets were packed with Parisians avoiding their apartments for a few more minutes. It was a rainbow of people bearing the heat of summer. Models and menials. Men, women, children. Arab women in headscarves pushing their babies. Young lovers stopping to check the menus of cafés open late. One last drink, perhaps, before they climbed the stairs to their apartments.

I turned over my phone every few minutes as I walked. Nothing. I had resisted sending Nadia another text, reaching out again.

But then I did.

I stopped on the Avenue Woodrow Wilson, thought for a moment, and started to text.

"I am so in the wrong," I wrote. "I would do anything to fix things. Please talk to me."

I pressed Send, and as soon as I did, I hated myself for my weakness.

"You are an idiot," I said to myself. Out loud. And I walked on, across the bridge, down side streets to my apartment.

Behind me, I heard footsteps, which was not exactly normal for this late at night, not typical in this place off the beaten tourist track.

I stopped on the first step of the stoop to tie my shoe, and I took a surreptitious glance back.

Fifty feet behind me, a big man with salt and pepper hair—a man I recognized instantly—was nonchalantly looking off into the distance as though he had nothing at all to do with me.

As though he had nothing to do with the wreckage of my life.

I stood up. I could go through my front door and leave him behind.

But this, of course, is not what I did, because that would have been prudent, and clearly I do not know how to do the prudent thing.

I turned, and with the speed of a thousand thousand sprints, of all the runs through Baghdad and London and Paris and Killeen, Texas, I bore down upon him.

"Are you after me, now?" I shouted in English, but whatever language he spoke, there could be no doubting the menace I bore.

I honestly thought I was going to hurt him, pay him back just the tiniest bit for my own pain.

I was going to mash him into the Paris pavement, and when I did, somehow, magically, the world was going to take that offering and return Nadia to me and everything would be okay.

Or something.

As I said, clearly I do not know how to do the prudent thing.

As I reached him, I threw a roundhouse punch with all my considerable momentum behind it.

In a movie, it would have taken his head off.

In real life, he simply sidestepped my punch, grabbed my arm, and used my own momentum to throw me down onto my back, knocking the breath out of me.

My head hit the sidewalk with a BONG like a bell ringing, and I went limp.

Then he kicked me. In the ribs. And in the face. And in the back. I felt ribs crack. I pulled myself tight into a fetal position, tight like I had held myself riding in a Bradley in Iraq, and I believed that this was quite possibly the end.

And then a voice shouted out of the darkness in French: "Antonio. No! Stop this!"

The salt and pepper man stepped back from me and said something in French about how I was the one who swung at him, what was he supposed to do? I lay grunting in pain. I rolled over, worked myself onto my hands and knees, which was all I could manage. My ribs were on fire. Each breath was a burning flame.

Footsteps drew closer, and I resolved to get to my feet, not to die on my knees. I was bleeding from my chin, and possibly elsewhere.

I had been in danger a hundred times, been in more than a couple of hopeless fights, but I couldn't remember the last time I had been hurt so badly.

I heard my father shouting at me to get up, but I could not crawl to my feet.

I dropped my forehead back to the sidewalk and waited for the end.

The footsteps stopped. A man sat down on some steps, fine polished Italian shoes just in my line of sight, crisp creases in his cuffed pant legs.

That was an expensive suit.

"I am sorry, Monsieur Jones," he said, in French. "Antonio exceeded his authority. You must have seemed a threat to him."

"I tried to be," I grunted, also in French.

"I am Ali," he said. "I believe you know my intended. Nadia."

My forehead was on the pavement. I could do nothing but wait. "You know that I do. Forgive me if I don't get up." I reached a hand to my chin. Perhaps it wasn't as bad as it felt. The curse of on-air vanity. I hoped I wouldn't need stitches. If I lived. "By the way, your French is very good."

He laughed. "It is perhaps my worst language. But you are kind to say so. Let's speak in English."

"Yes," I said, in English. "I am finding it hard to concentrate."

"Antonio has been following you all week," he said. "My mother knows that Nadia has been to your apartment. To dinner. To that saloon near the Opéra Garnier."

"Harry's New York Bar," I said.

"Even so. But she does not know the entire truth."

"The truth?"

"I have not told her," he sighed. "Because Nadia is perfect for me. She is smart, and ambitious, and from what little I know of her, someone who might be an actual partner for me. I have not found this often. And I have met many women."

"I'll bet you have," I said.

"My mother wants me to discard her. But I do not want to do this. I still want her to be my wife. I think she could help me."

"Help you do what?" I asked.

He sighed again, got to his feet, his shoes coming a step, then two closer to me. Given his style, I was imagining Omar Sharif, a little pencil-thin mustache. Surely this guy was too hip to have one of those Arab goatees.

"You think I am just another rich Saudi," he said, stopping a step short of my head. "I understand that. And you love her, or think you do. But understand: we will be wed, and after our wedding night, I will tell my mother that despite her concerns, Nadia was a virgin. Whatever has transpired between you, whatever else she has done in her life—I will preserve those secrets. I have no desire to ruin her. I need her. Do you hear me?"

I could not nod, my forehead cemented to the cement. I grunted.

"I know you do not believe this, but I will be good to her. I am not one of those Arab men who believe we are all superior to women, that they are fit to be nothing more than our servants. I have chosen Nadia for reasons beyond beauty and breeding. In time, who knows what feelings might grow between us? What we might accomplish together?"

He stopped, tapped his right foot a few times impatiently. "It benefits no one for me to let her go. Not my family. Not her family. And not her."

"It benefits me," I said.

"Ah," he said. "Yes. But does it?" I saw a hand touch the sidewalk, then Ali knelt at my side. "I have learned much about you, Monsieur Jones," he said. "And I believe you to be an honorable man."

Well, what does one say to that? You live your whole life hoping someone will offer such a judgment.

And then when it finally comes, it has to be from the future husband of the woman you adore?

It was too much. "What do you want?" I asked. I tried to struggle to my knees, and I felt his hand on my shoulder, holding me in place.

"Let her go," he said. "Step away. That is what I am asking you. One man to another." He felt how unwelcome his touch was and lifted his hand away. "If you love her, let her make her wisest choice."

"I want to see her," I said. "I want to talk to her."

"Very well," he said. "You deserve that much." He got to his feet. "I'm sorry, Monsieur." He began to walk away. "I do not blame you. For loving her. In another world, in another life—"

"All you are is rich," I spat.

He paused. I saw his shoes turn slightly, saw him momentarily consider turning back.

"I believe that I am more than that," he said. "That I too am an honorable man. I will have to ask Nadia for her trust. For yours. I know I have no right to ask that."

"She does not want to marry you," I insisted.

"Perhaps not at this moment. But she will," he said, and I could tell that he was finished. He had allotted more time on me than he had intended. "Good night, Monsieur Jones." He walked up to Antonio, spoke in a low voice words I could not follow.

Antonio turned in my direction. I tensed, awaiting the pain to come.

Instead, the big man tugged me bodily to my feet, pulled my arm over his shoulder, and half-carried, half walked me to my front gate. When we arrived, he rang the concierge's bell, once, twice, three times, and stalked away, leaving me parked against the wall.

"Oh sweet Jesus," I muttered. "Fantine will be so furious."

But no one else was there to hear me. When my landlady arrived in her robe a few moments later, the two of us were alone on the street.

Fantine took one look at me, saw the blood on my face, my broken posture, and she put her hands to her face. "Monsieur Calvin," she said. "What happened to you?"

"I was mugged," I told her, for that was certainly what it felt like, although my wallet continued to weigh down my back pocket.

"Do you wish me to call the gendarmes?" she asked.

"*Non*," I said. "*S'il vous plaît*. Help me to the elevator."

She got me into the elevator, took me up to my apartment, helped me open my door. "I can take it from here," I think I told her. I stumbled into the shower—the world's smallest shower—turned on the hot water, stepped in with all my clothes on.

And that's where I found myself, some hours later, the water long gone cold, myself pretzeled down into the bottom of the shower stall like some prisoner in a solitary jail cell too small to lie down in. I was shivering. Cold water in the summer in Paris is not so cold as it might be elsewhere, but it is plenty cold enough.

Somehow, I managed to tug myself upright, to extricate myself from the shower stall, to pull off my clothes, to dry myself.

But before I collapsed into my bed, I saw Nadia's message on my phone: "Meet me at Harry's at noon?"

"Yes," I managed to text back. "Merci." My very fingers hurt.

I looked at the clock—3 a.m. I was sore, each breath a trial, but I did not think I could sleep. I pulled on my running clothes, although there was no real possibility I could run in my current state. But I made my way downstairs, stepped out into the darkened street, and walked to the Pont de l'Alma Bridge.

There I stood at the place where Nadia had jumped into the Seine, where I had followed her, where my life had been transformed—for the better? I wondered, now. Would I always remember this as the place I found her?

Or the place I lost her?

I looked down into the water, the Eiffel Tower lit up, remembered everything that had happened, everything that had happened since. Pulling her from the water, my heart pounding with fear and exertion. Her sitting across from me at La Fontaine de Mars. The Cathedral tower. The fireworks. The walk to my apartment. The kiss.

Was it only a week ago—less—since I came to Paris? Since I met her?

Was it possible that I could lose her after finding her?

I leaned over, looked deep into the Seine. The water was dark, rippling beneath me, the lights from the Eiffel flickering in the current.

"Monsieur," a voice called behind me, "Don't do it!"

It was an Algerian tout, his hands full of Eiffel Tower souvenirs he had not sold, many of them blinking on and off. He looked at me with concern. He set down his Towers, stepped toward me.

"If you jump," he said, "you will never know what happened to you."

"Merci, Monsieur," I said. "I do not intend to jump."

"All the same," he said, "you seemed prepared to."

I straightened up, pushed myself back from the edge.

"No," I said. I shook my head. "I will not."

We looked at each other for a moment, just two human beings lost in the middle of the Paris night.

"Do you want to buy a Tower souvenir?" he asked me in English.

"Yes," I laughed. "I think I do."

I gave him ten euros for a silver Tour Eiffel lit up by flashing colored lights. He shook my hand, looked closely at me to make sure I had meant what I had said, and walked on into the darkness.

I brought the Tower back to my apartment, set it blinking on my bedside table, and fell onto the bed. I had barely pulled the duvet over me then I was asleep.

Khalid approached my bed, his hands worrying each other as he walked closer.

"Calvin," he called. "Calvin!"

"What?" I said. I sat bolt upright.

Yes. It was Khalid. All of his limbs in place. His head right where it belonged. Not a scratch on him.

In this dream, I started weeping, which is not, as you may have noticed, a thing that I ever do.

"Don't be so afraid, Calvin Coolidge," he said, although his voice was gentle, and his hand, when it rested on my shoulder, was reassuring.

"Elena is furious with me," I said. "She thinks I killed you." I gulped, trying to hold back those tears that would not stop. "I think she's right. I am so sorry."

"Oh Calvin," he said. "What was it you were saying? That there is so much you are not controlling?" He walked over to my window, looked out at the top of the Tour Eiffel, just visible over the building across the street. He let out a long sigh. Yes, he was most definitely alive. "It is beautiful here. Yes?" He remained at the window looking out over Paris. "You remember in the market? That little girl? I saw the explosives strapped on her. I saw her fear, that girl so like my own. I could not stand by and do nothing. I hope you understand this."

I nodded. "Could I have saved you? Her?"

He sniffed. Not a laugh, although close to it. "Are you almighty Allah, Calvin? Do you know everything? Control everything?"

"I am not," I admitted. "And I do not."

"I made a choice," Khalid said. "I did not wish to die. I did not wish to leave Elena and my children." He looked at me. "I did not wish to leave you." He turned back to the window. "But I could not live in such a world, not without doing whatever I could."

"I am sorry," I said. "I tried to tell Elena."

"That was never going to go very well," he observed, and true that.

"I miss you," I said. "Every day."

He turned back to me. "And I you, Calvin. We were a good team. We did good work."

"It was more than that," I said. "I didn't realize—"

He stepped forward, took my hand, raised it to his chest, placed it over his heart. "I know, Calvin," he said. "Please believe that I know." He let my hand fall, stepped back, and he smiled.

"Bury the bad," he told me. "Mourn the good."

I woke up. It was 10 a.m. and the bedroom was in full light. My face was dry, the tears, of course, only in my dreams.

I looked around the room, but I was alone.

I was so sore that I could barely move. The cut on my chin was minor, somehow, but my ribs were serious. The pain radiated out from them with every breath. I got painfully out of bed, willed myself upright. There might very well be a doctor in my future.

Ten o'clock was too early to drink, sadly. But not too early for painkillers. I had a few tablets left from a prescription for a wisdom teeth extraction two years previous, and I needed to do something, since I could barely move.

And I needed to move. I took two white Oxycontins, which I thought might be one too many. But I remembered my dentist's intake form, the pain continuum, a line which ran from "No Pain" on the far left to "The Most Pain I have Ever Experienced" on the far right.

And I was way down at the right-hand side of that continuum just now.

I was still in my running clothes, so I pulled on my shoes grunting, picked up my wallet and my iPhone, and limped downstairs and onto the street.

I punched up Imagine Dragons, turned *Night Visions* way up high.

I ran off to the southeast toward the Hotel Invalides, its dome gleaming in the morning light. I never ran this way, but I had some time to kill, and no desire to run back over the bridge. I did not trust myself.

Past the Invalides, I kept running. The song was "It's Time," the bass and drums ballistic. As I ran, the chorus came up: "It's time to begin, isn't it?"

I tried to figure this song out as I ran on. Was this a lament? A celebration—some sort of "I did it my way"? Frank Sinatra was big in my house growing up.

I don't ever want to change?

Or I can't?

Which sort of begs the question: Why begin something you can't finish?

Why begin anything at all?

I ran on toward Montparnasse, Imagine Dragons in my headphones, the pain in my ribs a steady but steadily more distant ache. Past the Café Montparnasse and La Rotonde and Le Dôme, past Mr. Hemingway and Mr. Baldwin and Ms. Stein and Mr. Picasso, and then left on the Rue de Rennes all the way back to the Seine. I checked the time—I still had plenty of it—and so I kept running.

My legs were aching, nothing compared to the pain of my ribs, and I was panting for breath. But this seemed to be the thing I needed to do. I had run the streets of Baghdad, where death was a knife's edge away, and now I ran the streets of Paris in the same way, pushed myself past the pain, past the exhaustion, past the remembering.

When I ran in Baghdad, I knew I was in danger, and I was in no less danger now, although the physical violence had faded. It still felt as though I could lose my life, as though I could suddenly disappear into the white light and be no more.

It felt like I could be lost in a heartbeat.

I ran past the four-tiered towers of Saint-Sulpice, past Saint-Germain, across the Seine at the Pont des Arts footbridge. The vista of the Louvre stretched in front of me, and at the top of the hill, well beyond it, I knew would be the Opéra Garnier.

And a few blocks from there, Harry's New York Bar.

I ducked through the long line of postulants in the courtyard of the Louvre, back and forth through the sidewalk walkers on the Avenue de Opéra.

I couldn't take another step.

And I couldn't not take another step.

And so I ran.

At last, at the Rue Daunou, I veered left, dodging traffic against the light. Past the Hotel Choiseul Opera, I saw the Harry's sign ahead, and I finally slowed to a walk, panting, my heart in my throat, the run catching up to me. I leaned up against the wall, trying and failing to catch my breath. It was not to happen. Perhaps this was the end, not last night. My heart would explode at Harry's New York Bar, and all my earthly problems be solved.

But no. I hurt. And I was going to live. Now. And later.

So I willed myself upright, pushed through the swinging doors of Harry's, and greeted Frederick.

"Monsieur Cal," he said. He looked alarmed, wondered if he should perhaps help me to a seat.

"Frederick," I said, taking a table near the bar. "I cannot tell you how happy I am to see you." I checked the time. 11:45. "A whisky sour, my good man."

"Oui," he said. "Coming up." He began fixing my drink, but he kept looking at me, questions in his eyes. At last, bartender etiquette be damned, he set his drink in front of me and asked a flood of questions:

"Where is Nadia? Is she to be married? How did you get that cut, those bruises? Did you confront the husband?" He paused, now practical bartender: "Do you require medical assistance?"

Wow. I raised a finger, thought better of it. "So. Let me explain. No, there is too much. Let me sum up. I attacked that man who has been shadowing us. He turned out to be more dangerous that I am on my best worst day. Nadia is coming. I think. I cannot say if she will be married. I think perhaps yes. I hope not. Honestly, I have no idea what is going to happen next except that I want to have a drink. And that terrifies me."

"The not knowing?" he asked. "Or the drink?"

I pushed the glass away from me. "Both," I said. I looked down at my hands, clasped in front of me. "Frederick," I said, "my father, my uncle, their father before them, they were all drunks. My father didn't drink all the time. But when he did, he hurt people."

"People?"

"No," I said. "Not people. Me." I sighed. "Before I came to Paris, I hadn't had anything to drink in a very long time. Which seemed to be a good thing. I am not a good drinker either."

"Then perhaps a bar is not the ideal place for you, my friend," Frederick observed ruefully.

I hiccupped a laugh. "Do you think?" I shook my head. "Yes. But it's a place I understand. I went to meetings. I went without a sip. We were ruined people there. But there are ruined people here too. I am comfortable with ruined people. I know their stories."

"Well. There will always be someone ready here to hear your confession," Frederick said.

"Even so," I said, crossing myself. "Bless me, Father, for I have sinned."

The front door swung open. Nadia walked in wearing her running clothes.

And carrying her dog leash.

She was so so beautiful.

It was a moment before she could look at me, and when she did, I immediately saw it in her face.

I did not even have to ask.

She had decided, and that decision did not encompass me.

Frederick recognized it too. He turned away, as though we somehow stood naked in front of him, as though this was not his to see.

She settled herself at the bar next to me, reached out her hand, touched my face gently. "He told me that he would not hurt you."

"He didn't," I said. "Not directly. I sort of, umm, attacked that guy who was following you. Us." I motioned with my eyes to the street. "Is he still out there? I'd like another shot at him."

She shook her head. "Oh, Calvin. You are better than this." Her hand left my face, fell to her lap.

"I'm not sure either of us knows that," I said. "I hurt you. Out of my anger. Terrible things bubbled to the surface. I am sorry. Now you're leaving me because of it."

"No," she said. "I know you are better than those bad words. I always knew that. I have never seen what you have seen, lived through your heartbreak." She turned to Frederick, who actually had his back turned to us, was somehow pretending to be occupied at the back bar. "Frederick," she said. "Please."

He turned around, that big bushy-headed man, and he could not look her in the face. "Nadia," he said.

"Make me a French 75, Frederick," she said. "Make it as though it is the last one I will ever drink."

A sad smile spread across his face. "That has always been my philosophy," he said. He went to work.

"Did you know that George Gershwin wrote *An American in Paris* at Harry's?" she asked me.

"I did not," I said, although of course I did.

"In the downstairs bar. Ali told me that."

"Ah yes," I said. "Not even Harry's is safe from Ali."

"No," she said. "You will always be safe at Harry's. Ali does not drink, and he does not hold grudges. But he wanted to understand this place. Why it is magical. Why something happened between us here."

"Something started here," I said. "But it became magical on a bridge. In a river. On a tower. And in my bed."

She nodded. "It was real. It is real." She took a deep breath, let it out slowly. "Calvin, I have decided to marry Ali. But not because I do not believe you are good and kind." And, she could not help saying, "And beautiful."

She blushed. Frederick turned away for a moment even though he had her drink in his hand. It was actually kind of charming.

"So are you going to tell me that it would never have worked between us?" I asked, more bitterly than I intended. "That we're from different worlds?"

She shook her head. "No," she said. "I am not going to tell you that. Because that would be untrue."

Frederick tried again, achieved delivery this time.

She raised her glass. "What shall we drink to?"

"I don't know," I said, and the despair was naked in my voice.

"We are not so different," she said. "I'm Muslim, you are not. I'm from Saudi Arabia, you are not. I've been sheltered in many ways, you have not. But I look at you and I think in many ways, we are the same."

"I don't care," I said. "Alike, different, it doesn't matter. I love you, Nadia."

Shit.

I had said it.

It was as though a huge weight had been released from my shoulders. There.

Her eyes glistened. She set her glass on the bar. "Be careful, dear heart," she said.

"I love you," I repeated.

"Calvin. This is one of those things that, once you say it, it can never be unsaid."

I reached out, took my whisky sour, took a sip. I was looking down at it, down at the bar, down at my battered knuckles. "I have never ever said those words out loud before," I said. "Not to another human. I should have. To my mother. My father."

"Maybe," she said, setting her drink down, "this could become a habit for you."

I laughed. It had taken me 35 years to get to this this point. It felt good. Only. What was missing?

Oh.

"You haven't said that you love me," I said.

"I am choosing," she said, her mouth tightening into a straight line, "from the options available to me."

"You have lots of choices," I said. "You could make another choice."

"It's been days, Calvin," she said. "Only days. I have known you only a little longer than Ali."

"You know me better," I said.

She smiled sadly, nodded. "I truly wish I could choose us. I do know that I desire your happiness. That I would rescue you from a rolling river."

"Don't make fun," I said.

She put her hand on her heart. Hope to die. "Never," she said. "You saved me. And you are saving me every day from now on." She laid two fingers on my forearm. "Please know that."

I turned away. Her fingers lifted. I knew nothing.

She looked down at my drink, ran her finger around the rim, smiled, took a sip.

"The next time you see me," she said, setting it back down on the bar in front of me, "I could be a pair of brown eyes behind a hijab. I wonder: will you know me?"

I looked at her. At her brown eyes, suddenly welling with tears. I was not the only one stricken by this choice.

"What do you think?" I asked.

"Yes," she said softly. "I think that you would."

We sat there for a moment in silence, the only sound Frederick cleaning and drying glasses behind the bar.

Over the kitchen door was that picture of Mr. Hemingway kicking a can down a road somewhere in Idaho. You could not see it in that exuberance, but knowing his history, the Black Dog was there, the pain that never goes away. The fear. The grief. The darkness at noon.

Nadia too was looking at the picture.

"Did you know that Mr. Hemingway's father killed himself?" she asked.

"Yes."

"And that Mr. Hemingway killed himself."

"Yes. He did."

She turned to me, laid a hand on my arm, squeezed. The pressure burned even after she lifted her fingers. "Don't you kill yourself."

"I won't," I said. "I keep right on. It's my curse."

"Your blessing," she said.

"Huh," I said. "You should talk."

"I have learned something, Calvin," she said. "Death is the end of the story. Life is full of surprises. You were a surprise." She looked down at the table. "Ali was a surprise."

"A good one?"

"I wanted to make a difference for my sisters in Saudi Arabia," she said. "To move the needle. You know this. Perhaps Ali can help with that. It is my decision, at least, to hope."

"Perhaps. God, I hate that word."

I looked up at Mr. Hemingway, back down at my stool, where Mr. Hemingway used to sit. Or did he?

Was that just a Harry's Bar myth? Honestly, how could anybody drink thirty whisky sours and go back to work?

How could anyone drink thirty whisky sours, period?

Maybe all of this was myth, lies that never happened.

And so, I wondered, suddenly exhausted, what was the point?

"Someday," I said, slowly, "it will be as though this never happened. Like a dream that I woke up from and can only remember based on how it made me feel. Joy. And pain. You are sitting right next to me. But you are already gone."

She took my hand, raised it to her lips, kissed it.

I would never see those beautiful lips again. Never hold that hand. Never walk through the streets of Paris with her or along the glistening Seine.

I thought that I could not bear it, this cascade of memories that would never be, the present becoming history.

And then I had a thought. No. A memory.

"When I was very young," I said, slowly, remembering, "my mother had a son. Cooper. He came too early. 25 weeks. Maybe less. I think they could save him now. I've reported on such things. But he looked more like a sonogram photo than a human being. When I saw him at the hospital, he was more blue than pink. More like a dying old man than a creature meant for this world."

I took her hand, or she took mine.

"Cooper lived for a week. When he was gone, we buried him. That graveyard plot holds him, and my mother, and my father, and there is a place for me there too, if I choose it."

"Why are you telling me this?" she whispered.

"It's been over 20 years," I said. "And I wonder: was Cooper ever really here? And if he was, then what was the point? Wouldn't it have been better that he never came than that he lived for a week and broke our hearts?"

She took my hand now in both of hers. "I see," she said. "Would it have been better if this had never lived?" She indicated the two of us and shook her head firmly.

No.

No.

"If you had not walked into this bar on Monday," she said, tolling on her fingers. "If you had not responded to my text on Tuesday. If you had not pulled me out of the river on Wednesday. If you had not given me your truths on Thursday. If you had not showed me your broken heart on Friday. If you had not told me that you loved me on Saturday. If none of this had happened?" She shook her head again. "Then I honestly think that the world would stop turning."

I turned away from her, looked down at the bar. "I would love to believe that," I said. For that was what it felt like. That this past week had significance. That it meant something.

That it meant everything.

Yet, here we sat, for what seemed to be the very last time.

She took a deep breath, and then, her voice quavering, she repeated something she had told me once when I stood in a high place, paralyzed, frightened, unable to move.

When without her I could not have taken another step.

"The Blessed Qur'an says that for those who believe, on them shall be no fear, neither shall they grieve." She let go my hand. Took up her leash. Brought her two hands together as though in prayer. "Don't be afraid, Calvin. And try not to grieve."

"Too late," I whispered.

She leaned in and kissed me on the cheek. Then she turned my face to hers, and she kissed me as though it was the last time.

Because it was.

"Ali is not you," she whispered. "But he is also not what I thought he was. Feared he was. He will hold my secrets, and my secrets will become his. And maybe he will help me change things."

"I would have held your secrets forever," I said. "I would have helped you change the world."

Her eyes were bright, and she leaned in toward me.

"Maybe someday," she breathed, as her lips brushed mine, "you will walk in those doors and I will be sitting here at the bar with my dog leash." She shook it sadly.

"*Inshallah*," I said. "Wouldn't it be lovely to think so?"

Because Mr. Hemingway has all the best words.

I closed my eyes, even while her lips were still on mine. I could not watch her go. I turned to Frederick as the doors swung back behind her, and when I looked up, he was weeping like a baby, his huge hand covering his face.

I took a drink from my whisky sour. I was lost, and alone, but somehow I did not feel as though I was going to fall into this glass and never emerge, as I had at other moments in my life.

Strangely, I felt that it was time to begin.

Not all of us had arrived at this point yet. Frederick was sobbing now, great wracking sobs. He was doubled over the bar when a couple of Japanese tourists pushed in through the doors, took in the scene, and fled. Maybe it was the same Japanese tourists from the other day. If so, I feared that their Yelp review would be unsparing.

"Don't be afraid, Frederick," I told him, gently. "Try not to grieve."

"*C'est impossible, Monsieur Cal,*" he sobbed. "What is lost—" He straightened up, wiped his eyes, his cheeks still glistening.

"That girl," he said.

"I know." I did.

"Your heart," he said.

"I know." I did.

"What will you do?"

I shook my head, sloshed my drink around in the glass, drank the last of it, and stood up.

It was time to begin.

"What I can," I said. "Merci, my friend."

15.

Paris

July 16, 2016
Saturday

The clock ticks and ticks. You know this. But we are not aware of it always, of the passing of time, of things coming to fruition. I left Frederick and the bar, walked to the Opera Métropolitain station, caught a train back south under the river, but I was not yet ready to return to my apartment. It was a sunny day, I didn't need to meet Ahmed for a bit for my Bastille Day story, and I felt that the bright afternoon sun might be a sign of some sort.

And also, of course, I did not want to sit in my apartment watching the clock, the slow progress toward 6 p.m., watching the approach of that moment after which some newly married couple might be taking sunset photos on some Paris bridge or another.

I walked along the Seine, past the book vendors and painters on the Left Bank, wondering, how is it even possible to walk when your heart has been ripped from your chest?

I was remembering that image from the ritual scene in *Indiana Jones and the Temple of Doom*. It is generally not a good thing to be the rip-ee.

And yet.

And yet.

As painful as this was inside and out—for every fiber of my being certainly now ached—there was a part of me standing to the side of the sodden mass of pain and heartbreak that was Calvin

Jones Jr. and recognizing that my hurt was not the most important thing on the planet.

That even as the earth around my feet slipped away, Nadia was perhaps for once standing in a place where she could live into her dreams for herself.

I hoped that for her.

Oh, how I hoped.

I wandered. There was so much of Paris I had not yet seen, and so little that I needed to do just at this moment. I walked back along the Rue de Rennes, and when I heard the bells of Saint-Sulpice, I wandered back toward them.

The square in front of the church was set up as a market with vendors and booths, but I walked past them all, toward the church itself, and I walked inside. The space was huge. The American Cathedral was a little jewel box of a church compared to this. Saint-Sulpice was massive, the ceiling towering, the far end of the church almost incomprehensibly distant, another continent. I slipped into a pew. Someone was singing a Mass in the far reaches, and it echoed through the church. I didn't know the words, but I could tell that something was happening. They were words ringed with meaning.

Across from me, beneath an ornate pulpit, a homeless man slept in the pew, his knees raised. I could just hear his snores over the chanting.

I checked the time on my Fitbit—1:15. Ahmed and I were supposed to meet at the studio at 2 and go out to film. I texted Father Cameron and asked if he might be available for an interview this afternoon, and he got back to me immediately.

"I'm at the church all afternoon. Just let me know when you're coming."

The sounds of the Mass echoed through the church, bounced around my head. I had never attended a Catholic service, so I didn't know what the priest was singing about, but the sound—and the beauty of the church—was soothing.

And that's not completely true. Kelly McNair and I went to a Catholic wedding once, in June 2015, she gorgeous in a mauve dress, me wearing my good blue suit and a floral tie. One of her sorority friends from SMU was marrying a tax attorney, which meant they inhabited a cloud city of wealth beyond me. The service was lovely. I remember the pipe organ, especially, and the thirteen bridesmaids in tulle. Apparently when you had that kind of money, no one worried about bad luck.

Kelly took my hand as the bride and groom exchanged vows, and she looked a little flushed, a little wistful. She kept looking over at me, maybe hoping I was absorbing the proceedings.

I let her hold my hand, but I wasn't feeling what she seemed to be feeling. What I felt mostly was discomfort—I had a reliable sense that I was the person in the church with the tiniest net worth—and I also realized that while women in general and Kelly McNair in particular might be moved by weddings, I was mostly thinking about how little I wanted to get married, now or ever.

Afterward, at the reception at the Petroleum Club in Dallas, Kelly and I danced under crystal chandeliers, and she lay her head on my shoulder.

"This was such a beautiful day, Cal," she murmured into my neck. "You know, I think my father might want to throw a wedding reception here."

"Hmm," I said.

"You know," she said, her finger coming up to caress my cheek, "we're not getting any younger."

"I do know that," I said. "I've got hair sprouting in places that hair is not supposed to appear."

She laughed. I knew that was not the response she was hoping for. I was in my thirties, she was in her late twenties, and apparently somebody who had living parents was feeling some small pressure to get married.

But I didn't love her.

I knew it then. I know it now. And love is so very hard at the very best of times, with the very best of people. So why on earth would you pretend?

My phone buzzed. It was Ahmed. He was in the office, wanted to know if I wanted to meet him on site.

"Yes," I said, softly. "Meet me on the Tour Eiffel lawn."

We could get some street footage from tourists, talk to people on the Debilly Footbridge, maybe, and then go to the Cathedral and get a short piece from Father Cam to wrap the segment.

A few pews ahead of me, an ancient woman was kneeling, her head on top of the pew in front of her as she prayed. I admired that, even though I couldn't do it.

Faith. Sometimes it's the only thing that keeps you going.

That, or doing a job.

Which was where I was headed now. As I walked, I thought about the questions I might ask.

I walked down past restaurants where James Baldwin used to eat, past the bar where Hemingway and Fitzgerald had drinks, past the hotel where Chagall lived and worked. My head was reeling a little, and not because of the whisky sour I had mostly finished.

The world was shifting beneath my feet, and I was wondering where it was going to deposit me when it was finished.

I found Ahmed on the lawn stretching southeast from the Eiffel Tower. Tourists were taking pictures with the tower in the background. For some reason, most of them wanted to be photographed jumping off the lawn, caught in midair with the tangible symbol of Paris behind them.

We talked to a few of them. I got more than a few blank looks. Some of the Americans didn't realize that France had been attacked.

We talked to a Parisian woman who was walking a path along the Champ de Mars headed home. We stopped her after she crossed the Avenue Joseph Bouvard. She shrugged her shoulders when I told her what interested us, what we wanted to talk about, a beautiful and totally Gallic reaction. What can you do?

"These people," she said. "They will not change our way of life. They can kill us. But they cannot change us."

On the pedestrian bridge near the Eiffel we talked to some of the Algerians who were selling trinkets to tourists. While they first seemed a little upset to have their commerce interrupted, they responded warmly when we asked them about Nice.

"We Frenchmen will not be daunted," said one of them, his hands karate chopping the air. "We will go on and live our lives. Shame on him! This monster. He makes us look bad, and he does not stand for us."

I talked to an elegant British woman near the Diana Monument off the Avenue de New York. It's actually the Flamme de la Liberté, the Flame of Liberty, a representation of our Statue of Liberty's torch, but since Princess Diana was killed in the tunnel just underneath it has become an impromptu memorial to her.

"Well," she said. "It is horrible, horrible indeed what happened." Her face turned dark, and her stiff upper lip grew stiffer. "But we shall not give in to these miscreants. Here, in Britain, anywhere in the world. They are on the wrong side of history. We shall overcome."

Which was a lovely, and I'm confident, unknowing echo of a song from the Civil Rights movement, and made me feel a little more assurance I was on the right track

Ahmed and I walked up Avenue George V to the American Cathedral to talk to Father Cameron. The black wrought-iron front gate was closed, so I called in, and in a minute or so he came out to admit us.

"Cal," he said, reaching out a hand to shake. "How are you?"

I shook my head. Too soon to say.

"Father Cam," I said. "This is Ahmed."

Cam inclined his head. "*Salaam Alaikum*," he said.

"Peace be upon you," Ahmed returned.

"I'm putting together a story on living with this terror," I said. "This grief. And I was wondering what your experience in the war—and what your tradition—might have to teach us about it."

"Come back with me," he said. "For the moment, there is no one in my office."

We passed back through the Dean's Garden, where an eternity past I had entertained the thought of tossing Nadia's monumental engagement ring into these hydrangeas. We entered a limestone building on the left, through a wooden door, and then stepped straight back into Cam's office.

He took a seat behind his desk. Ahmed set up the camera and I took a seat across from them. Since we were shooting with one camera, Ahmed would tape me asking the question, then Cam's response, then my response to it. Artificial, yes, but, except in the movie *Broadcast News*, it works.

"I'm talking with Father Cameron Gaines," I said, "who was a military chaplain in Iraq prior to coming to Paris to serve at the American Cathedral," I said. "Father, what advice do you have for those wrestling with their feelings about this terrorist attack?"

He was golden.

"Thank you, Cal," he said. "This is an important question, whether you're a person of faith or a person of no faith. We all live under an illusion of safety that was violently ripped away from us in an instant. It was always an illusion, but now that illusion is gone, and we're forced to reckon with it."

"And how do we reckon with it?"

"Community is essential," he said. "I tell my parishioners, 'We're going to be here for each other. I'm going to be here with you, no matter what happens.' This attack has brought up some really bad things for me, has shattered so much, that at this moment, I'm also really struggling with my faith and my belief in a good and loving God, and if you're struggling with that right now, please believe that you are not alone. All I can say is that when I wonder where God was in the attack, I remember this: Christians believe that God lost a son on this planet to a violent and painful death, so my feelings of uncertainty, anger, bewilderment, all that, are somehow known to the God I worship and pray to. Frankly, most of my prayers and worship right now are simply asking God, what the hell? Where are you? Do you know what we're going through down here?"

He shook his head. "But holy Scripture tells us that God does know, that God understands, that God is with us in the good times as well as the hard times. My faith insists that we believe that. But my heart is with everyone who is suffering right now, with all those who lost someone they loved in Nice, with all those who wonder how a loving God can stand by and let things like this happen."

This was not news. We don't air theology. But all the same, I asked. "You believe God doesn't stand by and let things like this happen?"

Cam shook his majestic gray head. "I believe God accompanies us in everything that happens. That rather than create a world where he shelters us from the worst things, he created a world where he can walk alongside us through those things."

I nodded. I would love to believe that. "So, practically, what should people in France do in response to these attacks?"

Cam nodded. "Don't give up," he said. "Live. Love. Form communities. The forces of evil have always attacked the forces of good. But our stories tell us that at the end of the day, they will not be successful. Dr. Martin Luther King Jr. used to argue that the moral arc of the universe is long. But that it bends toward justice." He nodded. That was a wrap.

"Thank you," I said. I nodded to Ahmed, who nodded back. We had gotten what we wanted.

"Thanks," Cam said. "Cal, I feel like this may be the most important work I've done since Iraq."

"You may be right," I said. Ahmed extended his hand, and Cam shook it. "I'll see you soon."

"Tomorrow? Come. We're doing that service for the National Day of Mourning."

"*Ay, caramba,*" I protested. "Don't ask for more than a person can give."

"You would be very welcome," he said, shaking my hand and holding it for a second before he released. "You know that. And you, Ahmed."

"Merci," Ahmed said. He did a little salaam, nodded.

"I'm still working on the service tomorrow," Cam said. "Can you find your way out?"

"Of course," I said.

I love it when people turn me loose inside institutions. Ahmed and I exited the building, walked across the Dean's Garden, and into what I guess they would call the cloister.

Which turned out to be a World War One memorial, where upon the walls were notations of every American unit that had fought in the war and their casualties at major battles: Cambrai, Château-Thierry, St. Mihiel, Meuse-Argonne. How many men each unit lost. And at the end of the hall, an angel commemorating these losses. It was stunning, really, the thousands and thousands of dead.

What kind of culture could allow this to happen? What kind of people would charge into certain death?

At the end of the cloister was a glass door and a button to open it. I pushed it gladly. Ahmed and I stepped out into the open space surrounded by stained glass and the ceiling high overhead. The woman at the volunteer desk waved at us and pressed some button that opened the iron gate.

And there, on the front steps, sat the dean of the cathedral, Clarice, a cigarette surreptitious in her hand.

"Ah, Calvin Jones," she said, patting the stair next to her. I plopped down.

I introduced Ahmed, told her what we were doing there, and then took a pull from her cigarette when she passed it to me. I shook my head.

"It's a horrible habit," she said, taking another drag. "But somehow, it helps me think straight."

"What are you thinking about?" I asked.

"I'm still working on my sermon for tomorrow," she said. "God help us, the prescribed Gospel text is Mary and Martha. It seems an awful match. Petty. But I think I may have found a route into this tragedy, a way to speak about Nice."

"Mary and Martha," I said. They were two sisters, I recalled, their brother was Lazarus, they were dear friends of Jesus. "From what I remember, that seems very—domestic."

"It does," she said. "At first, I thought there was no way to get to what we needed. But I think I've found a way to crack it open into something that touches all of us. That's all you ever hope for a sermon."

"Well, I hope it goes well," I told her, getting to my feet.

"Come and see if it does," she said. She saw my face, my dismay, and smiled. "I know. You don't want to be in church on Sunday. I'd guess that most of Paris doesn't. But I'd also guess that tomorrow we'll be full to overflowing, like the Sunday after 9/11 back when I was in Atlanta. People gather when tragedy strikes. And I want to offer them something."

"I haven't been to church in recent memory," I said. "I don't have a good history—"

"Balls," Clarice said, scritching out the cigarette on the step. "You don't have a history with us. Come. Listen. Decide for yourself if this is comfort or affliction."

I took her offered hand. "Okay," I said. "I can't imagine how you're going to find a way to make anyone feel better. Let alone me. But I would love it if you could." Gulp. "So maybe I'll see you tomorrow."

Ahmed and I stood on Charles V for a moment after Clarice went inside. "Do you have some thoughts?" I asked. "How to cut this?"

He nodded. "We got some good responses," he said. "And then Father Cameron's thoughts about how we move forward together." He nodded. "As a community. That is—solid. Helpful."

I agreed.

We recorded an intro and outro in front of the Cathedral where I identified myself and the network, said we were here on the day after the Bastille Day attacks, and I mostly got out of the way. It was good. We slapped five. And then Ahmed went off to edit this piece for 10 o'clock, and I wandered down Charles V toward the Pont de l'Alma Bridge, the place where my life changed, the place where I needed to see how—if—one could move forward after everything fell apart.

16.

Paris

———

July 16, 2016
Saturday

I said I was going to tell you the truth and only the truth, but it's clear to me that I've failed in that goal over and over again. My father was not a saint. Neither was he the monster I've recently made him out to be. I'm trying to find a way to show him to you—to explain to you how he made me, in some way, what I've become. How a person can love and hate someone in equal measure. But it's more complicated than I thought.

My father is more complicated than I thought.

Here's what brought me to that. After I sent Ahmed off to edit our work, I walked down to have an aperitif at a table outside Le Campanella, a café on the Rue Saint-Dominique. I thought it was going to be a simple transaction: I give them twelve euros, they give me a Kir Royale. But it turned out they had music playing back inside the café, and I recognized it immediately: "When Your Lover Has Gone," Sinatra, from his 1955 concept album *In the Wee Small Hours*, a whole disc full of hard sad music about living with a broken heart, if such a thing is even possible.

I am not, mind you, some hipster in skinny jeans ironically drawn to Sinatra. I imbibed him with my mother's milk, listening to my mom and dad as they swayed and sometimes danced to him. In the back of my mind, yes, maybe I wondered "Why not the Beatles? Why not the Eagles? Why aren't you getting it on to Marvin Gaye?"

But we know what we know, and that music was the soundtrack of my childhood.

In the early days, when my mom was alive, it was the happy albums, say, the 1956 *Songs for Swinging Lovers*, "You Make Me Feel So Young," and "Too Marvelous for Words," and "I've Got You Under My Skin." I remember coming home at dark from playing baseball with David Marshall and the neighborhood kids, walking in through the back door, seeing my parents dancing and laughing in the kitchen, hearing Frank's silken voice and perfect phrasing, watching them kiss, and offering my measured and thoughtful response: "Gross."

And my mom and dad would break apart as though I'd caught them doing something shameful.

The only shame, of course, is mine, for taking away that thing they found joy in. I think my mom had precious few things that brought her joy. My father had fewer still.

I asked him one time, when we were together in Iraq, about listening to Sinatra, which even for him seemed dreadfully unhip.

"Those were my dad's records," he said, raising his hands. What can you do? "He loved Sinatra."

I never asked him if he loved his father, if you could love someone who broke your heart.

Because I knew even then that you could, that sometimes it was the only option.

So I sat, and sipped, and ordered another Kir Royale, which was quickly becoming my drink of choice, and listened to Frank sing "Mood Indigo," and "What's New," and then Ella dropped by to sing "Someone to Watch over Me," and then it was Nat King Cole: "Gee it's great after being out late, walking my baby back home."

It was darker, although not yet full dark, and the waiters lit candles on the tables, and traffic on the street slowed, and people began to settle in around me to order not drinks but actual dinner, veal scallops and sea bass and salmon tartare, finished off with profiteroles and rice pudding and rum cake. And I just sat there seriously drinking by myself, which I had thought I had forgotten how to do, forgotten why I used to do it, and meanwhile my phone buzzed in my jacket pocket. I checked it to find messages from Jack and Kelly and Rob, messages that I ignored.

I ordered another Kir Royale, and yet another.

As I drank, I was thinking about that scene at the end of *The Graduate* where Benjamin Braddock gets on a pay phone and locates the church where his beloved is marrying another guy. I am a good journalist. In ten minutes, I think I could have found out where Nadia and Ali were staging their ceremony. And, like Ben, I am a strong cross-country runner. If it was inside the Paris city limits, I thought I could arrive in time to—

What? Bang my fists against a wall of glass at the back of the church?

No. More likely, to get my ass handed to me by Antonio or whoever was working security, because I was guessing that wherever Ali was, someone was always going to be working security.

And so I sat, and tried to drink that vision out of my head, because really all I could think about was Dustin Hoffman pounding his tiny fists against the thick glass, his face contorted with sorrow, shock, loss.

He looked like I felt, like I had run hard uphill, and to absolutely no effect.

As dusk approached, I pushed myself to my feet. I left a stack of euros on the table. Something compelled me to walk back north toward the river, and it wasn't until I walked onto the Pont de l'Alma Bridge that I realized why I was out there.

Nadia was married, and she and her husband were going to be taking pictures on a Paris bridge during the Magic Hour, pictures for social media, for the family back home, before she, as she had once feared, disappeared into her burqa. I know she had said that she expected they would be on the Alexandre III bridge, the statues a gilded background to her Elie Saab gown. But I thought, what if?

What if she decided to come back to the Pont de l'Alma, to the place where she might have ended it all and didn't?

What if she thought I might be standing there waiting for her? What if?

I will confess to you that there was nothing particularly rational about any of this. I was intoxicated, schnockered, really, irredeemably polluted from a succession of Kir Royales, which should not punch so far above their weight, and yet clearly they do.

I stumbled out across the bridge, the sidewalk packed with people stopping to take pictures of the Eiffel Tower, and made my way to what I will always think of as Our Spot, the place where two people once jumped into a river, one after the other.

I was standing there looking out to the place where I pulled Nadia to shore when I saw a flash of white to my left.

It was a bride, a photographer, and for a moment, my heart pounded so hard I thought it might precipitate me into the river. Then I realized that the bride was Japanese, and her groom was Japanese, and for a moment, that same heart seized up with disappointment.

And then, reality forked, and I imagined that bride as my Nadia, imagined her stepping toward me, imagined her taking my hand gently but firmly, the way she had once held it, high on the Cathedral tower.

What if?

"Don't be so afraid, Calvin Coolidge," Nadia said. Her hand indicated the Seine, the city, the world beyond. It could still be ours. "All we have to do is jump."

"Jump?" I said, because that did not suddenly seem like such a great idea, even inebriated as I was.

"You'd have to be crazy to jump off this bridge," she said, and I nodded my agreement. "No one will come after us."

"Okay," I said. "Let's do it."

I imagined us going over the side, the rush of air as we fell, the hard smack of water as we hit the river, plunged deep. I pulled us to the surface, gasped for air, kicked hard to pull us downstream along with the current.

The bridge, the people on it screaming, got smaller, until they faded from view. Downriver we floated, Nadia in my arms, the white billow of her bridal dress floating. I thought of Ophelia in *Hamlet*, buoyed up for a while by her gown. But this particular tragic heroine was not going to sink. I pulled for the bank, got my hand on a metal ladder set in the stone wall, pushed her up it. She got to the top, turned, held out that strong hand to pull me up to safety.

And it would be just that easy. We'd make our way back to my apartment, where we'd ignore every phone call, every text, every buzz of the door.

Because her wedding ceremony in Paris with Ali was just that, ceremonial. Her legal vows weren't to be exchanged until she was back in Saudi Arabia. But it seemed a shame to waste that phenomenal wedding dress. Father Cam would marry us, a tiny ceremony in the Dean's Garden that very same night. Or, hell, maybe Clarice would preside over a big ceremony in the nave of the Cathedral, the state flags hanging overhead, Allan blasting "Here Comes the Bride" or whatever on that monumental organ. That would take a little longer to plan. I'm sure we'd have to reserve the church. But didn't Rob say he was on the vestry? It could happen.

We'd start our life together, the two of us in my tiny apartment. Nadia would go to work for that international development agency with Allison. Or get on with the network as an English-language journalist. No. Too visible. Let's stick with the think tank so she could use her language skills and crazy smarts.

So she could change the world.

But two years later, our first child, Khalid, would be born, and we'd be forced to move into a bigger place: two bedrooms, a bath and a half, a newish building out in Suresnes or Saint-Cloud, one of those western suburbs on the other side of the river. And then we'd welcome our daughter, Anne, named for my mother, and Khalid and Anne could share a room, but as they got older they would need their own space. So we would move farther out from the city, a long commute in for me on the RER train, but still close enough to see our friends, to host the occasional apéro with Rob and Brigid, with Allison and her new girlfriend while the kids played on the back lawn.

We'd have people from the Muslim community over for Iftar, the Ramadan evening meal. I would fast with Nadia during Ramadan. Solidarity, of course. Not because I believed anything, although who knows? Maybe someday I would.

Nadia would pray at the mosque on Friday. Maybe some Sundays we'd haul the kids down to the American Cathedral, get off at the RER stop at Alma, walk up Avenue George V, sit in those wooden pews and marvel at the spangled light coming in from the stained glass windows and listen to God's voice as Allan played Bach.

We'd have lunch afterwards at one of those little cafés close to the Diana Memorial, as I guess Nadia would make me call it. Croque-Monsieurs for the kids. A Salade Niçoise for Nadia. I don't know what I'd have. Make it up. Fill it in.

Here's what matters: We're all together at the table, talking, laughing, the kids in their Sunday best, Nadia in a headscarf, her eyes twinkling as she looks around the table at our family, this improbable—this miraculous—love embodied.

I can see them, our beautiful brown-eyed children heading off to school speaking French and English and Arabic, can see the rainbow colors of their friends and their parents.

I can feel small arms around my neck, the butterfly kisses of Anne, who I would call Annie, and I would sometimes think about my mother when I held her close.

And I would hold my wife, Nadia, my dearest friend, my gift from the river, the woman who helped me make some sense out of this crazy world. I would hold her tightly as we danced in our small kitchen—because no matter how big our house in France, I'm guessing it would always be a tiny kitchen—to Sinatra, or the Eagles, or to Marvin Gaye.

"I told you," she would say, often, maybe murmuring it into my chest, because she is that much shorter than I am, "I told you not to be so afraid, Calvin. Isn't this a beautiful life?"

Yes.

Yes. A beautiful life.

But I realized now on the bridge, in a way that whooshed the breath from my lungs and dropped me to my knees, it would never be my life.

Nadia would have someone else's beautiful brown-eyed babies.

Some other loving father would get those butterfly kisses.

And that woman who helped me make sense of this crazy world? I would never see her again.

They're playing songs of love, Mr. Sinatra used to sing. *But not for me.*

The vision slipped away, no matter how hard I tried to grasp it. And I found that instead of embracing my wife, I was kneeling with my head against the glass of the bridge, my face wet with tears, calling her name.

The Japanese bride and groom were kneeling next to me. She had her hand on my forearm, and he looked as though he would like to put a hand on my shoulder but really wondered if I was crazy sad or crazy dangerous.

"Crazy sad," I managed to croak. I wondered for a moment if this was that Japanese couple who kept coming into Harry's Bar. If so, maybe they just expected this kind of emotional outpouring by now. Maybe that's what drew them.

Or maybe it was just the nakedness of my pain. It was universal. They recognized in it their own longing, their own fears, their own heartache.

They spoke softly, soothingly to me in Japanese. He was repeating the same phrase over and over, and while I didn't know what it meant, I liked the sound of it. And she was cooing, shaking her head, patting my arm.

Together, they helped me to my feet, although I found that I still could not stop weeping. I waved my thanks to them, told them that I was okay, although I clearly was a long way from okay, was in fact pretty fucking far from okay, and turned back to look out at the river. A long, packed tour boat from Bateaux Mouches passed underneath.

If I were Jason Bourne, I would drop onto the top deck, roll once and rise to my feet unscathed. I could flee this bridge and these memories. But Jason Bourne's story is another story that mine is not.

The bride tarried for a moment. "Nadia?" she asked, then pointed at me.

I nodded, tears dripping down my face.

She raised her hands to her heart, made a sad face, and said something I did not understand, but I'm sure was something like "I am sorry for your loss."

"*Domo arigato*," I told her. I bowed, and more tears dripped from my face as I inclined my head to her.

They bowed, formally, from the waist, and then went back to finish taking their wedding pictures. The light was still golden, I noted, the TV journalist still somewhere present in this drunken sodden mess of a man.

I wiped my face, wiped it again.

So this is what it felt like to lose everything.

My phone rang. Rock the Casbah. I was thinking seriously about changing that goddamn ringtone.

It was Jack. I wiped my face, as though he could see me, took a deep breath, let it out, answered.

"Well," I growled, "What is it, old man?"

"Oh, very nice," he says. "Where are you? I've had three texts from Kelly McNair in the last thirty minutes. She's come to Paris to see you and she says all she has seen of you is on the airwaves."

"Shit," I said. I shook my head. In my present state I did not want to see anyone, but at some point, I was going to have to talk to her. She deserved that much at least.

"I'll call her," I said. "Or text. Later. I'm a mess."

"Where are you, Cal?" my aunt said, grabbing the phone from Jack. "Are you okay?"

"No ma'am," I said. "I just came face to face with my heartbreak, and it kindly shook me." The bride and groom had finished up their shots and were getting back in their limo. They waved to me, and I waved back. "Congratulations," I called. I had no idea how to say it in Japanese, but they seemed to get my drift. The groom raised his hands together like a winning prizefighter and the bride blew me a kiss.

"What was that?" Jack asked.

"Oh," I said, "I'm on the Pont de l'Alma Bridge. Again. As ever." I waved as the limo pulled away. "I was just saying goodbye to these Japanese newlyweds who—well, it's a long story. I'm sure you didn't call to hear about my misfortunes."

"Why else would we call?" Jack said. "Do you need me to come and get you? To run interference with Kelly? I'll tell her you were called out of town. I'll tell her you don't want to see her. Whatever you need."

"I know you would," I said. "No. I've just realized how much I lost. Like, just now. This moment. I mean, I've been realizing all along. I lost things. We all lose things. But now—" It didn't really make sense to me, and I guessed it would make even less sense to sober people.

"Listen," I said. "Listen."

There was a moment, the river flowing beneath me, traffic passing on the road behind me.

"I am listenin'," Jack said softly.

I looked out at the river, flowing, flowing, and I shook my head, tried to shake some words loose. "My heart is broke, Jack," I said. "It's busted in a hundred pieces. And it feels awful. Like I don't know how I can live through it. Like I can't stand the pain of it. But it also feels good. Good. Because I wasn't sure there was still a heart there to break. And because I think she's going to be okay." I paused, shook my head again. "Nadia. You know?"

"Yeah," Jack said gruffly. "No. What can we do?"

"Oh, not a damn thing," I said. "Not a thing. Except this: Love me. All the way from Texas, if that's what it has to be. Just—don't stop loving me. You're all I've got."

"Well, son," he said, his voice cracking. "I believe you've got a lot more than us. But we can guarantee that."

"Thank you," I said.

The sun was setting. Soon the Tour Eiffel would light up. The crowd sitting on the Champs de Mars would ooo and ahh, and here, where I leaned on the bridge railing, this point on the Pont de l'Alma Bridge where Nadia tried to leap to her death and didn't, was perhaps the best place in Paris to watch that show, to see the tower lights reflected in the Seine, to observe the streetlights blinking on along the bridge with their soft glow, to see the boats, dotted with lights, as they slipped up and down the river.

"I guess this is going to be my life," I told Jack. "It's not the life I imagined. But it is pretty wondrous."

"Amen to that," Jack said. "Your aunt and I—we do love you, Jack. Always have. Always will. You tell us if you need anything."

"I need some wisdom," I said. "And I'm asking everyone I meet."

"I remember the thing we discussed that one time," Jack said. "Bury the bad. Mourn the good. See if you can do that."

"I will try, old man," I said. "I will try." I stood up. "Hug that beautiful bride of yours. I'm going to watch the lights come out."

And so I did.

17.

Paris

July 17, 2016
Sunday

Sunday morning in Paris. The city rouses itself gradually. The traffic is light. The cafés slowly fill with people wanting coffee, breakfast. And there I sat, at Le Grand Corona, the café from my vision, across the Avenue du Président Wilson from what I've been calling the Diana Memorial, waiting for Kelly McNair, who was not the tiniest bit psyched about being pulled out of bed so early on her first morning in Paris. But I had told her I was going to church at the American Cathedral, and that after, I had lunch plans, and sadly this was the only time I had available before I went out on assignment.

"Are you going to church with her? Lunch with her?" Maybe it was partly jetlag, but her text seemed really snippy. "I came all the way across the freaking ocean, Cal."

"I told you not to," I told her. Because, reader, I did.

"Can I meet her? The competition? This rescue project of yours?"

And while maybe I should have told her that all of that was over, that I was shattered, that Nadia was out of my life, I realized I'd never spoken her name to Kelly. And while a part of me felt like I did not want her thinking I was still available, the other part of me felt like I did not want her knowing that much about my pain. It felt too personal to share.

Which, I guess, said a lot about the relationship we did not have and never would.

"Meet me for breakfast," I said. I gave her the address.

"Is there a Starbucks close?"

"I doubt it," I told her.

"Do they have smoothies?"

"I doubt it."

"Jesus. How do people survive in this city?"

"Somehow they manage," I texted her. Smiley emoji x 3. "I'll see you at 9."

So there I sat at 9:15, a croissant, orange juice, and café crème in front of me, waiting for Kelly McNair to show.

My phone buzzed. It wasn't Kelly, though.

Allison.

"Lunch today?"

"Sure," I texted back. "I'd like that. Need it, I think. Are you going to church?"

"Of course."

"I guess I'll see you there. After I have this showdown with my ex at the Corona."

"Truly?" she texted. "Like you haven't been through enough for one week. Do you need a wingman? Is that what they say? The straights?" A perplexed smiley emoji followed.

I laughed. "I would not turn down your help. The extrication may be complicated. She has a very strong grip."

She sent more smiley faces. And I felt my own face slide into a smile.

The week hadn't been a complete loss.

"Was that her?" Kelly plopped down in the chair next to mine. She was wearing yoga pants and a designer workout bra, very low cut, an unexpected amount of cleavage. She was totally made up and put together, as ever, and she gave me a careful peck on the cheek, then turned to look out at the traffic circle, sighed as she pulled out her own phone and took a picture. "Ah, Paris. It is beautiful."

"It has its moments," I said. I was a world-weary Parisian now after a week. Maybe with an unfiltered cigarette dangling from my lower lip as I talked Existentialism with my anarchist friends, all of us clad in black berets. *C'est la vie.*

"Do you love it here?"

"I think maybe I do," I said. "It's not what I expected." This was not the best weekend to ask me that particular question. But I thought, maybe this might be home.

I helped her order a café crème and fruit for herself, and then she turned to me, put her hands together on her lap and leaned forward, which enhanced her already impressive cleavage, and asked, "So. Is this really happening?"

"This?"

"Are you really breaking up with me?"

"Kelly," I said. "I moved to another continent. That should have been a gentle hint."

She waved that away. "We look good together, Cal. We have a history. We have great sex. Don't you think all of that means something? Don't you think it's worth keeping?"

We did indeed look good together. I didn't tell Kelly that, on reflection, the sex was actually just okay. Which was fine. One of the few times I heard GI's talk about sex in Iraq—they spent a whole lot more of their time talking about food and about the heat—a Spec 2 was defending his decision to have sex with a woman who, in the eyes of his conversation partner, was a civilian caterer who seemed less than desirable.

"Sex is sex," he said. "The worst of it is still pretty good."

So there you go. Kelly was beautiful, and funny, and we looked good together, and the sex was still pretty good.

And I could not imagine spending my life with her, could not imagine connecting with her on any level that was not simply physical.

"Kelly," I said. "I am sorry. But it's over. I met someone. I fell for her. It changed me." All that was true.

She sniffed, and to my surprise, a tiny tear trailed down her perfect cheek.

She shook her head, as though she could knock my denial away. "Don't you remember that you proposed to me at the Amon Carter Museum?"

I laughed, then caught myself and eased it back. "You were tripping balls at the Amon Carter party," I told her gently. "In the car on the way home, you told me that John McEnroe had taken you out on the lawn and given you tips on your backhand." It hardly needs to be said, I'd guess, that Mr. McEnroe was never at that party in Fort Worth or even probably within a thousand miles of it.

Or that Kelly McNair did not play tennis.

She smiled. "I remain convinced that he did. And that you proposed to me. You were on your knees. You had a big diamond. Like, the size of my head." She shook her head more slowly now. "Oh. So maybe I did imagine it."

She laid her hand on mine. "But I wish you had, Cal."

"A diamond the size of your head?"

"Well yes. But no." She smiled sadly. "Asked me."

"You're a good girl, Kelly," I told her. "And someone will ask you. Here." I handed her the bag from Selfridge's. "I bought you some lingerie. I can't return it. So."

She took it from me, peeked inside. "Oohh. Would you like to see it on?"

"No thanks," I said. "It would be stunning. You are stunning. But—"

"So this really is the end," she said. Her head dropped. Her hands worried the bag, yet she did not want to set it down.

Kelly McNair really liked nice lingerie.

"What are you doing for the rest of the week?" I asked.

"Well," she said, "I missed Fashion Week," she said. "But I suppose I'll do some shopping. Hang out in cafés. Maybe meet some interesting man."

"Try the Ritz Bar. Or the bar at the Four Seasons," I told her. "Jay Z and Beyoncé are probably sitting there at this precise moment."

"Cal," came the voice above me, "darling," and there was Allison, as if I'd pressed a silent alarm. She looked beautiful, gray dress, gray Jimmy Choo pumps, matching Louis Vuitton handbag. Kelly looked at her and nodded in grudging approval.

"Hello," Allison said, holding a hand out. Kelly took it briefly, let it drop. "I'm Allison. You must be Kelly. Cal told me you were in Paris."

"So you're Cal's rescue project? I have to say, I imagined something different. Something more obviously shattered." *Meow.*

"I owe him a great deal," Allison said, patting my shoulder. She turned to me. "Are you ready?"

I nodded, left a stack of euros on the table. "Don't tip," I told Kelly. "They won't be impressed by it."

"Nobody tips," Allison said. "Except Americans."

"Well. I guess this is goodbye," Kelly said, and her voice was small, and even I felt the tiniest bit sad.

"Have a wonderful life, Kelly McNair," I said. "Find that man who will give you a diamond as big as your head. Find that man who will bring you to Paris for Fashion Week."

She snickered a little. Because those things so obviously did not resemble me. "Have a wonderful life, Calvin Smith. And if things don't work out with your Allison—"

Who cleared her throat.

"Sorry," Kelly said. "Sorry. Best of luck to you both."

I shook her hand. Two pumps, clear release. Maybe I should have felt worse. I had spent years of my life with this woman. Seen her naked on multiple occasions. I had even, if you believed her report, proposed to her that time at a museum in Fort Worth.

But the fact was, I had never felt for her the kind of love that seriousness required. And I knew I never would.

Do not marry someone you do not love.

So it was best we walk away.

She would have a great story. *He broke up with me at a little café in Paris . . .*

And I—I would have this. My life.

Older. Wiser. Sadder.

Alone.

Allison took my arm and turned me up the street toward the Cathedral.

"Thank you, thank you, thank you," I breathed to her as we walked past the Chinese Embassy.

"Life is hard enough," she said. "A little help from your friends, that's what we all need."

We entered the cathedral through the black wrought-iron gates, passed security into the cloister, and saw Father Cam, who was dressed in his robes. He took my hand, gave me a chaplain's examining eye.

"How are you bearing up?" he asked, remembering I'm sure our recent talks about Nice and terrorism. "And where is Nadia?"

I could see my face reflected in his expression. "Oh." He kept hold of my hand, shook it again. "Oh. I am so sorry, old man."

"On her way back to Saudi Arabia," I informed him. "I think she was married last night. Long story."

"You can tell it all at lunch. If you can tell it."

I nodded.

"And at least you're here," he said. "The church is full of people feeling broken and scared this morning. But something good is about to happen."

Allison turned to go into the church, but I lagged for a moment. "Forgive me, Father Cameron—"

"Just Cam, please."

My heart was pounding and I was feeling panicky, like the stone walls were closing in. "I don't know what I'm doing here. My past experience with church does not suggest that I'm going to find any meaning in this present darkness."

Cam looked around. He was being joined by a tall boy carrying a jeweled cross, two girls carrying candles, someone carrying a big bejeweled book. Time was running out. But still, he looked me in the eyes, saw my distress, and touched my arm.

"Listen to Clarice's sermon," he said. "I've read it. She went to the lessons for today and fought for good news."

"Her sermon?" I asked. My memories of sermons did not correspond with good news.

"A good sermon is like a conversation," he said.

"Every sermon I ever heard was just someone yelling at me," I said.

"Listen, Cal," he repeated. "And if you can, if you feel right about it, come up and take communion. It's a powerful action. It's an act of radical hope."

Clarice had arrived, and here was Nkwele, waiting for her. He kissed her fingers, then stepped away as the church people formed into a circle to pray. Cam nodded to me as he stepped into the circle, and I went on into the nave, where I found Allison, who was seated next to Rob and Brigid.

I looked at the service guide and didn't recognize much—it was just a multitude of words—but Allan was at the organ, and whatever he was playing, that Fauré, maybe, was beautiful, and the nave itself was beautiful, and it did feel like a gentle place to be at the end of a brutally hard week.

Other people apparently thought so as well. The Cathedral was full; by the time the procession began, every pew was packed, front to back, and they had to put out overflow seating in the rear. It was as though all of Paris thought it needed to be in church that morning. It put me in mind of the Sunday after 9/11. I did a story at Wilshire Baptist Church in Dallas, packed to the rafters on that morning, and it felt as though this congregation had a similar need, a similar hope that something good could happen, and so they had assembled from across the city.

In the Baptist church of my youth, everything built toward the sermon, which seemed to take up most of the service, so I was more than a little surprised when not halfway through the service, Cam processed into the middle of the nave and read a Gospel lesson about this time that Jesus visited Mary and Martha, about how Martha was pissed at Mary for not helping her fix dinner for Jesus and their guests, and then he walked back to the altar as Allan played, and then Clarice stepped up into the pulpit.

"*Bonjour,*" she said. "*Bienvenue à la Cathédrale Américaine. Je suis Clarice Washington.*" She paused. Looked out at those gathered. Nodded. "Good morning. I am Clarice Washington, Dean of the Cathedral. It is my great privilege to serve here at the American Cathedral of the Holy Trinity, and on behalf of the staff and members of the Cathedral, let me say to each and every one of you that you are most welcome this morning of all mornings, this national Day of Mourning, in this house of prayer for all people.

People murmured their thanks, their return welcome, settled into silence, and Clarice began to speak.

"'The world is too much with us.'

"That phrase by the British poet William Wordsworth has been ringing in my head of late, and perhaps this morning that phrase reflects some of your own feelings as well.

"Sometimes the world batters us and shatters us, breaks our hearts and shakes our hope.

"The world has lately felt to me like a dangerous and unsettled place. Terrorist attacks in Germany, Iraq, Pakistan. The Brexit vote, driven, so it seemed to me, by nativism, exclusion, and fear of the Other. The death of two Black men in America at the hands of police officers, captured on social media. The attack on White police officers at a Black Lives Rally in America by a Black veteran who said he wanted to kill them solely because of the color of their skin. And now, on Bastille Day, this horror in Nice.

"I have spent hours over the past few weeks walking, praying, hoping for some clarity as I walked alongside the Seine with the music of the Irish rock band U2 in my ears."

I liked that image. And wondered why I hadn't run into Clarice yet on my morning runs.

"We have gathered this morning hoping for understanding. In the Anglican tradition, we come together to worship, we read the Scriptures together, and we trust that the preacher will help us discern God speaking into the silence that is our heartbreak.

"And so, as we do, I came to the lectionary texts prepared to wrestle on all our behalves this morning, to seek some understanding, to find some good news in the midst of this present darkness."

She looked down at her notes, then out at all of us. "Some of you know, I think," she said, "that I grew up in Alpharetta, Georgia, a small town to the north and east of Atlanta. The divisions between Black and White, the divisions between male and female, were very clearly demarcated there. There were places you were welcome and others where you would never be welcome, decisions made before your birth because of the color of your skin and the arrangement of your chromosomes.

"One of those places where a woman was not welcome," she went on, "was in the living room on Sunday afternoons. That's when the men watched football while the women cleaned up and drank coffee and gossiped and waited impatiently to go home." I remembered a similar arrangement in Texas. My folks used to have friends over to watch the Dallas Cowboys play on Sunday, the men in the living room drinking beer and hooting, the women sipping coffee and whispering in the kitchen.

"But there was something wrong with me," Clarice said in her deep beautiful voice. She laughed, sadly. "Not only was I too tall, and too skinny, and too dark skinned, all things I was deeply conscious of, but I loved football too much. Our own Atlanta Falcons, of course, but also the Cowboys and the Packers and the

Broncos. I could name the starting quarterback on every team. I could tell you why Roger Staubach was better than Craig Morton, why John Elway was the greatest quarterback ever. And yet, I wasn't welcome in that room where football games were playing on our only television screen."

She shook her head. "Perhaps this seems like a matter of little import. But in our Gospel lesson today, in which Mary transgresses the boundaries of her culture to sit and learn at the feet of her rabbi, something is happening. I despaired about how to take this lesson and preach from it on the Sunday after the Nice attack. I wondered where we might find comfort in what looks like a domestic story of woman's work and woman's spaces, of Jesus inviting one of these women to cross over into the space he occupied.

"And I will tell you," she confessed, "I would have given anything to have back last week's Gospel text of the Good Samaritan." A little chuckle at that, for reasons I didn't get. Some inside Jesus joke. "The Good Samaritan, people, is *the* great lesson in a time of suffering, fear, worry." She shook her head. It was not to be. "I could have pulled in Augustine's admonition that every human being is our neighbor. I could have quoted William Gladstone, who said, essentially, that the ground on which we stand is not White ground or Black ground, Christian ground or Muslim ground, gay or straight. It is *human* ground. I could have channeled the Reverend Doctor Martin Luther King Jr., who retold that parable of the Good Samaritan on his last night on earth, who called on his listeners to respond to danger with dangerous unselfishness. I could have cited the great writer and priest Barbara Brown Taylor, who says that Jesus is calling us all to come near enough to recognize that our neighbor is, simply, anyone anywhere who needs our help.

"Last week's Gospel shatters walls and it breaks down preconceptions. It is truly radical. But please do not be misled by the seeming domesticity of our Gospel this week. In its own way, it is just as radical, just as clearly indicates the Kingdom Jesus came to inaugurate, just as powerfully speaks hope into a world demarcated by divisions."

She paused to see how we were hearing this. I was, I will confess, a little surprised. Clarice said she had found a way to move from Martha being miffed at Mary to Bastille Day, to the horror in Nice, and so far I couldn't see how she could possibly get there. It looked like trying to get from John Wilkes Booth to Kevin Bacon in Six Degrees of Kevin Bacon: impossible. Let alone how the NFL might ever fit into all of that. But I looked at Allison: she was listening raptly, and seemed to believe that something was about to happen, and so I looked up at Clarice, and I settled back in faith, trusting the messenger, if not the message.

"My older brother Tyrone, of blessed memory, was the Black male presence in my home growing up. Like many young Black men of my acquaintance, he came to a premature and violent end. As I tell you about him now, he has been dead for over twenty years. But I remember him still with love, with gratitude, and here is one of the reasons why:

"Although tradition dictated that the living room be reserved for Black men on Sunday afternoons, Tyrone invited me to come and sit on the floor in front of him and watch football.

"Now please understand, his friends did not want this. They felt it violated sacred boundaries. They pushed back, hard, told me to my face that they did not want me there. 'Girl, this ain't your place!' Called me stupid or worse, begged Tyrone to change his mind."

Clarice's eyes were glistening now, although her voice was steady. "But my brother loved me more than he cared about following the rules. He was willing to give offense to his friends to make space for me.

"It's so important for us, looking at the Mary and Martha story from these many centuries removed, to understand that Martha is not put out about the fact that Mary isn't helping her fix dinner, although that is what she says. No: she is outraged by Mary's brazen behavior. Mary is sitting in the part of the house where women in first-century Palestine were not supposed to be, behaving as though she is a man.

"More importantly, Mary sits at the feet of Jesus, like a student in those days. And this thing that Mary is doing, again, is taboo. Rabbis educated other men; women were separated and excluded. And yet, Jesus invites Mary, pushes back against the grumbling of the men, lets her sit at his feet and learn. Jesus loved her more than he cared about following rules.

"So, when I reflect on these disciples of Jesus, the first thing I see is those young Black men in my living room. It is hard not to imagine them muttering and murmuring, putting Mary down, calling her out. She does not belong there."

She smiled thinly. "That is what I see at first, because that is my own history. So. Maybe the disciples agree with Martha that what they are seeing is shameful.

"And maybe they don't.

"Because here's the thing: Unlike those young men parked in front of our television set in Alpharetta, Georgia, those disciples of Jesus had been exposed to a larger world. Maybe by this point in their journey they had seen enough impossible things, listened to enough radical teachings, to recognize that this barrier, these rules, simply represented more of the lines that Jesus has come to cross. As in the Parable of the Good Samaritan, which teaches that we are called to reach out a hand even to those who ought to be our enemies, as in the teaching of Paul that in Christ there is no distinction between male or female, Jew or Gentile, maybe the disciples—and we—are finally starting to see that this is exactly what Jesus is all about.

"Maybe on this evening in first-century Palestine, as Martha cooks and Mary listens, they are understanding what Jesus has been teaching, the same lesson, by the way, that Bono of U2 was singing over and over again into my ears as I walked this week, heart-torn, along the Seine:

There is no them.
There is no them.
There is only us.

"Only us." She paused, looked out into a huge space full of people nodding, and I discovered to my surprise that I was one of them. I knew that U2 song, "California," had run along the Seine to it, and some part of me wanted to live in a world where those words could actually be true.

"It is this Jesus," Clarice said, raising her hands high in the air, "the Jesus who calls us to dangerous unselfishness, the Jesus who tells us that we love and serve God by coming near to those in distress, the Jesus who teaches that there are no parties or sides, that, beloved, we all stand on *human* ground—it is this Jesus we meet this morning in the home of Mary, Martha, and Lazarus.

"And it is this Jesus who restores our hope, refuels our strength, and sends us out renewed to love and serve a world that desperately needs some good news this morning—and every morning.

"AMEN."

Allison was sniffling beside me as Clarice climbed down from the pulpit and took her seat. She was not alone. There was a spirit of awareness in that space, a common connection. We had come hoping for something. And, in those minutes she had spoken, Clarice had somehow gathered that something for us. With us.

"Wow," I whispered to her as Clarice sat down. "Is she going to go back up now and tell us we're all doomed or something?"

Rob shook his head. "You are in the wrong place for that sermon," he whispered back. "You'll have to live with this one."

"Wow," I repeated. We got to our feet and started to recite a creed. I found it in the program, read along, said some of it out loud. I thought that maybe you had to believe all this stuff to say it. What did "one holy catholic and apostolic church" even mean?

But maybe saying it was how you came to believe it.

After prayers we greeted each other—"Peace be with you," is what everyone said to me, and so I shook hands and said it back to them, peace being a very good thing—and then afterward, Father Cam and Clarice went up behind the big altar at the far end of the nave in front of that wondrous altarpiece.

"What happens now?" I whispered to Allison.

"We celebrate the Eucharist," she said.

"What?"

"Communion," Rob said, leaning across Brigid. "You used to call it the Lord's Supper. You don't have to receive it. You can just sit here."

I saw Cam doing something that looked very much like setting a table, and then Clarice stepped up to the altar, turned to the congregation, looked out, I thought, directly at me, and announced, "Wherever you are in your journey of faith, you are welcome at this table."

And I was decided.

"What do I do?" I asked Allison.

"Come with me," she said. "You take the bread. You sip the wine."

"Why?" I said. "What does it mean?"

She started an explanation, then shook her head as she saw that Clarice was preparing to speak. "It's a gift for the brokenhearted," she whispered.

She held up a finger as I started to ask. More explanation could come later.

Clarice began to sing. Chanting, I now know. "The Lord be with you," she sang, and the congregation answered her.

Her voice carried, it soared, it echoed like that priest chanting in Saint-Sulpice.

It reminded me of the voices of the muezzin, calling from the minarets in Iraq.

I began to understand why people pray.

"Wow," I said again.

I stood when Allison stood, knelt when she knelt.

I followed her down the aisle to the altar rail.

I held my hands out for the bread, which was actually more a stale cracker that crunched sadly in my mouth.

I sipped the wine, red, strong. It made me cough a little.

"Port," Rob muttered on the way back to our seats. "Fortified wine. To kill germs and all that." Vestry talk.

If I was expecting magic, then the bread and wine were not that. I was not transformed, different, a brand-new human without fear.

But something had happened. Something about kneeling alongside Allison, Rob, Brigid, the others. Something about Clarice's voice as she told me, "Calvin, this is the Body of Christ, broken for you." Something about the electric shock of her touch as she placed that tiny wafer on my palm and squeezed.

Something about getting to my feet, blinking, as though a flashbulb had gone off in front of my eyes.

I was still gathering, getting my mind around what we'd done, about how this vast room full of individuals had become something more, something larger and yet more connected, as Cam tidied up at the altar, as Clarice offered a blessing, as people around me crossed themselves, as the priests and choir processed to the back of the church.

Allison bowed as the cross was carried past, and reflexively, although I could not have told you why, I bowed with her.

"What just happened?" I asked, but Allison shushed me again as Father Cam stepped forward from the back of the nave.

"Alleluia, alleluia!" he shouted. "Go in peace to love and serve the Lord."

"Thanks be to God," was the response from those around me. "Alleluia, alleluia!"

And then we were done. People looked around at each other, some of them likewise seeming a bit dazed. We had walked into the Cathedral as hundreds of broken individuals. But for moments, there, it felt as though we were simply one. One community. One family, even.

That we had been seen and known and understood.

That there was only us.

Now, of course, the family was breaking up, like any family after Sunday dinner. We drifted out, singly or in groups. People began to walk through the black wrought-iron gate onto George V, turned left or right to the river or the Champs.

"Lunch?" Allison asked, turning to the three of us. "La Fontaine?"

"I've got to host the welcome coffee in the Dean's Garden," Rob said. "You kids go on without us." He turned to Brigid, and they nodded some agreement. "Come for an apéro tonight?"

"Sure," I said. "I would like that."

"Yes," Allison said. "And perhaps dinner after? I've got reservations at Excoffier."

"Oh," Brigid said. "Of course. Can you make it four?"

"*Certainement*," Allison said. "Cal and I will drop by and make it so."

Brigid embraced Allison, and then she took me by the arms, held me for a moment. "And how are you, Calvin?" she asked.

"People are going to have to stop asking me that," I said.

"That bad?" Rob asked.

"You saw our broadcast last night," I said. "Father Cam told us, 'Live. Love. Form communities.'" I looked around at the four of us, broken people all, and yet I nodded. "That seems to be the thing to do."

Nkwele was standing near the gate, and Allison and I shook his hand before we departed.

"Did you understand her sermon?" I asked Nkwele in Arabic.

He smiled at me and shook his head. "In my culture, things belong where they belong. I do not understand all this concern about boundaries." But he looked over at Clarice shaking hands and embracing people as they exited. "But I did not come to listen to her sermon. I came to stand by her on this day. To say that, as I think she said, love is stronger than hate."

"*Salaam alaikum,*" I told him.

"And peace be with you, little man," he laughed.

"I am just not that little," I complained as we walked out onto Avenue George V.

"Oh, do be quiet," Allison said, putting a finger up to my lips and smiling to take the sting from it. "Not everything requires commentary."

"Okay," I said. "For you." And she slipped her arm through mine as we walked off toward the Seine on that beautiful Sunday afternoon.

18.

Paris

July 14, 2017

I would not have believed any sort of happy ending possible on that Sunday a year ago when we walked out of the American Cathedral, even though, like the disciples, I was perhaps beginning to see the world in a new way. But as Allison and I walked down the avenue toward the river, my phone buzzed, and I knew somehow that it would be Nadia.

Certainement.

I stopped in front of the Chinese Embassy. Allison stopped beside me.

"Cal," she said. "What?"

I held up a finger.

I took a deep breath.

I pulled out my phone.

From this moment on, my life would be different.

"My dear Calvin," Nadia's message said, "Ali and I leave Paris this afternoon. But I must thank you, now and forever. Whatever comes next, you handed me on to it. I will not forget."

"Half a mo," I said to Allison. God. I was British. "It's her."

"Nadia?"

I nodded. "The very same."

"Oh my God," she said, wrestling for the phone. I showed her the message. "What are you going to say?"

I considered half a dozen responses, typed a few words a dozen times, discarded each false start. I ran through formal, informal, angry, loving, regretful, cheery, despondent. It was too much. 144 characters couldn't even begin to address what Nadia, what this week had meant. What they still meant. 144 characters was not enough, would never be enough.

Yet it was all we had.

So I went small, trusting her to read between the lines.

"As you handed me on," I texted. "Please take care of yourself. And should you ever require help walking the dog…"

She was typing a reply. Dot dot dot. A smiley face came first. And then this:

"You will be the first to know."

I nodded. That was how we had begun. I started to respond, but she was already ahead of me:

"I have decided that I will be like James Bond."

It was hard to ask, but I had to know. "Broken?"

"No." There was a pause, dots as she responded. "Brave."

"Because," I texted back, a catch in my throat as I typed, "that is where the bravery is."

I thought perhaps that was it, the last word, but as usual, I was wrong.

"I love you, Calvin Jones. Pray for me, I beg you. Please do not forget me."

Allison looked at me, stricken. And indeed, there were tears in my eyes now. But I was smiling as I typed an answer I could not have sent even a week previous:

"I will pray for you. You have my word. As I beg you will pray for me, dear one. Je t'aime, Nadia Al-Dosari. Je t'adore. Now. Forever. Adieu."

I pressed Send. And that was it, I knew. The end.

The end of us.

And yet—

And yet.

"Oh, Cal," Allison said, reading over my shoulder. "It's—"

She couldn't find a word that fit, that answered, that fixed anything. Because there wasn't one, and she knew it, and I knew it, and I'm sure Nadia knew it, for my phone remained dark.

I slid it back in my pocket. We walked on to the river. I looked across at the Tour Eiffel, at the crowds around us, people from all over the planet united in the act of taking selfies.

I leaned over to look at the river. "That dock," I said, indicating the stone wharf on the right, downriver, where the house boats were moored. "That's where I pulled her out of the water. Where I see the homeless man taking a bath every morning when I run. I should ask his name. Find out if he's hungry. I don't know why it never occurred to me to do that."

Allison leaned in close and embraced me, and I was glad for her. When we broke the hug, I put an arm around her shoulder and we started walking across the bridge.

"Let's eat," I said. We walked on to La Fontaine, where we had a lovely lunch. I asked her about her perfect match. She told me that she was looking for a woman who kept her hair short, who saw through the deceit of Vladimir Putin, and who loved macarons from Ladurée.

I told her I would keep my eyes open because I was pretty confident such a woman must exist.

And then I told her about a time shortly before my father shipped out to Iraq when I walked into the old family home in Killeen to find him sitting in the dark and listening to Frank Sinatra: "In the wee small hours of the morning, that's the time you miss her most of all."

"I think about her too," I spoke up, surprising my father. "I miss her. All the time."

He sat up, startled, as ashamed as though I'd caught him masturbating.

"What are you doing here?" he asked.

"I had an interview with a colonel on base," I told him. "I didn't mean to surprise you. I'm sorry. I should have called ahead."

"Oh," he said. He reached to turn down the stereo. "It's okay. I just didn't know you were coming. That's all."

My father and I never talked easily with each other, nor did we that afternoon. I asked about the deployment coming up. He asked if it was true that I'd be heading over to Iraq, how the network envisioned what was coming, whether I was excited or nervous.

Then we sat for a long time in silence. I could feel the vacant spaces in that room, in that house, and I felt for my father, but I did not know what to say to him, what truthful words he could hear from me that he would not bat away like flies.

At last, he got to his feet, Sinatra still crooning quietly, sadly, in the background, "When Your Lover Has Gone," and my father held out his hand. "I'm sure," he said gruffly, "that you have places you need to be."

And I could have told him no. That no one else was looking for me.

That this was actually the most important place that I could possibly be.

That I loved him, despite everything, and always would.

But I didn't say any of those things.

I pushed myself to my feet, shook his hand, let it drop.

"I'll see you, old man," I told him. "Keep your head down."

"And you," he said.

We said goodbye.

"You miss them both," Allison said when I finished, and I nodded, for of course I did, missed them and many more, and we toasted those we had loved and lost with the good Fontaine house red, and at the end of our lunch, we walked back out into the Paris sunshine.

We put that day behind us, and the next, and the next, and now, here we are.

It is some months after that week when I first arrived in Paris, when I began to uncover what lay in the shadows of the City of Light. I have moved on from my woeful family history, where we began this story, to the Pont de l'Alma Bridge, where I suppose it ends on another bright July afternoon, to this place I must return again and again until I understand my story, or at least can let it rest in that peace where stories go when they have served their purpose.

Not that there isn't much to report, or that more hasn't happened. In the year since I lived those events, Rob and Brigid have regained their true affection for each other, and have embarked on a second honeymoon that hasn't quite ended. I see them once a week socially, but I am glad they are taking this time to cocoon and to move forward together.

I see Frederick weekly at Harry's, if not more often. He's become a valuable source for me, and I actually put him on the network payroll, which makes my drinks a business expense, I hope. He's dating a Japanese woman who was somehow brave enough to step into the bar. He tells me she has a cute friend, also Japanese, who has seen me on the air and wants to meet me, but I am not ready for any such thing. Not yet.

Allison herself met a lovely woman from the Ukraine, Erika, who shares her contempt for Vladimir Putin and her love for macarons from Ladurée. Especially the bright green pistachio ones. Erika sometimes comes to church with Allison on Sundays, and I have heard Allison introduce her as her girlfriend, stop, blush, smile at Erika, leave it be.

And I cannot help but hear about Ali, Nadia's Ali, although I am not Facebook stalking him or anything like. I just can't help it, being a journalist and all. I know things. It turns out that Ali is one of the progressive Saudi leaders pushing to liberalize the kingdom. He was behind the plan to bring movie theaters back to Saudi Arabia, and I read that Ali is pushing for women's rights to drive a car, as well as other shamefully liberated prospects.

I think that I may have misjudged him, as painful as that is to admit.

I think perhaps he might be a good husband for the woman I love.

But enough of that. The less I think about Ali, the better I sleep at night, and there is much to celebrate without losing sleep. For many of those I love, there has been some sort of a happy ending. Something good has grown out of these high weeds and dangerous seeds.

And as for me?

Well, what does a happy ending even mean? Does it mean getting what you wanted? Or does it mean getting what you needed, even if you lost some of the things you loved in the process?

When I began this story, I promised a tale that was complicated and difficult and beautiful, and I confess that I didn't know if Paris was going to feel to me like a place I lost myself or found myself, could not know until I walked through this story alongside you.

Now I know.

Now I know the American Cathedral, and a little more about the Episcopal tradition, where I have learned the piece of liturgy about "those we love but see no more," a line that could apply to my mother and my father, to Khalid and Elena, to Darla Trent and Kelly McNair even, for I loved even those as well as I could, which was not, frankly, very well.

It could apply to Nadia, who I loved more than I can say, and who I cannot yet think on without bruising my heart, although that phrase gives me comfort, reminds me that I am far from the first to love and lose.

I am apparently an Episcopalian now—"a Whiskeypalian," my Uncle Jack grumbles, presumably rolling his eyes—but I assure him that this move has been good for me. I have found a community outside the newsroom or Harry's Bar. We pray together. We work together. Rob and I cook breakfast for the homeless once a week.

I curated a forum for the Cathedral recently on religious violence, gathered Jewish and Muslim and Christian leaders and guided them in conversation, and it was a thoughtful and surprisingly well-attended program, considering that many Parisians think bigotry against religions is the last acceptable prejudice.

I have come to believe that maybe there is something larger than myself and my little desires, something that resides in and beneath the river, in and behind the clouds, in and inside the faces of those I meet, and that Something must be a force of love and justice, for I have found that I need to believe in a force of love and justice if I'm not going to jump off a bridge and disappear forever into the depths. This life can and will break your heart.

But now when I pray to that Something, I do not feel that my words are dropping into some bottomless pool. I feel that they are somehow being marked, even if my exact desires may not be met. I feel that I am getting what I need rather than what I think I deserve.

For so long I could not pray. The only concept I had been given of prayer was that of a Coke machine. You put in your change and pressed a button and expected something to be delivered. And so often I got nothing. Or a Tab when I explicitly asked for a Sprite.

But that is not prayer, Father Cameron has told me. Prayer is not about whether you get what you want. It is about aligning my heart with the heart of the universe. He told me, "Bono says prayer is about getting on board with what God is doing instead of asking God to get on board with what you are doing."

And you know me: I do love me some Bono.

So now, to my great surprise, I pray. For Nadia, of course, but also for my friends in Paris, and for the life of the world, and that the work I came here to do might have meaning. I pray so regularly that people might mistake me for a devout Muslim, which would be fine with me. I have met many Children of Mohammed who put my own infant faith to shame.

And now I know the Seine, which is the heart of this great city, and will ever be my beating heart, a place where I risked something big for something good, even though I did not get to keep it.

I walked beside the Seine hand in hand with someone I loved, I watched the moonlight flicker off its waves, I saw the Eiffel Tower reflected, and I still walk or run alongside it every day. Sometimes, although it is *très* expensive, I have an aperitif at a café on the river before going out to dinner, and while I keep one eye on the rainbow mob passing by, I keep the other on the river.

I do not tire of the Seine, and I do not believe it is tired of me.

And now I stand here looking down at it from this place where I have stood so many times, and first, I am amazed that I ever jumped from this bridge into that water far below. That I ever could jump from it.

Because, honestly, this is way too high for anyone to even consider such a thing. It is terrifying. I don't think I could do it now if President Macron himself were to topple over.

But second, I am soothed and touched that at one magical moment in my life, I stepped off this bridge as naturally as stepping off a curb.

I did it without thought, without regret, and without fear.

I have lived most of my life afraid to stride into the river. I was afraid it would sweep me off and carry me away, because, truly, I have lost more things than I wanted, watched them carried away downstream for good, which seemed to me to be a very great tragedy. And so, I thought, maybe it was safest to sit on the bank, safest even on the hottest day of the year just to dip a toe into the current.

But the river remains the river, whether I jump in or not.

And it turns out that there are greater tragedies than losing something you love.

There is the tragedy of not loving enough, of being so afraid you will lose everything that you refuse to care about anything.

I will never commit that sin again, *Inshallah*.

Now I stand here and watch, but I have known the river, and the river has known me, and I can never fear it again.

The waters surge away toward the sea, ripples and rivulets that touch the land and change it and leave it behind.

But the memory of every touch remains.

Those we loved and lost are not gone. Not really. They are just— elsewhere.

And someday we may walk into Harry's Bar, let's say, and find them sitting there, smiling.

They already may have ordered a drink for us.

That, at least, is my fervent hope.

This is Calvin Jones, reporting from Paris.

 Au revoir.

ACKNOWLEDGMENTS

Over the course of the years I worked on this book, I spent a lot of time alone reading, thinking, traveling, and writing, but so many people were a part of this project that it would be criminal not to name and acclaim them for their important contributions. Sometimes I've simplified or changed real things to improve the story; I do use actual places and institutions fictionally in this novel. And sometimes it's entirely possible that despite my care, I just screwed up. Any mistakes, errors, or misspelled French words, of course, are my responsibility entirely.

I owe my firsthand knowledge and love of Paris to the American Cathedral in Paris, a fictional version of which appears in these pages. The Most Rev. Lucinda Laird, the past Dean of the Cathedral, invited me to stay in the cathedral's tower apartment during a European speaking tour in the Fall of 2013. In 2014, my wife Jeanie and I honeymooned in the tower, and I've returned every year since except during the Pandemic. I could not have written this novel without my many months at the Cathedral. I am grateful for the chance to serve now as the Cathedral's Canon Theologian, and to regularly read, write, teach, and preach in Paris. And it is one of my greatest honors to have preached a version of Clarice's sermon at the Cathedral on the Sunday following the Bastille Day attack in Nice for the National Day of Remembrance in 2016. I also wrote and read at the American Library in Paris, a great writer's institution for the past century, ate at every single restaurant mentioned in these pages, and made numerous visits to Harry's Bar. I think Frederick would know me on sight and start making a Manhattan. With Bulleit rye, of course.

One of the reasons I write is that I want to know things. To that end, I read widely and asked lots of questions to try to find out about a war correspondent's life, to understand what it was like to serve in Iraq and Afghanistan during the 2000s. NPR journalist John Burnett talked with me about his time in Iraq, as did former military chaplain the Rev. David W. Peters. Both men wrote fine books about their experience, which I read, as well as combat memoirs and war studies by Matthew Gallagher, Thomas E. Ricks, Mark Owen, Dexter Filkins, and others. David Peters offered me his thoughts on what my fictional Father Cam might offer as a pastoral response to the terror attack in Nice, and I used them almost verbatim. They were that good. *The Greater Journey: Americans in Paris* by David McCullough, *The History of the American Pro-Cathedral*, by Cameron Allen, *This Side of Paradise* by Scott Fitzgerald, and *The Sun Also Rises* and *A Moveable Feast* by Mr. Hemingway offered background and atmosphere about Paris and the Riviera.

My teaching home for thirty-plus years, Baylor University, offered me time to write, including a research leave which I spent partly in Paris, and a summer sabbatical during which I finished the first draft of this novel. I am grateful also for travel funding which took me to Paris in the pursuit of other research, and acknowledge the University Research Committee and the Dr. Benjamin Brown IV Fund for Interdisciplinary and Collaborative Scholarship for those further chances to immerse myself in French life, and the Baugh Family Foundation for the grant which saw me completing the final revisions of the book in Switzerland. I also gratefully acknowledge the support of friends and colleagues at Baylor, including my dean, Lee Nordt, my department chair, Kevin Gardner, and colleagues Tom Hanks, Hulitt Gloer, Richard Russell, Joe Fulton, Dianna

Vitanza, Deanna Toten Beard, and my students, past and present. I love Baylor and serve her gladly.

My wife, Jeanie, has shared many of my adventures in Paris, has made my life better than any story, and is the one woman for whom I'd willingly jump off a bridge. I've actually done it before. But Jeanie also offered me insights from her ten-year career as a TV journalist, saved me from needless mistakes (again, any you discover are my own), and helped me create time and space to write this and every other book, the greatest gift a writer can receive. Thank you, my love.

Terry Nathan, of Blessed Memory, offered me his lake house in the Texas Hill Country to write, and much of this book was drafted or revised there. I cannot fully express my gratitude to Terry and his daughter Alison Nathan Huxel for the opportunity to work without interruption. This book became possible because of that gift.

Toward the end of this process, Amal Wilemon read the book to consider how I had represented her Muslim faith and culture. I am grateful for her engagement and her encouragement. It was important for me to accurately and fairly depict all of this rainbow cast of characters, especially in a book that wrestles with the spectre of religious violence. I'm also grateful for Beth Malcolm and Amanda Vaughn who read with a thoughtful female critical sensibility and offered suggestions.

I listened to Mumford and Sons, Imagine Dragons, Travis Meadows, Matthew Perryman Jones, Jeremy Messersmith, U2, Bruce Hornsby, Phoebe Bridgers, Fauré, Duruflé, and the soundtrack to *La La Land* as I worked. This music took me directly to a deep emotional place as I wrote and edited, and would be a proper soundtrack for this work—along with Mr. Sinatra, of course.

We stand on the shoulders of giants. I owe practical storytelling debts to the writers of *Casablanca*, to Damien Chazelle, who wrote and directed *La La Land*, and to Rolin B. Jones, who talked with me about writing the funeral scene in my favorite episode of *Friday Night Lights*, "The Son," as well as to James Baldwin, Richard Ford,

Walker Percy, Margaret Atwood, Pat Conroy, Anne Tyler, Phil Clay, Tim O'Brien, and Ben Fountain. Brownie points will be awarded if you can tell me what those debts might be. That's the teacher in me.

I also give thanks for engagement with my friends who tell stories, with my friends who love stories, and for all of you who have read this story. I could not do this work without you.

Thank you.

Greg Garrett

Leukerbad, Switzerland
Easter, 2022

ABOUT THE AUTHOR

Greg Garrett is the author of five novels, two books of memoir, and more than twenty works of nonfiction. His first novel, *Free Bird*, was a *Publishers Weekly* First Fiction selection and a Best First Work of Fiction from the *Rocky Mountain News*. *The Prodigal*, cowritten with the legendary Brennan Manning, received a starred review from *Publishers Weekly* and has been translated into Spanish, Portuguese, German, and Dutch editions. His other novels are *Cycling* and *Shame*; all have been critically acclaimed. In his life as a nonfiction writer, Greg writes about race, faith, politics, and culture. He serves as the Carole McDaniel Hanks Professor of Literature and Culture at Baylor University, and lives in Austin, Texas, with his wife, Jeanie, and their daughters, Lily and Sophia.

ABOUT PARACLETE PRESS

Paraclete Press is the publishing arm of the Cape Cod Benedictine community, the Community of Jesus. Presenting a full expression of Christian belief and practice, we reflect the ecumenical charism of the Community and its dedication to sacred music, the fine arts, and the written word.

The Raven, to ancient peoples, represented light, wisdom, and sustenance, as well as darkness and mystery. In the same spirit, Raven Fiction reflects the whole of human experience, from the darkness of injustice, oppression, doubt, and pain to experiences of awe and wonder, hope, goodness, and beauty.

Learn more about us at our website:
www.paracletepress.com
or phone us toll-free at 1.800.451.5006

SCAN
TO
READ
MORE